THE WALLS
OF JERICHO

THE WALLS OF JERICHO

A NOVEL

JACK FORD

BASCOM HILL PUBLISHING GROUP >> MINNEAPOLIS, MN

BASCOM HILL
PUBLISHING GROUP

BASCOM HILL PUBLISHING GROUP
322 FIRST AVENUE N, 5TH FLOOR
MINNEAPOLIS, MN 55401
612.455.2293
WWW.BASCOMHILLBOOKS.COM

ISBN-13: 978-1-62652-325-8
LCCN: 2013948435

DISTRIBUTED BY ITASCA BOOKS

COVER DESIGN AND TYPESET BY JENNI WHEELER
EDITED FOR BASCOM HILL BY ROBERT CHRISTIAN SCHMIDT

PRINTED IN THE UNITED STATES OF AMERICA

THIS BOOK IS DEDICATED TO MY
MOTHER, PEGGY WHITE, FOR ALL SHE
HAS DONE FOR HER CHILDREN.

"By faith the walls of Jericho fell down after they had been encircled for seven days."

HEBREWS, 11:30-31

"Yes, Mississippi was. But, Mississippi is, and we are proud of what we have become."

MYRLIE EVERS-WILLIAMS

WIDOW OF SLAIN CIVIL RIGHTS LEADER MEDGAR EVERS

OCTOBER 1, 2002

PROLOGUE

Lafayette County, Mississippi
July 21, 1960

The headlights snapped off as two vehicles turned onto a narrow gravel road. A new model, two-tone Buick sedan coasted to a stop in a small clearing, followed closely by a rusty, battered, black Chevy pickup truck. The soft ticking of their idling engines was swallowed up by a chorus of night sounds from the surrounding trees and thick foliage.

Across the clearing, about a hundred yards away, stood a small church. Its weathered, single-story wood frame was topped by a sagging tapestry of patched and rusty sheet metal, crowned by an old steeple that somehow managed to preserve a shabby dignity despite its precarious list to one side. Although it was approaching midnight on a Thursday, the old building was ablaze with light and alive with noise, as the soulful strains of a lively Negro spiritual wafted through the thick folds of the heavy Mississippi summer air.

Two young men climbed out of the truck, each holding a longneck beer bottle, and sauntered over to the Buick. Both looked to be in their late teens, scruffy and lean, hair unkempt, dressed in worn jeans and dingy white t-shirts. The driver leaned against the car and took a long pull on his beer.

"So," he said, gazing toward the church, and then glancing down at the man in the driver's seat of the Buick. "What now?"

The two men inside the Buick were also in their teens and were also drinking beer. But, instead of old jeans and t-shirts, they wore khaki pants and short-sleeved white button-down shirts. The driver was bobbing his dense thatch of reddish-blond hair up and down to the sound of Roy Orbison's "Only the Lonely" drifting from the radio, while his passenger sat slumped in the seat, a baseball cap tugged low over his forehead. The driver reached over and turned the radio down.

"We wait," he answered, between sips of beer.

Across the field, inside the Morning Star Baptist Church, the rollicking, hand-clapping rendition of "Ain't That Good News" wound down as the minister rose from his seat on the altar. Reverend Calvin Butler, dressed in a dark suit despite the oppressive heat, was a slight man with an oval, boyish face. A pair of horn-rimmed glasses framed deep-set, intelligent eyes that, tonight, glowed with evangelical excitement.

Raising his hands to silence the congregation, he smiled at the three dozen or so men, women, and children who had gathered to listen to their guest. The last of the clapping died away.

"Brothers and sisters," Reverend Butler began. He paused a moment until the crowd had hushed. "Brothers and sisters," he repeated, this time more forcefully. "Let us thank our brother, Elijah, once again for driving all this way to visit with us tonight."

He smiled down at the man seated next to him. "And we thank you, brother, for the good work you're doing for us—and for all the colored folks in this state—to teach us to stand up for ourselves and to register to vote."

Another burst of clapping erupted, punctuated by shouts of "Amen!" and "Lord bless you, brother!"

The visitor, Reverend Elijah Hall, who looked to be no older than thirty, nodded to the crowd. His dark, handsome, square face, glistening with perspiration, looked like it was cut from polished ebony marble. A slight smile tugged at the corners of his mouth.

"Brother Elijah," Reverend Butler continued, his voice now rising and pulsing with rhythmic energy as he gestured toward the congregation. "We want you to know—we want everyone in this county to know—colored folks and white folks alike—that we believe! That we believe in your mission! That we believe that God has blessed us by sending you to join us tonight! To teach us—to help us understand—all of us, men and women, boys and girls—that it is time! To help us to understand, as that great court in Washington told us, that separate is *not* equal! And to help us to understand that to be equal, we need to be heard!" he shouted.

More applause and shouts of "Amen!" and "Yes, Lord!" burst through the small, stifling room.

The minister plunged forward, this time not waiting for the congregation to quiet down.

"It is time," he repeated. "Time for the colored folks of this county to stand!"

"Amen!" the congregation answered.

"Time for us to speak up!"

"Amen!"

"Time for us to be heard!"

"Amen!"

"Time for us—all of us—come Election Day, to vote so that our voices can be heard—not just inside this house of God—but throughout this state and this nation!"

This time the room exploded into a cacophony of clapping, foot stomping, whistles, and shouts of "Amen."

Elijah Hall stood, and Reverend Butler wrapped his arms around him, holding him in a long embrace, while the congregation launched into another chorus of "Ain't That Good News," their voices raised to God, tears streaming down their cheeks.

I got a crown in that kingdom—ain't that good news?
I got a crown in that kingdom—ain't that good news?
I'm gonna lay down this world
I'm gonna shoulder up my cross
I'm gonna carry it home to Jesus—
Ain't that good news, my Lord, ain't that good news?

Thirty minutes later, the last of the gathered crowd had said goodbye and the minister and his visitor stood together in the doorway.

"Are you sure you won't stay the night with us?" the minister asked.

"Thank you, Reverend, but no. I need to be in Jackson tomorrow night for another meeting and I'd just as soon get a head start tonight. I've got a cousin lives about an hour from here and he's expecting me. I'll get some sleep there."

"Well then, you'd better get started," Reverend Butler said, looking up into the night sky. "Feels like some rain's comin'. Lord knows we could use it, but I don't want you gettin' caught up in a storm this late."

Hall extended his hand. "Thank you, Reverend, for your hospitality. And for gathering so many of your folks tonight."

"No, Elijah. It's us who thank you. What you're doing is God's work. These people—our people—need to hear what you have to say. Need to know that other folks just like them are ready to stand up and vote. It's God's work," he repeated, placing his hand on Hall's shoulder, as they walked to his car. "And we thank you for it."

Hall climbed into his rickety black Ford sedan and fired up the engine.

"Take care now. And be careful drivin'," the minister said softly.

"I will, Reverend. God bless you."

Hall tugged at the gearshift on the steering column and the car chugged away from the old building.

Reverend Butler watched the taillights disappear into the night and then turned back into the church, closing the door behind him.

A moment later, across the field about a hundred yards away, two sets of headlights blinked on and then also disappeared into the night.

The road was narrow, dark, and winding, more a country lane than a highway. Elijah Hall was hunched over the steering wheel, peering cautiously out through his dirt-streaked and insect-speckled windshield into the blackness ahead. He had traveled about three miles from the church when he noticed a set of headlights some distance behind him. Glancing up occasionally at his rearview mirror, he could see that the other vehicle seemed to be gradually closing the distance between them. Elijah slowed down a bit and pulled slightly toward the soft shoulder on the right, hoping the car would pass him. *Might as well let him go on ahead and light the way for me*, Elijah thought.

The other car drew closer, then swung out around to the left and accelerated. Elijah glanced over toward the passing vehicle but was startled at the sudden flash of a second set of headlights in his rearview mirror. Just then, the first car swerved sharply back in front of him. With Elijah jerking the steering wheel hard to the right, the Ford slid off the road and onto the shoulder, throwing up a fishtail of dirt and gravel. The car came to rest, its engine stalled and smoking, with the front tires settled into a low drainage ditch.

The driver behind him quickly hit the brakes and wheeled in behind Elijah, bracketing the old Ford between the two mysterious vehicles.

For a long moment, there was no sound or movement. Elijah, nearly blinded by the headlights behind him, started to push open his door when he saw the silhouettes of two men approaching the front of his car. Two more figures appeared behind him. He pulled his door shut.

"That there was some serious careless drivin'," a voice said.

"Yeah, you coulda got us all killed drivin' like that," another voice chimed in.

Elijah shaded his eyes, trying to make out the faces of the men through the glare of the headlights.

"Don't you go lookin' at us, nigger!" snarled one of the men.

"Here! Quick! Put these on," a voice urged the others in a harsh whisper.

There was a rustling outside the car door. Elijah tried to sneak a look at the men but could only make out the four figures in a tight huddle. Then, suddenly, his door was yanked open and two sets of hands jerked him out of the car. Struggling, he was pinned up against the hood. As he tried to twist away, he felt a heavy blow to his stomach that seemed to suck all the air out of his lungs. He gasped and then groaned as he was punched a second time, the blow a vicious shot to the kidney. Doubling over, wrapping his arms protectively around himself, Elijah sagged down to his knees as the men holding him released their grip.

"Goddamn, nigger, can't you take a punch?" cackled one of the men.

"Shit, no," laughed another. "This here ain't no hard-workin' field nigger can take a little beatin'." The man lashed out with a hard kick that drove Elijah over onto his side. "This here's some sissified preachin' nigger. Probably ain't even from 'round here. Ain't that right, boy?" he said, driving his boot once more into Elijah's side.

Elijah Hall grunted in pain and tried to turn away from his attacker. As he rolled onto his back, he saw that the four men had formed a circle around him. The headlights cast a gauzy, spectral glow on the figures as the circle tightened, only dark eyes visible through the slits in the burlap hoods they wore.

One of the men, the driver of the Buick, reached down and grabbed Elijah by the shirt, yanking him up into a half-sitting position.

"Listen here," he sneered. "We all don't need no more nigger voters in this county. And we don't need no more of your kind showin' up and makin' noise about all you niggers and your civil rights. You understand?" he said, flinging Elijah back to the ground. He kicked the preacher in the stomach and stepped away.

"We all got some civil rights, too. And one of them rights is to kick the ever-lovin' shit outta you to make sure you don't ever come back here again. Boys," he added, nodding at their prey, who was now trying to scramble away.

The two jeans-clad teens took turns planting their boots into the preacher's sides as he tried to roll away, covering his face with his arms, gasping and groaning from the force of the blows. Suddenly, the fourth attacker leaned into the scrum and stomped on the preacher's back, driving him flat onto the ground. Then he stepped back and turned toward the others.

"Stop!" he yelled. "That's enough!"

"What the fuck's your problem?" hissed one of the men, glaring at him. "You some kinda nigger lover?"

"Shit, I ain't no nigger lover," he spat. "He deserves a fuckin' beating. But y'all gonna kill him," the teen said, turning toward the leader. "And I damn sure didn't come along for no killing."

Before the leader could answer, the same teen turned and, once more lashing out with his foot, caught the groaning Elijah squarely on the side of his head. "There! He got the damn message, now leave him be. C'mon, let's go."

But, before he could move away from the twisted, writhing figure on the ground, one of the Elijah's arms suddenly shot out, grabbing the teen's leg, pulling him to the ground. Struggling to keep his balance, the teen fell sideways, slamming into Hall's car and tumbling into the drainage ditch. As he stumbled to his feet, his burlap hood slipped off and he looked directly into the fierce, defiant eyes of the beaten and bloodied preacher.

Elijah rose to his knees, swaying unsteadily, his gaze locked on the eyes of the young man who had stopped the beating.

The shotgun blast shattered the heavy silence of the muggy night.

The preacher's body pitched forward, arms splayed out, legs twitching, his head and shoulders sliding into the roadside ditch, a bloody crater gouged across his back.

"Jesus Christ!" screamed the teen, scrambling backward, his white shirt splattered with Elijah Hall's blood. He turned toward the others, his eyes searching and frightened.

The leader stepped into the milky halo of the headlights, a shotgun in his hands, tendrils of smoke curling up out of the double barrels.

"What the hell . . . ? Why'd you shoot him?" the blood-splattered teen pleaded. "We were just gonna scare him—not kill him!"

"I shot him 'cause he saw your face," the leader answered coldly.

"But he only saw *me*. Not all y'all."

"Yeah, but maybe I don't trust you to keep your damn mouth shut if he talked—and someone came lookin' for you," the shooter answered, a steely edge to his voice. He looked both ways down the empty road, and then nodded toward the body. "Leave him be. Let's get the hell outta here. Now!"

Two of the attackers jumped back into the truck while the leader raced to the Buick, pausing as he swung the car door open.

"Now!" he screamed at the fourth teen, who stood transfixed, staring down at the smoldering, crimson gash in the preacher's back. He slowly peeled his gaze away from the body and staggered back to the car.

The Buick lurched out onto the road, followed by the pickup truck. As they roared away, rain began to fall, first as a soft pattering, then a steadier thrumming, finally bursting into a raging torrent, silver sheets of water pounding down on Elijah Hall's body as jagged streaks of lightning split the dark, angry sky.

CHAPTER 1

Jackson, Mississippi
2002

The door to the liquor store creaked open and a man sauntered in, a long-barreled revolver in his hand. At first, the old man behind the counter did not bother to look up, his eyes locked on the small television screen perched next to him. The gunman quickly scanned the two narrow, packed aisles, overflowing with bottles and cases of beer. Satisfied that they were alone, he sidled up to the counter.

He was tall and rangy, dressed in jeans, scuffed cowboy boots, and a tattered hooded sweatshirt. Heavy, gray-flecked stubble covered a long face, with skin like worn leather, an angular jaw, a hawk-like nose and cold, dark eyes. Leaning over the counter, he gently nudged the clerk under the chin with the gun barrel.

"Sorry to interrupt your show there, bud, but I'm in a bit of a hurry."

The clerk, a withered and stooped old black man with a crown of tufted white hair, looked up slowly, pulling his chin carefully away from the gun. There was only a brief flash of fear in his eyes, replaced swiftly by what seemed to be defiance. He locked eyes with the gunman and spoke softly.

"What y'all want?"

"I think I'll just take everything you got in there," the gunman answered, nodding toward the cash register. "All of it. Throw it in one of them bags. And hurry it up."

The clerk shuffled over to the cash register, his eyes still locked on those of the stick-up man.

"Ain't much here," he said.

"No problem. Whatever it is, it's more'n I got right now."

Grabbing a paper bag, the clerk stuffed a handful of bills inside and tossed the bag across the counter.

"Thanks," the robber said, a big smile creasing his face as he picked up the bag. Reaching across the counter, he grabbed a bottle of Jack Daniel's, and then waved the gun in the man's face.

"Now don't go bein' no hero and do something stupid, ya hear?"

The clerk said nothing, just glared.

The scream of the sirens reached them a moment before the flashing lights came racing into the parking lot outside the store.

The would-be robber turned on the clerk. The smile gone, his face now twisted in anger.

"You call the fuckin' cops?" he screamed.

"This the third damn time this month someone tryin' to rob me. Yeah, I called the fuckin' cops," the old man said angrily, nodding toward a switch near the register. "What you gonna do now? Shoot me?"

"Hell no, I ain't gonna shoot you," the man said, his eyes frantically searching the inside of the tiny store. "You got a back door?"

"Nope. Only way out be the same way you came in."

The robber stepped behind a shelf packed with cases of beer and peered out the grime-streaked window. He counted at least three police cars outside.

"Aw, shit," he snapped. Shaking his head slowly, he tossed the paper bag on the counter, walked to the rear of the store, and sat down on the floor, his back against the wall. Twisting off the bottle cap, he took a long swig of the Jack Daniel's.

"Might as well just make myself comfortable for a spell," he said calmly to the clerk, "and enjoy some of this." He raised the bottle and took another long pull. "Don't think I'll be gettin' my hands on much of it for a while." He closed his eyes, leaned his head back, and exhaled deeply.

"Damn, Ricky Earl," he mumbled to himself, "now you fucked up big time."

Outside, two more police cars came flying into the parking lot, overheads flashing, sirens blaring.

Ricky Earl took another drink.

CHAPTER 2

"Professor?"

The young black woman's hand shot up as she peered out from behind the screen of her laptop.

The man pacing the stage of the small lecture hall looked up in the direction of the question.

"Yes?" he answered.

"I don't think I understand. How did the courts allow the Sovereignty Commission to exist?"

Professor Jefferson Trannon stopped his pacing and paused thoughtfully before answering. One of the youngest professors on the faculty of the Law School of the University of Mississippi, Trannon was a favorite of the students. He was trim and athletically built, dressed in jeans, loafers, and a white button-down shirt under a blue blazer. With long brown hair, swept back from his forehead and curling up at the collar, framing an angular, ruggedly handsome face which was highlighted by sparkling blue eyes, he looked younger than his thirty years—more like an older student than a professor.

"It was a very different time," he began, scanning the earnest young faces arrayed before him. "And Mississippi was a very different place. The Sovereignty Commission wasn't just a collection of angry racists.

It was actually an official government agency, created by statute and funded by taxpayers."

Another hand shot up. "Funded by taxes? And nobody had a problem with that?"

"Nope." Trannon paused. "Well, not most folks, anyway."

"Did anyone ever try to challenge the Commission's work?" another student asked.

The professor shook his head and shrugged. "As I said: different time, different place."

"So, Professor," a student in the first row asked, chuckling, "is this discussion some kind of a marketing tool to get us to buy your book?"

Trannon smiled. He had recently published a book about the history of the Sovereignty Commission, titled *Shades of Darkness: The Secrets of the Mississippi Sovereignty Commission*. It was a scholarly look at the creation and workings of the Commission, based on previously sealed files that were finally made public in 1998. The book was well reviewed, gaining him some notice in legal and academic circles. It had also garnered him, to his surprise, some hate mail—and even some actual threats—which, more than a year later, had finally slowed to a mere trickle.

"No, but that's not a bad idea," he said with a sheepish grin. "Might have to add it to next semester's required reading."

He looked around the lecture hall. Thirty young and searching faces peered back at him, nearly a third of them black. *Different time, different place*, he thought.

"So, here's the deal on the Commission," he said, the smile now gone. "A quick synopsis, so you don't actually need to buy my book. Established by a law passed in 1956, it was part of Mississippi's response to the Supreme Court's school desegregation ruling. You remember *Brown v. Board of Education*? Not a very popular decision down here back then, as you might've guessed. Anyway, the Commission's function—at least, officially—was to 'protect the sovereignty of the State of Mississippi.'"

Another raised hand. "What did that mean, 'protect the sovereignty'?"

"Well, theoretically, their mission was to keep the federal government out of Mississippi's business. And that sounded fine, especially in a place where the notion of states' rights is so revered. But in practice—well, the mission wasn't so politically noble. The bottom line is that the real job of the Commission was to preserve segregation—by any means necessary."

"But how could a government agency get away with that? Even back then?" asked a young black man from the center of the room.

"Because it was just that—a government agency. The governor acted as chairman and the attorney general and a bunch of state legislators were part of the Commission. Plus, the state provided a budget of about a quarter-million dollars a year—or more than one and a half million dollars in today's money."

"For what?" came a question from the back of the room. "What *exactly* did they do?"

"Well, for starters, the Commission created a vast network of spies and informers. Staff members included a number of former cops, state police, and even some FBI guys. Their job was to track down and keep an eye on so-called 'racial agitators' and others who supported desegregation. But it didn't stop there. Sometimes 'keeping an eye on someone' turned into harassment, threats, and even violence."

"And they got away with that?"

"The Commission was so powerful and its connections to local law enforcement and government so strong—" Trannon paused and looked around the lecture hall, "—that it simply did whatever it wanted. And nobody asked any questions. At least, nobody who was in a position to do anything about it." Shrugging his shoulders, he added, with a rueful half-smile, "Hard to imagine in this post-Watergate, cable news, Internet world. No questions asked."

"So, what happened to it?" asked the young black woman who had started the discussion.

"Finally, as the civil rights movement gained some traction, it became just too much of an embarrassment—even for Mississippi. Funding got cut in 1973, and the Commission officially shut down in 1977. But state lawmakers ordered all of its files sealed until 2027."

"How could they do that?" the young black woman erupted angrily.

The professor shrugged again. "As I said before: different time, different place. But the ACLU and some other organizations decided to jump in. After a decades-long court battle, most of the records were unsealed in 1998."

"Most?" someone asked. "How come not all?"

"Good question. Not entirely sure of the answer. The federal judge who issued the order to unseal the files—more than 130,000 documents, by the way," he flashed another rueful smile, "I know because I looked through most of them—held back information on forty-two people. The judge's order kept their names and information secret until they die. But with no explanation of why. Kind of mysterious, isn't it?"

"Was anybody ever prosecuted?" asked another voice from the back of the room.

"Nope. The really nasty stuff—murders, beatings, burnings—could never be proven. There were always stories and rumors, but nobody would ever come forward to testify. And most of the major players are dead now. So the Sovereignty Commission has receded into the past, just another ugly footnote in the chronicle of the civil rights struggle."

"That sounds pretty good. Is that the last line in your book?" asked a grinning front-row student.

"No. But it does sound pretty good, doesn't it? Have to remember that if there's ever a second edition," Trannon said, grinning back at him. "Okay, folks, that does it for today," he said. "Make sure I hear from you soon about paper topics. See all y'all next week."

As he was gathering up his notes, Trannon was quickly surrounded by several students.

"Hey, Professor," said a young man, who had the square, solid build of an athlete. "We've got a flag-football game Thursday afternoon against the business school geeks. You in?"

Trannon looked up, cocked an eyebrow, and seemed to ponder the question. "We got anybody in this law school with a better arm than that chicken-wing of yours?" he asked good-naturedly.

"'Chicken-wing'?" exclaimed the young man in mock indignation. "Man, with your over-the-hill wheels you could run for two days and still not outrun this cannon," he said, flexing his right bicep.

Trannon chuckled. "Okay, Robert. I'm in."

"Great. See you then," the young man said as he hustled out of the classroom.

"Professor?" Two of the female students—one black and one white—who had been so curious about the Sovereignty Commission, approached. "We've got a favor to ask," they said in unison, broad, slightly flirtatious smiles splayed across their faces. "We're in charge of the job opportunities symposium next month," one of them said, "and we're hoping we can get you to be on the panel? And to come to the cocktail party the night before?"

"Happy to help out," he said, being careful to keep his return smile as professional as possible. "Just get me the details."

"Thanks so much," said one.

"See you next week," said the other as they both backed out of the room, still beaming.

Glancing at his watch, Trannon grabbed his notes, stuffed them into an old leather satchel, and rushed out the door.

CHAPTER 3

The cramped, cluttered office was not much bigger than a storage room. A small wooden desk was wedged into a corner, surrounded by bookshelves stuffed with legal texts, case books, and what seemed like reams of loose paper, some cascading down to the floor. Two diplomas from the University of Mississippi—one from the college and the other from the law school—were hung on the windowless walls, together with a photo of the 1992 Ole Miss football team and a framed copy of the book cover of *Shades of Darkness*.

Jeff Trannon tossed his satchel onto the chair and grabbed the handful of phone messages that had been left on his desk. A slightly perplexed frown creased his face as he read one of them. The message was from a *New York Times* reporter who wanted to speak with him about his book. Funny, he thought, that a reporter would want to talk with him at this point—more than a year after the book came out.

Damn, Trannon thought, looking at his watch, *I'm going to be late.* He stuffed the messages into his jacket pocket and hurried out of the office. Moments later, he emerged from the front doors of the building and took off at a jog across the Grove, the legendarily beautiful center of the Ole Miss campus.

The University of Mississippi had been home to Jeff Trannon for nearly a third of his life. He was born and raised in the surrounding town of Oxford, and it was the only college he had ever dreamed of attending. A local high school football star, he happily snatched up a scholarship offer to play for his hometown Rebels and enjoyed a modestly successful career, playing in every game his last two years as a wide receiver and special teams standout. Following graduation, he stayed on at the law school, where he worked his way onto the *Law Review* and graduated with honors.

Spurning offers from some of the more prestigious law firms in the state, he instead took a job as a prosecutor in the local district attorney's office. By the time he left the job five years later, he had developed a reputation as a tough, but fair, prosecutor—well liked by the cops, judges, and even the defense lawyers he worked with. A year with a big firm in Jackson had quickly convinced him he wasn't cut out for private practice, with all of its hourly billings and internal politics. So he came back home to Oxford and the law school at Ole Miss. Although there were times that he missed the inside of a courtroom, he had to admit to himself that he had quickly fallen in love with teaching and writing.

As he emerged on the far side of the Grove, he could see that a crowd had gathered outside of the Lyceum, the main administrative center, and the geographic and historic heart of the university. Erected in 1848, it was the university's first building. An elegant and stunning Ionic Greek Revival structure, the portico fronting the red-brick façade was guarded by an array of six enormous fluted columns, with a mirror-image six more columns gracing the rear. Although much of the town of Oxford, including the courthouse, had been burned by Union troops in 1864, the Lyceum and the other university buildings had been spared the torch by serving as hospital facilities for Union forces.

Arriving at the front of the Lyceum, Jeff joined the crowd as it snaked around the building toward the rear. As he turned the corner, he spied the dean of the law school standing in the front of the gathering, near the podium, waving and gesturing to an empty seat next to him. Weaving his way through the crowd, Jeff reached the front row and settled into the empty seat.

The dean, a dapper man dressed in a seersucker suit, sat down next to him, offering a small, ironic smile.

"Glad you could make it."

"Sorry," Jeff offered somewhat guiltily. "Class ran a little late."

Glancing around, Jeff saw that about two hundred people were assembled around a monument that featured a life-sized sculpture of James Meredith, the courageous young man who, in 1962, had been the first black student to enroll at Ole Miss. Most were milling about, talking, while others had already claimed their seats.

Turning back toward the dean, Jeff noticed an attractive young woman standing near the Meredith statue. She appeared to be examining the quotes inscribed in the marble walls of the memorial and scribbling into a reporter's spiral notepad. As he strained to get a better look at her through the shifting crowd, an official stepped up to the podium.

"Ladies and gentlemen," he said, leaning into the microphone. "Please take your seats. The ceremony is about to start."

CHAPTER 4

The University of Mississippi has played a unique role in the passion play that has been the civil rights movement in the Deep South. In 1962, it found itself at the epicenter of the shocking violence that marked that movement, at once both the face and voice of decades of racial anger, intolerance, and fear that were woven throughout the fabric of Dixie.

The segregationist South was reeling in 1962, buffeted by the winds of change ushered in by a parade of legal decisions fueling the increasingly active struggle for racial equality. Following the 1954 decision by the United States Supreme Court outlawing segregation in public schools, small legal skirmishes were giving way to actual pitched battles as civil rights opponents fought to prevent the Court's pronouncement from becoming a reality.

One of those pitched battles took place before the gracious, historic columns of the Lyceum in late September and early October of 1962. When the smoke, quite literally, cleared, two people had been killed, twenty-eight United States Marshals had been shot and wounded, dozens of other law enforcement personnel had been injured by tossed bricks, bottles, even Molotov cocktails—and the first black man to be enrolled in Ole Miss's history had walked up the Lyceum steps, passed through the sacred columns, and entered the tradition-bound symbolic heart of the university.

James Meredith was an Air Force veteran who sought to be the first to shatter the racial barrier at Ole Miss. Following a protracted legal battle, which was ultimately resolved in his favor by the United States Supreme Court, and due to the continued resistance by the Governor of Mississippi, Meredith needed the help of federal forces to compel the school to honor the law and allow his admission. He then spent two tormented semesters on campus, harassed by many and shunned by nearly all, before graduating in August of 1963.

Looking around him, Jeff was struck by the irony of it all. Here they were, gathering to celebrate the courage of James Meredith, at the same site where many had gathered in an attempt to frighten him off—and even kill him—during those turbulent and troubled days in 1962. *Different time, different place*, he thought, yet again.

A hush came over the crowd as the Chancellor of the university stepped up to the microphone. In many ways, the Chancellor was the living embodiment of the path that his university had traveled over the past decades. A big man, he had been a stalwart on some of the great Ole Miss football teams during the late 1950s and early 1960s. Although raised in the era of Southern athletic and social segregation, it was his vision and leadership that had helped transform the university, in one of the great historical ironies, from the smoldering center of anti-integration fervor into a beacon of racial harmony and reconciliation.

"I want to thank you all," he said, scanning the crowd, "for joining us today as we gather to remember an important time in our history, both as a university and as a nation. It was forty years ago that a courageous young man defied the time and the tides of hatred by walking into this building and declaring that he would not be moved. James Meredith taught us then about the virtues of honor and perseverance and justice. And he also taught us a great deal about patience and forgiveness, as he endured the trials and tribulations of his difficult time as a student here.

"But we have learned much from his teachings, though the learning process was often painfully slow. You only need to stroll today across this beautiful campus, which means so much to so many of us, to witness the true integration—not just of color but of culture and spirit—that is the legacy of James Meredith." He paused for the applause that rang out from those before him.

"We gather here today to celebrate yet another step in the journey begun by that one man some forty years ago. Today, we come together to announce a substantial gift to the Institute for Racial Reconciliation, which, as you know, has been a leading force—since its inception—in the study of our past and the important racial dialogue leading into our future. This generous gift will allow the Institute to expand its facilities and, as a consequence, expand the scope and quality of its programs as it heads into the next decade of the twenty-first century." Again, applause.

Looking around the crowd, the Chancellor spotted Jefferson Trannon and nodded in his direction.

"Before I introduce our most gracious benefactor, I want to note the presence of a special guest. The name of William Trannon is one that every Ole Miss Rebel, young or old, recognizes. One of our all-time football greats, an exceptional lawyer, a former dean of our law school, and the youngest-ever chief justice of the Mississippi Supreme Court, William Trannon was one of the early champions of civil rights in this state. His wisdom, and his great courage—in the face of scorn and even violence—were responsible for vast changes in the legal landscape that helped to usher in the laws that allowed the civil rights movement to take root and flourish. He is, indeed, one of the greatest leaders of this university and this state. Although Justice Trannon could not be with us today, his son, Jefferson Trannon—who we are proud to have on the faculty of the law school—is here representing his father."

There was an earnest wave of applause as Jeff rose and, with a raised hand, acknowledged the Chancellor and the crowd.

"Jeff, please extend our best wishes to your father and let him know that we all look forward to seeing him again soon. Actually, we could probably use him on the field this Saturday when Alabama comes to town," the Chancellor said to laughter from the crowd.

"Now," the Chancellor said, raising his hands to quiet the gathering, "I'm honored to introduce the man whose generosity is the reason for our celebration today. Senator Tillman Jessup has served in the legislature of the great state of Mississippi—as did his father and grandfather before him—for more than two decades. And," he added with a smile, "if what we've all been hearing lately is true, he'll be continuing that service from the governor's mansion fairly soon." Another burst of applause. "During all of this time, he has worked tirelessly to improve the lives of every citizen. Also during this time, he and his family have made significant donations to various social and academic causes, once again doing their best to improve the quality of life in our state. Although Senator Jessup chose to attend that other university over in Starkville," the Chancellor said with a chuckle, "we here at Ole Miss have, nevertheless, always looked at him as family. And so, we're delighted today to introduce, with our deep thanks, an esteemed and generous member of our family—Ladies and gentlemen, Senator Tillman Jessup!"

Rising from his seat in the front row, Senator Jessup waved to the crowd, acknowledging the hearty applause, as he walked to the podium and shook hands with the Chancellor. He was a tall, thick-bodied, square-faced man with a florid complexion and light brown, wavy hair that was just beginning to surrender to touches of gray at the temples. Dressed in an expensive dark suit, with a white shirt, bright red tie, and matching red handkerchief flowing from his breast pocket, he looked every bit the rich, successful Southern politician.

"Thank you, Chancellor, for those very kind words," he said in a deep, easy drawl, smiling at the crowd. "My wife, Kendra Leigh, and I, as always, are delighted to be back here at Ole Miss and to be a part of this celebration." He nodded toward his wife sitting in the front row. "As everybody knows, she's not only the beauty but also the brains of this marriage. As the Chancellor noted, I got my degree from Mississippi State but she—," he shot a glowing smile her way, "—she was the smart one. A Rebel cheerleader, president of the Tri-Delts, and the Ole Miss Homecoming Queen her senior year—I certainly married well!" he said to an explosion of laughter and good-natured applause.

Kendra Leigh Jessup, stylishly ultra-thin, dressed in a severely tailored blush rose-colored suit, her blond hair swept up and framing a face that easily conjured up the beauty of a '60s campus queen, turned slightly and offered a quick, imperious wave to the gathering.

"We're happy," he continued in a more solemn tone, "to play our small part in advancing the work of this fine institution. As we look at this monument to James Meredith, we're reminded of a dark time in our history. But we're also reminded of the progress we've made, not just here at Ole Miss but throughout this great state of ours. Thank you, then, to the staff of the Institute for Reconciliation for their devotion and hard work in advancing this cause. And thank you to all of you who have gathered here today to make your voices heard in this continuing struggle."

Smiling and waving, Jessup made his way back to his seat and joined his wife.

"Shortest speech I've ever heard from him," Jeff whispered to the dean.

"Don't worry," the dean replied quietly. "You can be sure he's not finished working this crowd."

After a few more words from the Chancellor and the President of the Institute, the event wrapped up. Many of the attendees drifted off toward the steps of the Lyceum where a cocktail bar had been set up.

Jeff was wandering through the maze of guests, hoping to locate the attractive woman he'd seen near the monument, when he heard his name called. Turning, he saw Senator Jessup approaching, his wife following a few steps behind.

"Good to see you again, Jeff," Jessup said, grasping Trannon's hand and delivering a hearty clap to his shoulder.

"Good to see you too, Senator."

"You remember Kendra Leigh?"

"Yes, indeed. Nice to see you again, ma'am."

Mrs. Jessup responded with what struck Trannon as a rather empty, uninterested smile, especially for a politician's wife, and offered a brief handshake. She began to say something, but was cut off by the booming voice of her husband.

"So, how's the ol' judge doing?"

"He's doing fine, sir. Thank you for asking."

"Well, you make sure you tell him that Kendra Leigh and I were asking for him."

"I certainly will. I know he'll be glad to hear that."

Turning to his wife, Jessup said, "You remember what his daddy did to us his senior year? A one-man wrecking crew," he said, turning back toward Trannon. "State had a pretty good team that year, but 'Fast Willie' just turned that game into a track meet. Had three long touchdown runs—and another called back. Your daddy sure could run," he said, shaking his head. "Fastest boy—colored or white—I ever saw on a football field."

"Yes, sir. I've heard quite a lot about that game over the years." Jeff smiled. "Especially from you State folks."

"Well," Jessup said, nodding and smiling to someone over

Trannon's shoulder as he grabbed his wife's arm. "You be sure to send him our regards."

"I will," Jeff answered, but by the time the words were out of his mouth the senator had moved on to jovial handshakes with a new group of admirers.

Jeff worked his way through the crowd, politely fielding questions and greetings for his father, and then circled around to the front of the Lyceum and headed off toward his office.

CHAPTER 5

The lawyer glanced up from the file in front of him as the door to the cramped cinder-block conference room swung open. A burly, unfriendly-looking guard filled the doorway, and then stepped aside as a prisoner, clad in an orange jumpsuit, stepped into the room. Shuffling, in that manner peculiar to jail inmates, his feet clad in white socks and blue shower sandals, the prisoner ambled over to the small metal table in the center of the room and dropped into the plastic chair across from the lawyer.

"Mr. Graves," the lawyer said, struggling to lift his bulk out of the chair as he extended his hand. As he stood, the prisoner could tell that the lawyer was short, easily fifty pounds overweight, and stuffed into an ill-fitting, worn blue suit. "I'm Travis Murray. I've been assigned to represent you."

"Well, ain't this your lucky damn day," the prisoner chuckled, grasping the lawyer's hand. "I go by Ricky Earl."

"Okay, Ricky Earl," Murray nodded, scanning some papers in the folder. "Why don't we get started by talking about these charges? Says here that you walked into a liquor store, pulled a gun, and robbed the guy behind the counter." He looked up. "True?"

"Yep, pretty much," Ricky Earl answered.

"Any reason?"

"Just needed some money," he shrugged. "Been seriously strung out for a while. Thought I'd make a quick hit and get outta town." He shrugged again. "Didn't count on the old man bein' some kinda fuckin' hero."

"Okay," Murray said, scribbling some notes on a yellow legal pad. "Well then," he looked up, "here's our biggest problem. I talked to the prosecutor's office this morning. Wanted to get some idea what they were looking for to make this go away. Afraid the news isn't good."

"Didn't think it would be. So, what's the bottom line?"

"The bottom line is . . . they're looking to max you out. Life, no parole."

Ricky Earl was silent for a moment. "No chance to carve off some time?"

"Nope. Seems they got a bit of a hard-on for you. Guess it has something to do with your sheet," he said, holding up a computer printout. "Fifteen priors tend to get prosecutors a little riled up."

"Actually, it's only thirteen, but then who's really counting?" Ricky Earl smirked. "No help that the gun wasn't loaded and I gave up without a problem?"

"Sorry. I tried all of those arguments but no dice. Unless you've got something really good that we can bargain with," Murray held up his hands in a gesture of surrender, "there's not much that we can do except plead for some mercy at sentencing."

"What's the chance of that?"

"Honestly? Not much, I'm afraid. We drew a real hard-ass judge and you're, unfortunately, way past 'three strikes and you're out.' Wish I had better news, but by now you know how the game's played."

Ricky Earl was silent for a long moment, looking off into the distance.

"Ricky Earl? You okay?"

His eyes slowly came back into focus. "Yeah. Sure. Not like I wasn't expecting this," he answered, lost in his thoughts.

"So, what should I tell them? You want to plead and take our chances? Hope that by saving them from a trial we just might catch a little break?"

Ricky Earl again didn't seem to hear.

Murray leaned closer across the table. "Ricky Earl?"

"Yeah, sorry. Just thinking," he said softly, leaning back in his chair, folding his arms across his chest. "I'm gonna need a little time to sort this all out. That okay?"

"Well," Murray answered, gathering up his file and stuffing it into a briefcase, "I guess they'll be all right with a few more days, given what you're looking at." He slid his card across the table. "Call me next week with your answer. But don't wait too long. We don't want to piss them off any more than they already are. Okay?"

"Sure," Ricky Earl answered, picking up the lawyer's card and slipping it into his pocket.

CHAPTER 6

North Lamar Boulevard in Oxford, Mississippi, is a gracious vestige of the Old South, a broad, leafy street marked by large, elegant old homes adorned with graceful porches and majestic columns. The street radiates out from the center of Oxford and has long been—together with its sibling, South Lamar Boulevard—home to the upper echelon of the Oxford community.

Jeff Trannon had taken the short walk from the campus and had paused before one of the more grand structures, a three-story mansion with striking pillars and wide verandas wrapping around the front and sides of a home that seemed right off the movie set of *Gone with the Wind*. Its breathtaking beauty was marred only by a rather odd blemish—a corner of the veranda apparently damaged by some long-ago fire, the old charred, unrepaired remnants visible even from the street. This was Jeff Trannon's boyhood home. Indeed, it had been the home to three generations of Trannons and was still the residence of his father, the revered retired chief justice of the Mississippi Supreme Court.

Jeff strolled up the long walkway, took the steps two at a time, and pushed open the massive oak door. The interior was of classic Southern plantation-style design with a wide center hall running from the front to the rear of the house, a sweeping staircase on the right followed by a series of French doors lining the hallway that opened into an expansive living room, a smaller sitting room, a music room, and a library. Beyond these rooms, the hall emptied into a large kitchen that ran along the rear veranda.

A woman, wearing a housedress and apron, peered around the corner from the kitchen and smiled when she saw him in the hallway. She was petite and elegant, her charcoal hair, shot through with streaks of white, was pulled tightly back in a bun, framing a round, soft face with skin the color of caramel. Elizabeth Worthington had been with the Trannons as long as Jeff could remember, not just a part of the home, but also a part of the family. Although, with her unlined face and refined carriage, she appeared to be in her fifties, Jeff was certain that she was at least in her mid-seventies, perhaps even older. Since the death of Jeff's mother after a long illness, and the retirement of his father, she had become even more of a presence inside the rambling old home.

"Hey, Jefferson," she said, welcoming him with a warm smile and a pat on the cheek. Since his mother had passed away, Elizabeth was now the only person who always called him by his full name. "Didn't know y'all were dropping by this afternoon. Everything okay?"

"Fine," he answered, bending over to give her a quick kiss on the cheek. "Just came from a reception up at the college and thought I'd drop in on Dad. Lots of people were asking for him."

"That's nice," she said, wheeling and heading back toward the kitchen. "He's in the library."

"How's he doing today?" Jeff called after her.

"About the same," she answered, disappearing around the corner.

Jeff crossed the hall and pushed open the doors to the library. Stepping inside, he thought about how he'd always loved this room, with its immense marble fireplace, flanked by oak-paneled walls and carved bookshelves. Once, as a child, he'd tried to count all the books stuffed into every corner of the shelves, but gave up as he neared one thousand, wondering if even the great man—his father—had actually read all of them. More than any other part of the house, this room would always be what he recalled when he thought of his father. The books everywhere, the tidy desk with stacks of papers and legal pads and sharpened pencils, all arranged carefully and in a specific pattern like pieces on a chessboard, reflecting both the wide-ranging curiosity and the precise intellect that had made his father such a commanding figure as a lawyer and a judge.

William Trannon was sitting in a tufted leather wing chair in front of a broad window, looking out on the big magnolia trees guarding the side yard. Jeff crossed the room quickly and patted his father tenderly on the shoulder.

"Hey, Dad. How you doing?" he said gently.

His father, dressed as usual in charcoal-gray slacks, blue blazer, and white button-down shirt with a crimson and blue striped tie, stared quietly out the window. A sad smile creased Jeff's face as he dropped into the matching wing chair next to his father.

It was barely three years ago when Jeff began to notice the changes in his father. At first, they were not terribly alarming—a name forgotten, a story repeated, an appointment missed. Just normal signs of getting older, Jeff had thought. But then the embarrassing events seemed to come more rapidly and were more obvious. And soon the whispers began. Stories of confusion during judicial conferences, embarrassing lapses during conversations, and, finally, an episode of such bewilderment on the bench during an oral argument that a judicial colleague ordered a recess. When the hearing resumed, the chief justice's chair was empty.

The downward spiral had been swift and merciless. William Trannon—legendary athlete, brilliant scholar, ardent advocate, wise jurist, and paragon of all things good and noble—had Alzheimer's disease. His days were now spent in a chair, staring aimlessly, that imposing mind imprisoned in an enveloping shroud of confusion. He spoke rarely and only offered all-too-brief flashes of recognition of family and friends.

Jeff had made it a regular part of his schedule to visit often. He would talk with—or, more precisely, *at*—his father about current events and legal news and what his old friends were up to. He no longer expected any real reaction from his father to any of those stories, and he rarely received any. But surprisingly—and, Jeff thought, perhaps miraculously—the only subject that ever elicited a reaction from his father, even if it was merely a widening of his eyes or a slight nod of the head, was talk of the Ole Miss football team.

"So, Dad," Jeff began, leaning over to intersect his father's unfocused gaze, "Alabama's comin' to town this Saturday." No reaction. "They're pretty good this year," Jeff continued. "Got a new coach and he's got 'em playing like the Bear's old teams."

And then, for a brief moment, at the mention of the legendary Alabama coach, Bear Bryant, there was a spark in his father's eyes, some flicker of awareness, at once both tantalizing and heartbreaking, that whisked across his face and then vanished, like a glimpse of summer lightning on the far horizon.

"Could be a good game," Jeff continued. "We looked real solid last week. New quarterback's coming along and the defense's been playing well. Game's on television, so I'll remind Elizabeth to put it on for you." He made a mental note to do so, as he followed his father's gaze out through the window.

"Just came from the college," Jeff offered after a few silent minutes had passed. "A ceremony up at the Lyceum outside by the Meredith memorial."

As he mentioned James Meredith, Jeff glanced over to a framed photo that hung on the wall next to the fireplace. It had always seemed odd to Jeff that, with all of his father's honors and accomplishments, only two photos graced his library walls. One was of the 1962 Ole Miss national championship football team—his father, the number twenty-seven emblazoned in white on his blue jersey, seated in the first row. The other was a grainy black and white newspaper photo of a young James Meredith sitting in an Ole Miss classroom, surrounded by a sea of vacant desks—except for one. The lone student sharing the resounding emptiness of the classroom with Meredith was a young, earnest, and determined-looking William Trannon.

"Lot of folks showed up for the ceremony. Had to sit through some speeches, but it wasn't too bad. The Chancellor even suggested that we could still use you on the field Saturday," Jeff chuckled. "Anyway, they all were asking for you."

Jeff looked over, searching for a response, knowing there would be none. Finally, he sighed deeply, sat back in his chair, and shared the silence with his father.

CHAPTER 7

The attack came from behind, without warning. First, a swift, crushing punch to the kidneys sent Ricky Earl Graves stumbling to his hands and knees. Then a fusillade of fists and feet drove him sprawling to the ground. He tried to roll away, wrapping his elbows protectively around his head, searching for some escape from the hammering blows. But the cordon of furious black men only tightened around him, flailing away at their target.

Then, just as suddenly as the beating had started, it was over. The attackers rapidly melted back into the receding throng of other inmates in the prison recreation yard.

A pair of prison guards jogged over to the bloody figure still writhing in pain in the dirt. While one guard was calling the medical unit on his radio, the second rolled Graves over. Both eyes were already nearly swollen shut and blood streamed from his mouth and nose.

"Just stay still. You'll be okay," the guard said, scanning the yard. "What's an old man like you doin' beefin' with them black boys?"

"I ain't beefin' with nobody," Graves mumbled, spitting out a mouthful of blood.

"Then what the fuck was that all about?" the guard asked.

"Somebody told them niggers that I used to be in the Klan. They been threatenin' to kick my ass ever since." Graves groaned, pain streaking up from his damaged ribs as he struggled to take a breath. "Fuckers finally got me."

"Got ya pretty good, too," the guard said. "Don't you go tryin' to move till the doc gets here."

"Think I'll be able to park in the medical wing and away from them fuckers for a while?"

"Probably, by the looks of you. But not forever," the guard answered. "Some advice? Most of the assholes in here don't give a shit if you was in the Klan or not. Some might even think you're a hero, if you were. But if *those* boys think you're KKK," he nodded toward a group of black prisoners now watching intently from across the yard, "then you better get yourself some friends to watch your back."

"Ain't got no friends in here," Graves said, his words thick and slow through his bloodied lips.

"Well then," the guard answered, "you just better find some someplace. Before we go carryin' you outta here in a pine box."

CHAPTER 8

"So," Jeff said, both surprised and pleased, "didn't I see you yesterday at the memorial ceremony outside the Lyceum?"

The woman sitting on the other side of his desk inclined her head slightly and nodded. She didn't look at all like the hard-edged, big-city journalist Jeff had expected when he had agreed to an interview with the *New York Times* reporter who had called him again that morning. And he certainly hadn't expected his interviewer to be the same woman he'd found so intriguing at the previous day's ceremony. She was dressed in a conservative dark skirt and matching jacket. A waterfall of thick, curly, auburn hair cascaded down to her shoulders, surrounding a pretty, oval face, with high cheekbones and radiant, penetrating green eyes flanking the only imperfection in an otherwise striking appearance: a slightly crooked nose, sprinkled with freckles, that looked like it might have been broken sometime in her past.

"So then, why were you there? And why this interest in the Sovereignty Commission?" Jeff asked, thinking that she was even more attractive up close than she had appeared from a distance.

"And I thought *I* was the one who was doing the interview," Ella Garrity said, through a small, playful smile.

"Sorry," Jeff said. "I don't often get a request from a paper like the *New York Times* to talk about my book. Just wondering why a reporter would want to come all the way down here to interview me."

"Fair question," she nodded. "I'm working on a series about race relations in Mississippi, a kind of 'then-and-now' look at where the state's been and what kind of progress has been made. That's why I was at the ceremony yesterday. And I'd come across your book when I was doing some research on the Sovereignty Commission and thought your observations might be helpful."

"Happy to help out. First off, how much do you know about the Commission? I don't want to bore you with stuff you already know."

"Well, I do know a good bit about its history and structure. I'm actually from Mississippi."

"Really?"

"Why so surprised?"

"Don't know," he shrugged. "I guess when I think about the *New York Times* I don't think of reporters from Mississippi. How'd you end up there?"

"I went to college up north—"

"Where 'up north'?" Jeff interrupted.

"Yale."

Jeff raised an eyebrow and nodded, impressed. "So we couldn't keep you down on the farm?"

"Afraid my folks were intent on sending me away. And it was quite an adventure for a little girl from a small town down in the Delta. Don't get me wrong, I loved Yale. But a part of me did miss tailgates, sundresses, and football games down South," she added.

"Guess it really is in the blood," Jeff said, warming up to her.

"Guess it is," she said, the hint of a wistful smile momentarily appearing. "Anyway, after graduation I knew I wanted to be a writer so I took the first newspaper job that would have me. Wrote community news and obituaries for a small weekly in Connecticut. Then I caught on with the *New Haven Register* and, after a few years there and some stories that got noticed, I found my way to the *Times*."

"Pretty impressive resume," Jeff said. "Especially for someone so young."

"I'm actually quite a bit older than I look," Ella shot back, her emerald eyes sparking, clearly not delighted by the reference to her age.

"Sorry," Jeff replied quickly, raising his hands defensively. "Didn't mean that as any kind of criticism. Actually meant it as a compliment."

"No problem," Ella answered, the flash of annoyance extinguished as quickly as it had appeared. "Anyway, getting back to the Sovereignty Commission, I was especially curious about whether you had talked to anyone associated with it when you were doing your research."

"Not too many of them left, I'm afraid," Jeff said, shaking his head. "Found a few still alive, but they were mostly just clerks and secretaries who'd been pretty young when they worked there. Couldn't really give me any details or background on the work the Commission did. Most of my research came from the documents."

Ella nodded. "I had the same results." She paused a moment, then leaned forward. "Did you ever hear anything about any so-called 'investigators'? Guys that did the dirty work?"

"Yeah, I heard a lot about them. And found some names in the documents, too. But none of them are still alive, at least none that I could find."

Ella leaned back in her chair, her lips pursed, quiet for a moment.

"Why're you asking about investigators?" Jeff asked. "Did you find any?"

"No. Not yet, anyway."

"Do you have some leads? Someone who's still alive?" Jeff asked.

"Not really a lead. More like just a rumor. About a former investigator who's still around but doesn't want to be found."

"Any details?"

"Not really. Heard the rumor from a couple of different sources. But nothing concrete. Both thought that the guy had made it clear a long time ago that he didn't want to talk. *Ever.* To anyone. Apparently, he may be one of the bad guys who knows where a lot of skeletons are still buried."

"Literally?"

"Maybe. Who knows? But I'd love to track him down and ask."

Jeff leaned back in his chair, his fingers steepled in front of his face, and thought a moment. "Why do you think he'd even meet with you—if he's still alive—much less actually talk with you?"

"Can't hurt to try. Worst-case scenario is he refuses to see us."

"'Us'?" Jeff asked, shooting her a quizzical glance.

"I thought, given your interest in the Commission, you'd jump at the chance to talk with someone who was on the inside. Also," she said, flashing her most engaging smile, "I could use your help trying to find him. Figured you know your way around."

Jeff looked at her carefully, considering her request, and then nodded slowly. "Okay, I'm in."

"Great," she said, as the smile faded quickly, now all business again. "So, where do you suggest we start?"

"I'll reach out to some law enforcement folks I know. See if we can find any new leads. And we should take another look at some of the Commission documents. Did anybody mention a name?"

"Just one. Thought it might be something like Hollingsworth or Hollingsly."

"Well, at least that gives us something to run with."

"Hopefully." She paused a moment. "One more question?"

"Sure."

"Thomas or Davis?"

Jeff looked at her, puzzled.

"Which one are you named after—Thomas Jefferson or Jefferson Davis?"

Jeff chuckled. "Neither, I'm afraid. Named after my grandfather. Although my guess is, as an old and proud Mississippian, he'd probably have said Davis."

"Sorry, just my reporter's curiosity. Although some people might call it nosiness.

"And, by the way," she added, a brow arched and a twinkle in her eyes, "you don't look that old yourself. For a professor."

"Okay, okay. My apologies again." Jeff raised his hands in mock surrender. "I promise—no more mention of anyone's age."

CHAPTER 9

"I wanna make a deal."

Travis Murray looked up from Ricky Earl Graves's file, puzzled. "Make a deal? What're you talking about? You already pled out and got sentenced."

Graves leaned across the visiting room table toward his lawyer, his eyes and lips still bruised and swollen, his face crisscrossed by stitches. "I gotta get outta here."

"Ricky Earl, we talked about this when we first met. That was the time for you to come up with something to trade with the prosecutor. But you said you had nothing. And, given your record, you would've needed some pretty good shit to work any kind of real deal. We're just lucky the judge didn't max you out."

"Yeah, real fuckin' lucky," Graves sneered. "If I live to be eighty-five and catch a break from the parole board I might get over the wall and get to die all alone in some fleabag motel. Some fuckin' luck."

"So why're we having this conversation now?"

"Because I don't wanna die in here. And I sure as hell don't wanna die with some jailhouse nigger's shiv stuck in my gut."

"Look, I understand," the lawyer said, a note of sympathy in his voice. "But it's too late. Your case is done. Unless you miraculously come up with some big-time information, there's really nothing more

I can do for you."

"Well, that's the thing," Graves said, lowering his voice even though they were alone in the prison visiting room. "I happen to have some pretty big-fuckin'-deal information. And now I'm ready to trade."

"Okay. So tell me what you've got," Murray said, not sounding the least bit convinced.

"It's about a murder," Graves answered.

"What murder?"

"An old murder. Back in the sixties."

"Give me details," Murray said, pulling out a legal pad.

"A nigger preacher got killed tryin' to get other niggers to register to vote. Happened outside Oxford. Got a lot of publicity but nobody was ever charged. Never even had any suspects."

"And how do you know about the killing?" Murray asked, scribbling notes on his pad.

"'Cause I was there."

The lawyer's head shot up. "You were there when he was killed?"

"Yup."

"Did you kill him?" the lawyer asked quietly.

"Nope. But I saw it happen."

"So, who was the killer?"

A wicked smile crossed Graves's face. "Well, ya see, that's the big-fuckin'-deal information that's gonna get me outta here."

"Maybe. But we're talking about a long time ago. Who knows if there's still any interest in a cold civil rights murder case?"

"There'll be plenty of interest in this case. Trust me."

"Why're you so sure?"

Graves smiled again. "Because the killer of that nigger preacher is the same man who's gonna be the next governor of the state of Mississippi."

CHAPTER 10

"Tillman Jessup? He's the killer?" Murray asked, shocked.

"Yup. Tillman Jessup's the one killed that preacher. Back in '60. And now they say he's a shoo-in to be the next governor." Ricky Earl chuckled. "Ain't that gonna surprise a shitload of people!"

The lawyer dropped his pen and leaned closer to his client. "Ricky Earl, you bullshittin' me about this?"

"No, sir. This the God's honest truth. Ol' Tillman's the one pulled the trigger and wasted that nigger."

"And you were there? You saw the whole thing?"

"Yes, sir. Was standin' right there next to him when he fired. Like to scare the shit outta me."

"Okay then, let's back up a little," Murray said, picking up his pen and scribbling furiously on his pad. "Tell me how it happened. Everything."

"Well, a bunch of us was just hangin' 'round drinkin' beers and bullshittin'—"

"How many of you were there?" the lawyer interrupted.

"At first there was a whole gang, maybe ten or twelve," said Graves, his gaze shifting away from the lawyer and focusing on something off in the distant past. "Most of us just got out of high school and we was all just hangin' 'round a barbeque joint shootin' the shit, lookin' to pick up girls. Anyway, by the end of the night there was just four of us left. Me and one a my buddies, and Jessup and another guy. We kinda knew each other from school but we wasn't real close-like with them."

"Wait a second," the lawyer demanded, looking up from his writing. "Who were the other two guys?"

Graves shook his head slowly. "That ain't important now. My buddy and the other kid ain't with us no more so they ain't gonna be no help."

"But if we're going to convince a prosecutor that you're telling the truth, they're going to want to know who else was there."

"Nope," Graves said, shaking his head sternly now. "I ain't gonna bring those boys' names into this. They ain't with us and there ain't no reason for their families to be troubled now after all these years. Ain't gonna do it."

"Okay, well, we'll deal with that issue down the road if we need to." Murray scribbled another note, and then looked up. "So who came up with the plan to kill him?"

"Shit, we never planned on him gettin' killed. We mighta been a little crazy back then but we wasn't that damn stupid."

"Then how'd it happen?"

"Still ain't quite sure after all these years. We was drinkin', like I said, just hangin' 'round in the parking lot, and we got to talkin' 'bout what was goin' on with all the niggers and them folks from up north comin' down here to agitate and all." Graves paused to pull a pack of cigarettes from his shirt pocket, popped one out, tapped it three times on the desk, and fired it up. After a deep drag, he turned his attention back to the lawyer.

"Ol' Tillman seemed 'specially worked up over all them voter registration rallies. I remember him sayin' that the niggers 'round here don't have the sense to come in from the fields in a lightnin' storm, so how they gonna be expected to vote like a white man?"

"I don't understand," the lawyer said, puzzled. "So how'd you go from this drinking in a parking lot to a murder?"

"Just hold on," Graves said between drags on his cigarette. "I'm gettin' there. Anyway, like I said, after a while, the other boys drifted off and it was just me and my buddy and Tillman and the other boy. Finally, I got a little tired of listenin' to him bitchin' so I said 'Why don't you just quit your talkin' and do somethin' 'bout it?'"

"What did he say then?"

Graves chuckled a bit. "Tell you the truth, he seemed a little pissed off that a redneck like me would be callin' him out, him bein' a rich college kid and all. So he got real uppity and said 'Like what?' So I told him there was one a them rallies goin' on right then out at the nigger church and maybe we should head out there an' put the fear a God in the nigger organizer. Teach him a little lesson."

"What'd he say to that?"

Graves thought a moment. "Lookin' back on it, I think he kinda felt hisself backed into a corner. You know, was he just a big-mouth blowhard or did he really have the balls to do somethin'? I figure he didn't want to look like some pussy in front a the likes of us rednecks, so finally he says, 'Well then, let's us go teach that nigger a damn lesson he won't forget.'"

"What about the other boy? What'd he say?"

"Didn't say nothin'," Graves answered, shaking his head slowly. "Didn't seem real interested, but he was ridin' with Tillman so I don't think he really had much of a choice without lookin' like a pussy hisself."

"So what happens next?"

"Me and my buddy jumped into my truck and the other two got into Tillman's car and we headed out to the church."

"What was the name of the church?"

"Shit, I don't know. Don't think I ever knew it as anything other than the nigger church. Anyway, once we got out there we just hung 'round till the rally ended, then we followed the preacher out onto the highway.

We ran him off the road, pulled some old feed bags from my truck over our heads so nobody'd recognize us, yanked him outta his car, and started roughin' him up a bit. And that's when things got outta hand."

"How?"

"Well," Graves said, twisting his face in thought. "It kinda happened real quick-like. First, the boy with Tillman tried to stop the beatin' and we all got pissed at him. Then the stupid fuckin' nigger pulls the boy's hood off and right then Tillman fuckin' freaks out."

"What'd he do?"

"He grabs a damn shotgun out the back of his car and blows the fuckin' nigger away, right there on the side a the road. So now we're all screamin' at him, yellin' 'Why the fuck did you do that?'"

"What'd he say?"

"Well, that's the thing. Up till then, I just figured him for a big-talkin' rich kid. But now, with this nigger lyin' dead in the road, his head down in a ditch, blood all over the fuckin' place, Jessup's all cool-like and starts orderin' us all around. Says get in the cars and get the fuck outta there. Later, we pulled into a parking lot and when I asked him again why he killed the fucker, he looks at me real cold-like and says he wasn't gonna run the risk of his life bein' ruined if the preacher identified any of us. And then he said, lookin' straight at me and my buddy, if we ever breathed a word of what happened, he'd make sure we ended up on the side of a road just like that fuckin' preacher." Graves paused a moment and looked directly at his lawyer. "And you know what?"

"What?"

"I believed him. I believed he'd kill us. Or maybe have us killed. And I've believed it till this day."

"So why tell the story now?"

Ricky Earl shrugged. 'Cause I reckon I ain't got much to lose anymore, do I?"

CHAPTER 11

Downtown Oxford, Mississippi, known for generations as "The Square," is a charming ode to all things Southern. At the center, as with so many Southern towns, is the old courthouse, standing sentry for a century and a half over the comings and goings of the county seat of Lafayette County. Built in 1840, the venerable structure had been torched and destroyed by the Union Army of General A. J. Smith in the waning days of the Civil War. Rebuilt in 1872, ironically through federal government funding, it is a striking and majestic building with two wings flanking a central edifice graced by large windows, balconies, and double doors along the outside of the second-floor courtroom, archways topped by pillars adorning the two main entrances, and an imposing clock tower crowning it all.

A number of roads, including North and South Lamar Boulevards, radiate out from the courthouse, like spokes on a wheel. The Square itself is an eclectic collection of elegant old buildings surrounding the courthouse, housing upscale stores, restaurants, and impressive offices. Many of these structures are fronted by New Orleans-style balconies with finely carved wooden or wrought-iron balustrades, and graceful galleries that shade the sidewalks.

Jeff sat on one such balcony that wrapped around the second story of a bookstore directly across from the courthouse. It was one of his favorite haunts on the Square, a quiet oasis where you could sip a sweet tea and page through a new book while enjoying the hustle and bustle of the activity below from a cozy distance. Paging absently through a newspaper, he wondered why he had been summoned here in the middle of a workday. Ella and he had been busily scrolling through Sovereignty Commission records on computers in the law school library, searching for some mention of an elusive investigator named either Hollingsworth or Hollingsly, when he'd received a curious and cryptic phone call from a former colleague begging Jeff to meet him immediately. Unwilling to come to the law school, the caller had suggested meeting at the bookstore.

Looking up at the sound of a screen door slamming shut, Jeff saw his friend, Travis Murray, shuffling out from inside the store, a file under his arm and a glass of iced tea in his hand. Murray dropped into a rocking chair next to Jeff and offered a sheepish smile.

"Thanks for meeting up with me. Sorry it was such short notice."

The two men had been friends since Jeff's early days as a prosecutor. Murray was a criminal defense attorney and a good portion of his clients were indigents assigned to him by the court. After their first few cases together, Jeff had quickly realized that Murray's heavy-set, rumpled appearance belied a sharp legal mind and a kind soul, a combination that was not always found in members of the criminal bar. Despite being on opposite sides of a number of cases, they had developed a respect for each other that blossomed into real friendship. Since Jeff had quit practicing law and gone into teaching, Murray had called him occasionally for advice on a case, but today's call had been different.

There had been an urgency in Murray's voice and a troubling unwillingness to provide any details on the phone that had caused Jeff to immediately excuse himself from Ella and their research to race down to the Square.

"Been a while, Travis," Jeff said, leaning over to shake his friend's hand. "How've you been?"

"Okay," Murray shrugged. "Still dealing with the same shit. Working out deals, some trials, trying to pay the bills. You remember."

"Yeah, I remember," Jeff chuckled. "That's why I got into teaching."

"You were smart. Regular paychecks and no clients to deal with. Sounds pretty good to me."

"I'm enjoying it. But I've got to admit, there are times when I miss the courtroom. Not a lot of times—but some. Anyway," Jeff said, his smile fading, "what's all this mystery about?"

Murray leaned closer, his gray, wire-brush eyebrows furrowed as he looked around anxiously. Satisfied no one was close enough to overhear their conversation, he slid a dollar bill across the small table between them.

"What's this?" Jeff asked.

"It's your retainer."

"Retainer? What for?"

"So that this conversation stays confidential. Attorney-client privilege."

"I don't get it," Jeff said, puzzled. "You want me to represent you?"

"No, not me. I'm retaining you to be co-counsel on a case."

"Travis, what the hell're you talking about?"

"I need your advice. And your help. I might be in the middle of something that's way too big for just me and I got to figure out how to handle it."

"Okay, slow down," Jeff said calmly. "Let's start at the beginning. First of all, are you in any trouble?"

"No, no, it's not me. It's a client."

"Well, that's good to hear. With all this mystery shit, you had me scared there for a minute. So, who's the client and what's it all about?"

"The client's nobody," Murray said, relaxing a bit. "A big-time loser, rap sheet longer than your arm. He's doing thirty years on an armed robbery, but he's old enough that he's probably only leaving prison in a box."

Jeff shook his head, still puzzled. "I don't get it. What's the big deal then?"

"The big deal isn't the client. The big deal is the person he wants to dime out on an old murder." Murray stopped and looked around again.

"So," Jeff said, a slight smile turning the corners of his mouth, "are you going to give me this name or do I have to guess?"

"This is confidential, right? You're in?"

"I'm not sure how 'in' I am but, yeah, this is confidential."

"Okay, so here's the deal. My guy says he was there when a black preacher—a civil rights organizer—was murdered back in 1960. The case was never solved. No arrests, no suspects, nothing. And here's the kicker." Murray paused, his eyebrows arching. "He claims the killer was none other than the next governor of this great state—Tillman Jessup!"

"Is this a joke?" Jeff asked, staring incredulously at Murray.

"No joke. This is for real. My guy's given me the whole story. Says he was there and saw Jessup do the shooting. I checked out the details of the old murder—there wasn't a whole lot out there since there wasn't much of an investigation—and they seem to square with what he told me."

"And you believe him?"

Murray thought a moment before answering. "Yeah, I believe him," he said solemnly.

Jeff sat back in his chair, shaking his head. "I don't know, Travis. If this is true—and that's a big 'if'—and if we can actually prove it—and that's probably a bigger 'if'—I just don't know . . . ," he said, his voice trailing off.

"Look, Jeff," Murray said, leaning closer, "if this is true—and I think it is—someone has to do something about it. We can't just let a killer become the next governor."

"But, Jesus Christ, we're talking about Tillman-fucking-Jessup! And a forty-year-old murder! And some scumbag lifer! Who the hell's going to believe him?"

"I do, Jeff," Murray said quietly. "And, if you talk to him, I think you will, too."

Jeff was quiet for a moment, then looked directly into his friend's eyes. "I guess that's what I'm afraid of."

CHAPTER 12

"So," Ella asked, "what are you going to do?"

Jeff and Ella were walking through the Grove at the center of campus. After the conversation with Travis Murray, Jeff had returned to the law library, where Ella was still poring over the records of the Sovereignty Commission. Realizing that he'd need a media ally if he took the case, and already feeling that she was someone he could trust, he asked her to come outside to talk. After she acknowledged that their entire discussion would remain completely "off the record" until he declared otherwise, he had related his conversation with Murray to her.

"I'm still not sure," Jeff answered.

"Then why tell me the story if you're not sold on it yourself?"

"Like I told Travis, if we go ahead with this, the media'll be all over it like flies on molasses. And we'll need to try to control it. At least in the beginning."

"Wait a minute. I didn't say anything about being 'controlled,'" she said, anger flaring. "The only thing I agreed to was keeping the story off the record until—"

"Whoa! Calm down. I didn't mean that we'd try to control *you*. I only meant that by working with you we could control when the story broke. That way, you get the exclusive, and we have the story reported first by somebody we trust will be fair and honest. You help us and we help you. Deal?" He grinned and thrust out his hand.

"Deal," she said, a smile slowly working its way across her face as she shook his hand. "But I'm still curious. Why tell me the story if you're still not sold on it yourself?"

"It's not so much that I'm not sold on the story. I'm just not sold on whether I want to be a part of it."

"So you do believe it? That Jessup is a killer?"

Jeff gnawed on his lower lip thoughtfully before he answered. "I've known Travis a long time and I trust him—and he believes it."

"But that's not my question. Will the court direct the witness to answer the question," she said, mimicking a cross-examiner, a playful glint in her eyes. "Do you believe it?"

"I guess I believe that Travis could be right. That it could be true. But I won't know for sure until we talk to his client."

"What'll you do then, if you believe him?"

"I'm not sure," he answered softly.

They walked silently, strolling through the Grove until they ended up at the front of the Lyceum. Without saying anything, they both sat down on the steps between two of the sculpted columns. After a while, Ella turned to him.

"Why did you decide to come here for school?" she asked.

"Never really thought about anyplace else," Jeff answered, gazing about the grounds. "Just always assumed this was where I belonged. When they offered me a football scholarship I cancelled my other recruiting visits and signed on right away."

"But what about your father? He must cast a pretty imposing shadow around this place. Didn't you ever worry about that? About living in that shadow while you were here?"

At fiirst, Jeff didn't answer. Then, still gazing out over the campus, he nodded his head slowly.

"I guess there was a time that I thought about going someplace else. But then I realized that, no matter where I went, I was still going to be 'Willie Trannon's son.' And, after a while, I figured I was okay with that. Look," he said, turning to face her, "he's done some pretty incredible things with his life. And I've got enormous respect for that. I really do. So I decided to stay here and try to carve out my own little niche." He was quiet for a while. "I guess this just always seemed like home. Plus, around then was when my mom first got sick." He shrugged. "So I stayed."

"And . . . ?"

"And what?"

"Are you glad you stayed? Even with that shadow always around?"

"Yeah," he answered softly. "I guess so. Shadow and all."

She stared at him, searching his face as he continued to look off into the distance. Then she touched his arm gently.

"Sorry. That's all probably none of my business. Just the curious reporter in me, I guess. Anyway," she said, her tone all business, "what's the next step?"

Jeff snapped out of his reverie and quickly stood up. "I've got to decide if I'm in or not. So, I guess we need to go have a talk with Travis's client."

"And then?"

Jeff sighed. "And then we both decide if we're ready to turn this damn state upside down."

CHAPTER 13

"You sure it's a good idea, bringin' a reporter in on this?" Ricky Earl Graves asked, eying Ella suspiciously.

Jeff and Ella had traveled with Travis Murray to visit his client at the prison. They were seated around an old metal table, the top scarred by the carvings and absent scrapings of a legion of bored, angry, and frustrated prisoners. Through the heavy security-glass window embedded in one of the cinder-block walls, they could hear the echoes of the shouts, slamming doors, and overhead speakers that made up the symphony of routine prison sounds.

"Yeah, it's a good idea," Murray answered. "Like I said, if we go forward with this the media will be all over it. Ella's agreed to help us get our story out, in return for an exclusive about how it all went down."

Ricky Earl shifted his gaze from his lawyer back to Ella, this time with an admiring glint in his eye. "Well, if you say so, Counselor. Plus, she's a damn sight better lookin' than anybody else been to visit me. Okay, ma'am," he nodded. "Glad to have you on the team."

"Thank you, Mr. Graves—"

"Ricky Earl," he interrupted.

"Okay, Ricky Earl," she said smoothly. "I appreciate the compliment. And I'd agree that I'm certainly a damn sight better looking than these two," she said with a wry smile, tilting her head toward Jeff and Murray. "But," she added, her tone now more professional, "you need to understand something. I'm not 'part of your team.' I'm not some publicity flack. I'm a reporter. And my job is to tell the story, objectively, in a way that's fair to everyone. Understand?"

"Sure do," said Ricky Earl. "No offense meant."

"None taken," Ella said.

Ricky Earl chuckled. "But I still hope we get to visit often. Bein' my age and in my condition, just sittin' in a room with a pretty girl's 'bout the best you can hope for."

Ella nodded.

"Okay, then," Murray jumped in. "Jeff, as I mentioned, will take the lead. He spent some time as a prosecutor, so he's got the contacts and knows most of the people we need to talk to."

His eyes narrowing, Ricky Earl turned toward Jeff. "You related to the judge?"

Jeff nodded. "He's my father."

Ricky Earl looked to Murray. "That help us?"

"Not directly," said Murray. "But people certainly know and respect Jeff's family. And they respect him, too."

"Sounds like it can't hurt," said Ricky Earl, still focused on Jeff. "But tell me, Mr. Trannon, why'd someone like you want to get involved with someone like me? I can understand Miss Garrity, here, wantin' a story; and Travis, well, he's my lawyer. But what's in it for you?"

Jeff locked eyes with Graves for a long moment. "I'm not here to 'help' you, Ricky Earl. Tell you the truth, I don't really like you or your kind. If I believe your story and I do get involved, it's not to help you. It's not even to hurt Tillman Jessup. It's only to make sure that someone—no matter who he is—doesn't get away with murder. Even after all these years."

"Well, that sounds right noble," Ricky Earl said, a slight smirk creasing the corner of his mouth. "And I'm okay with that. Don't need me any new friends. Just want to get outta here. So," he said, looking around the table, "now that we've gotten the pleasantries outta the way, what's next?"

"How about you telling us your story. Everything, from start to finish," Jeff said.

"Sure will," said Ricky Earl, pulling out a pack of cigarettes from his shirt pocket. "Hope y'all don't mind if I smoke. Got a feelin' we might be awhile."

Two hours later, Ricky Earl leaned back in his chair, stubbed out his last cigarette, and tossed it into an ashtray, along with the ten others he had smoked while he told his story and Jeff and Ella had peppered him with questions.

"So," he said, spreading his hands out in front of him. "That there's 'bout it. Funny thing," he added, almost wistfully, "whenever I think back to that night, I can always hear 'em all singin' inside the church. And I remember thinkin' back then, while they was all clappin' and hollerin' some song about 'good news,' that we had some mighty bad news in store for that there preacher. Anyway," he said, looking around the table, "what do y'all think?"

Jeff tossed his pen onto a legal pad filled with his scribbled notes. He took a deep breath and slowly exhaled. "Well, Ricky Earl, I think I believe you. But there're some things I want to check out, first, before I'm ready to sign on."

"You go right ahead. I ain't goin' nowhere. One thing I got is plenty of time."

Jeff leaned toward the prisoner, his arms on the table. "You sure you don't want to tell us who else was there that night?"

"Nope," Ricky Earl said sternly. "Ain't gonna do it. Like I told Travis here, first time we talked. Those boys ain't with us no more and I ain't gonna put their families through none of this. No, sir," he shook his head. "Ain't gonna happen."

Jeff looked pointedly at Murray. "Okay, then. We'll just have to figure out how we'll deal with that later."

"Ricky Earl, you ever talk about this to anyone else before?" Murray asked. "Any family or friends? Maybe one of your lawyers?"

"Nope. Like I said before, I surely did believe that Jessup woulda done to me what he did to that nigger preacher if I'd talked."

Jeff looked at Murray. "Too bad. If he'd told the story to anyone, we might've been able to use it as a prior consistent statement if we ever got to a trial."

Ella looked puzzled. "'Prior consistent statement'?"

"It's a bit complicated," Jeff said. "The evidence rules will sometimes allow you to introduce the fact that a person has told the same story that he's telling on the witness stand now, to someone else at an earlier time—a prior consistent statement—to support his credibility. So, if the other side is claiming that your witness is lying, that he's just making up a story—"

"Well," Ricky Earl interrupted, his face twisted in thought, "there was one fella."

"Someone you told the story to?" Jeff asked anxiously.

"Yep. Don't know how much help it'll be though."

"Why?"

"'Cause he ain't the kinda guy who'd be likely to want to help out, that's why."

"Who is he? And when did you talk with him?"

"It was back a few days after the killin'. A guy showed up at my place late one night. Introduced hisself and showed me a badge. Said he wanted to talk to me 'bout the death of one of them there nigger agitators. Them's his words—'nigger agitators.' Right away, that seemed a little strange to me, but I just said I didn't know nothin' 'bout it. Then he looked at me real cold-like and said that he wasn't no cop and, as far as he was concerned, every one of them there agitators should be shot, too. So now I was real confused about who he was and what was goin' on. Then, I nearly shit when he told me he knew I was there when the nigger got gunned down, that he knew who all else was there, and that it was his job to make sure that no one else ever found out 'bout it."

"You sure he wasn't a cop who was just jerking you around—trying to get you to confess?" asked Jeff.

"Yeah, I thought maybe that was it, at first. But then, well, there was just somethin' 'bout him. First of all, he seemed to know everythin' 'bout that night, all the details. He told me he'd talked to one of the others—he wouldn't tell me who—and that he knew who'd done what. But he said his job was to make sure the whole fuckin' thing would just go away. No cops, no investigation, no charges—no nothin'. But he said that, first, he needed me to tell him exactly what happened. And then he said he needed me to forget about the shooting forever—and to forget that I ever met him. Then he pulled his suit jacket aside so I could see a big ol' .45 he was carryin' in a shoulder holster, and said to me that if I kept quiet everythin' would be fine. But if I ever so much as whispered anything about the killin', in twenty-four hours I'd be deader than that there nigger."

"And you believed him?" asked Jeff.

"Damn straight, I believed him. So, I told him everythin'. And damned if the whole thing didn't just go away, just like he said."

Jeff thought a moment. "Did he tell you his name? Or who he worked for?"

"Not so sure about who he worked for. Said it was some kinda special government agency."

Jeff and Ella exchanged knowing glances.

"And a name?" asked Jeff again.

"I sure do remember that. It was Hollingsly. A. J. Hollingsly."

CHAPTER 14

The drive from Oxford to the Morning Star Baptist Church took about ten minutes. Jeff and Ella headed out of Oxford on Highway 6 and then turned off onto a narrow, two-lane road that meandered through fields of reddish dirt studded with copses of pine trees. Jeff had discovered that the Reverend Calvin Butler, who had been the pastor of the church back in 1960 and—apparently—the last person, other than his killers, to see Elijah Hall alive, had retired some years back but was still associated with the church as a senior pastor. During his decades as the church leader, he had become a powerful force in the county, revered by his black congregation and, ultimately—as the shackles of segregation loosened—respected by the white community, as well.

As they drove, Ella took in the fields, punctuated by occasional small, ramshackle farmhouses and rusting farm equipment.

"This area probably looked pretty much the same back in 1960 as it does now," she said quietly.

"Certainly hasn't changed much since I've been around," Jeff agreed.

"You think Reverend Butler will be much help?" she asked, still gazing out the window.

"Don't know. Might be in his eighties by now, or close to it. I guess it depends on how sharp he still is."

"And how much he wants to help. Or doesn't," she added ominously.

As they rounded a small curve, they came upon the church, set back about fifty yards from the road. It was a squat, cinder-block building with two large windows flanking a broad set of steps leading to the front double doors. The one-story structure had a shingled roof capped by a drooping wooden steeple, a rather incongruous, aged appendage to what looked like an otherwise fairly new edifice.

On the steps sat an older, frail-looking, white-haired black man, dressed in a dark suit. Rising stiffly as they parked in front of the church, he walked toward them, hand outstretched in greeting.

"Welcome," he said in a strong, deep baritone voice that belied his slight build. He wore a pair of horn-rimmed glasses that magnified his still alert, penetrating eyes. Jeff and Ella took turns shaking his hand, both struck by the strength in his grip.

"Thank you for agreeing to see us," Jeff said.

"Glad to meet you, Mr. Trannon. Your daddy's been a friend for a whole lot of years. How's he been doin' lately?" the pastor asked.

"Pretty well, sir. Thanks for asking," said Jeff.

"Well, you be sure to pass on my best to him. And you, Miss Garrity," he said, turning to Ella and offering a broad smile, "it's a real pleasure to meet you, too. Seen some of your articles over the years. Happy to have you both come visitin'. C'mon inside where we can get a little more comfortable."

Reverend Butler led them up the steps and into the church. It was surprisingly cool and dark inside, given the midday Mississippi heat and humidity, even at this time of the year. They found some chairs in a corner and settled into a small circle.

"So," Butler said, squinting intently at both of them through his glasses. "You said you wanted to talk about Reverend Hall's murder. Why?"

"Well," said Jeff. "We're looking into the details and thought you might be able to help us out."

"I might be. But you still haven't answered my question. Why?" he asked again, his eyes still smiling, but his voice stern, laced with the authority of many years of sermons.

"Well, sir," Jeff began, glancing quickly at Ella and then turning to Butler. "We're actually involved in an investigation into his murder."

"Investigation?" interrupted Butler. "He was murdered near forty years ago. And there were no suspects even back then. I don't mean to sound rude, but what possible kind of investigation could you two be conducting now?"

"Fair question," said Jeff. "And I could see why you'd be puzzled. Let me explain. First, I want to share some information with you and I'd be much obliged if you'd consider it confidential between us."

Butler stared at Jeff intently for a moment, and then nodded his assent.

"Okay then. We've come across some information about Reverend Hall's murder. Information that may well help to solve his killing."

"What kind of information?"

"We've found a man who was there when it happened."

"One of the killers?"

"Well, he's not the one who pulled the trigger, but he was there."

"And he's told you how it happened? And who was involved?"

Jeff nodded.

Butler was silent for a moment. "Why would this man come forward with this information now?"

"I wish I could tell you it was out of the goodness of his heart. But it's not. He was recently sentenced to a long prison term and he's looking for some way to get his time cut down. He's hoping that, in exchange for his story and his testimony, he might get some kind of deal."

"You'll pardon me if I suggest that your description of this man doesn't immediately fill me with an abiding sense of trust," Butler said, a small, wry smile working its way across his deeply creased, oval face.

Jeff shrugged. "That was exactly our feeling at first. But after hours talking with him . . . well, we think he's telling the truth."

Butler sat back in his chair, his gaze focused on the altar in front of the church. After a while, he turned back to Jeff and Ella. "You know," he said softly, "in a way, I've always blamed myself for Elijah's death."

"Why?" asked Ella gently. "You couldn't have known what was going to happen to him."

"I never should have let him drive back so late. Not around here. And not in those days. I should have insisted that he stay overnight." He shook his head sadly. "He'd be alive today if I'd insisted. I truly believe that. Believed it for forty years now."

They all sat in silence. Then Butler sighed, sat up, squared his shoulders, and looked directly at Jeff. "I'd like to talk with this man."

"We might be able to arrange that. But first, we need your advice."

"About?"

"About whether we should go public with this. And whether we should push to prosecute the killer."

Butler looked at them both carefully. "You haven't told me who the killer is, yet."

"No, sir, we haven't. That's the problem."

"Why such a problem? A killer is a killer, no matter how long ago it happened."

"That's true," Jeff answered. "But in this case, the killer is a very important man."

Butler leaned forward. "Mr. Trannon," he said, his voice now that of a preacher offering a glimpse of truth to his congregation, "do you read your Bible?"

"Perhaps not as often as I should," Jeff answered somewhat sheepishly.

"And you, Miss Garrity?" Butler asked, turning toward Ella.

"A great deal when I was younger. Not so much now," she confessed.

Butler raised a critical eyebrow and asked, "Do you remember the story of Joshua and the Battle of Jericho?"

"Sure," said Jeff.

"And what do you remember about the story?"

"Well," Jeff answered, thinking quickly back to his Bible lessons as a young boy. "Jericho was a fortress city besieged by Joshua and his Israelite army. But rather than take the city by force, Joshua ordered the priests to surround the city. Once they were in place, they sounded their trumpets and the walls came crashing down. So Joshua was able to conquer the city without a fight."

Butler looked to Ella who quickly nodded her agreement with Jeff's memory of the Bible lesson. He then smiled kindly at both as he shook his head.

"I'm afraid you both suffer from the same limited recollection of the story that has afflicted most of my flock over the years."

Both Jeff and Ella appeared puzzled.

"You're correct that the great warrior, Joshua, a successor to Moses, had surrounded the city of Jericho, which was a stronghold of the Canaanites. But the destruction of the city didn't occur immediately. Joshua ordered his priests to lead the troops in a march around the city once a day for six days. As they circled the city, the priests sounded their trumpets. Then, on the seventh day, Joshua ordered the priests and the army to circle the city seven times, again blowing the trumpets. And on the seventh time, Joshua ordered all to 'shout, for the Lord has given you the city.' And as the trumpets blew and the people shouted, the walls of Jericho came tumbling down." Butler looked pointedly at Jeff and Ella. "Do you see, then?"

Jeff and Ella seemed confused.

"Do you see, then, the meaning of the story for us?" Butler repeated.

"I'm afraid I don't," Jeff answered, still puzzled.

"For years, I've preached about Joshua and the Battle of Jericho.

I've told my people that the Bible offered us a parable through the story of Jericho, a parable that helped us to understand our own battle against the fortress of racism and bigotry. A parable that taught us how to bring that terrible fortress tumbling down." He looked again carefully at Jeff and Ella, sensing that they were still uncertain about his meaning.

"Our struggle for civil rights, and against the brutality of racism, wasn't won in a single great battle. It's taken us many years, and great suffering and loss by many people, to fight our battle. And, in some ways, it's still being fought today. But what the story of Joshua and Jericho teaches us is that our battle against racism can be won, not by a single blow of brute strength, but by the constant sound of the trumpets of righteousness and the voices of good people seeking change. We've conquered the evil of bigotry not with weapons, but with God's will. Not by force—but by faith."

Butler looked at them carefully. "What I'm saying to you is, it doesn't matter how important this man who killed Elijah may be. He needs to pay for his crime. The trumpets of justice need to be blown, even now, forty years later. What's left of the walls of Jericho, the fortress of racism and hatred, needs to come tumbling down. And you two must sound those trumpets."

After a moment, he smiled at them gently. "Now, come and tell me your story."

About an hour later, they left the church and walked to Jeff's car. Butler had listened carefully as Jeff and Ella described Ricky Earl Graves's story of the murder of Elijah Hall. He had asked just a few questions and, when they had finished, simply nodded his head and said, "Thank you for coming to me."

Butler offered his hand, first to Ella and then to Jeff. "What will you do now?" he asked both.

"I think it's time now for me to talk to the district attorney. Try to convince him that Ricky Earl's telling the truth and that it's time to go after Tillman Jessup," Jeff said.

"That, I believe, shall be quite an interesting meeting," Butler chuckled.

As she started to climb into the car, Ella suddenly stopped. "Just one last thing," she said to Butler. "We meant to ask you this earlier. Do you, by any chance, remember the songs being sung in your church the night of the murder?"

"Songs?" Butler asked. "Is that important?"

"Could be," Ella said. "I realize it's a long time ago but . . ."

"Miss Garrity," Butler interrupted. "I remember every moment of that night as if it was yesterday. And I'm sure I will until the day I leave this earth. Of course, I remember. We were singing one of my favorites: 'Ain't That Good News.' Haven't sung that song since," he mused. "Rather sad, isn't it? Singing about good news just minutes before a good man would be murdered."

Ella shot Jeff a glance, and then said to Butler, "Yes. Very sad."

CHAPTER 15

"So, why this interest in an old murder? You working on a new book?" asked the man sitting at the head of the large, ornately carved conference table.

Gibb Haynes was the district attorney for the Third Circuit Judicial District, an office he'd held for as long as Jeff could remember. Tall and lanky, with his thinning hair slicked back from a face that was all hard angles, he had been born and raised in Oxford and was proud to claim—as he did each time he stood for re-election—that he never saw any good reason to leave his hometown. An Ole Miss grad, from both the college and the law school, he was that most unusual combination, even now in his late sixties, of both a talented prosecutor and a consummate politician. Equal parts "good ol' boy" and polished campaigner, he had made it his practice, over the years, to personally handle many of the high-profile cases in his office, while also making it his practice to court all of the publicity he could possibly generate. Friends and foes alike joked that Gibb Haynes had never met a reporter or photographer he didn't like.

Haynes had given Jeff a job as a prosecutor right out of law school and, even though Jeff knew the job had been a favor to his father, he had worked hard and quickly earned the respect of his boss and his colleagues. In short, Jeff liked the old man and admired his honesty and how he ran his office.

Jeff grinned and shook his head. "Nothing as simple as a new book. I wish it was."

"So then, what?" asked Haynes, a smile on his face but a glint of hard curiosity in his eyes.

"What if—hypothetically speaking—I had a guy who could give you all the details about the murder of Elijah Hall, including the name of the shooter?"

"That was way back in 1960. Anyone still alive to prosecute?" asked Clayton Poole, the sheriff of Lafayette County, a square-shouldered, square-jawed, crew-cut wearing, big block of a man, who was sitting to the right of Haynes.

Jeff shifted his gaze to Poole. He had worked with the sheriff during his time as a prosecutor and respected him. Despite his gruff demeanor, he was a good cop who always played by the rules. Jeff nodded.

"The killer."

District Attorney Haynes leaned forward in his chair, his eyes narrowing. "Well then—hypothetically speaking—I'd be very interested. But how does your guy know about this?"

"He was there. Saw it all go down."

"So he's an accomplice?"

"Technically, yes. On a felony murder basis. He was there and roughed the victim up, but says he had no idea anyone was going to get shot."

"Isn't that what they all say?" Poole said disdainfully.

"Yeah, but this time I happen to believe him."

"Okay," said Haynes, leaning back in his chair and steepling his fingers together. "Let's say, hypothetically then, that your boy's telling the truth. Who's the shooter?"

"Well, that's where this all gets really interesting." Jeff paused and looked hard at the district attorney. "Suppose I told you that the killer was Tillman Jessup. Hypothetically."

Haynes said nothing for a long moment and simply stared at Jeff. Finally, he shook his head slowly. "C'mon, Jeff. You serious?"

"As a heart attack," Jeff said solemnly.

"*Our* Tillman Jessup?" Haynes said incredulously. "The next damn governor?"

"One and the same."

"What the hell? You got to be kiddin' me, right?"

"I wish I was, Gibb. But my guy seems to be legit. He's got all the details. I pushed him hard looking for holes, but his story never changes. Even volunteered to take a lie detector."

"Jesus Christ . . . ," Haynes muttered, his voice trailing away into silence.

"I know," Jeff said softly. "That's what I thought, too."

Haynes took a deep breath and slowly exhaled. "Okay, so before we go any further in this hypothetical conversation, who's your guy and what's he looking for to tell his story?"

"Name's Ricky Earl Graves. A big-time loser, lots of convictions, mostly drugs and burglaries. Took what's essentially a life hit as a multiple offender on an attempted armed robbery of a liquor store." Jeff shrugged. "Wants a shot at parole so he doesn't have to die in prison. Maybe do a few more years, then get over the wall."

"Okay, first question. What's a lowlife like him doing hanging around with someone like Tillman Jessup? Even forty years ago?" Poole asked.

"Both grew up here in Oxford. Didn't run with the same crowds back in high school but he says they kind of knew each other from around town."

"Any other witnesses?" asked Haynes.

"Nope. He says there were two others with them when the murder took place but they're both dead now."

"So, no corroboration? Just this guy's word? Jesus Christ, Jeff. You expect me to try to take down the next governor on a forty-year-old murder charge, based on nothing more than some shitbird swearing that he was there and Jessup did the shooting?" said an exasperated Haynes.

Jeff nodded. "I know it sounds bizarre. But if this guy's telling the truth—and I think he is—our next governor would be a cold-blooded murderer. You going to let that happen without at least looking into it?"

"Jesus Christ," Haynes repeated softly, sagging back into his chair. He was quiet for a moment, and then turned to look at Sheriff Poole. "What do you think, Clay?"

Poole looked at Jeff, his eyes narrowed to slits, then grunted. "Hell, sounds like the most damn fool thing I ever heard. But if Jeff here believes this particular shitbird, seems to me it can't do no harm to at least have a little chat with him."

Jeff raised both hands palms up and looked first to Poole, then to Haynes. "That's all I'm asking. Talk with him. Check out his story. Seems to me he's got some details that only someone who was there would know. Run him on the box to see if he's telling the truth, if you want. Then decide."

"Jesus Christ," Haynes said yet again. "You know what kind of shit storm you could be cranking up?" he asked Jeff. "Damn, Jessup's the most popular politician we've had in Mississippi in a long time."

"You think I don't know that? You think I don't wish I never heard of Ricky Earl Graves?" Jeff answered sadly.

Haynes stared off into the distance for a while, then looked back at Jeff and sighed deeply. "What the hell. Never been much of a fan of Jessup and don't owe him a damn thing. We'll talk to your boy, but no promises." He turned to Poole. "Clay, let's us have that little chat with Mr. Ricky Earl Graves. You set it up. Let Jeff know when and where. And let's bring Terrell Jackson in on this." Then he turned back to Jeff. "You okay with Terrell runnin' the investigation?"

Jeff nodded.

"I hope you know what you're gettin' yourself into, boy. I'll be stepping down soon, no matter what, so it don't matter much to me. But you're still going to be around for a long time. And if we take on Tillman Jessup but don't end up taking him down, my guess is he ain't going to be in a very forgiving mood. Ever."

CHAPTER 16

The only light in the darkened room came from a log fire crackling in the cavernous stone fireplace. A man sat quietly in an old, deeply creased leather armchair, the firelight flickering and dancing around him. At first, he seemed not to hear the ringing of a cell phone sitting on the small table next to his chair. Then, he slowly placed the empty glass in his hand on the table, next to a nearly empty bottle of Jim Beam bourbon, and reached for the phone.

"Yeah," he rasped, his whiskey-soaked, cigarette-stoked voice bearing witness to nearly eighty years of hard drinking and hard living.

"Heard from a few friends that some people been askin''bout you," said the voice on the other end.

The old man grunted. "What kind of people?"

"The kind of people you ain't gonna want to talk to."

"Like who?"

"Like a newspaper reporter and some professor from Ole Miss."

"What're they lookin' for me for?"

"Don't know. All's I know is that they been asking around. Wonderin' if anybody knows where they can find you."

A. J. Hollingsly sat silently for a moment, contemplating the news. He had spent the last fifteen years of his life holed up in this log cabin tucked in the hill country of northeast Mississippi, avoiding the searching spotlight of an inquisitive few—mostly journalists—seeking to plumb the depths of one of the last of the old-time segregationist crusaders. Protected by a small but rabid network of like-minded friends, he usually managed to discourage any attempts at engaging him in conversation. Most times, a simple warning attached to a stern "no thanks" was enough. But sometimes that simple warning wasn't quite sufficient to dampen the curiosity of those seeking to find him. In those cases, a more pronounced form of discouragement was required. After that, none had continued to search.

He sighed heavily. "Why don't you tell some of the boys to let 'em know that I ain't interested in having no conversations with them. Not now or never. Just a little bit of persuadin', mind you. Don't wanna create no problems if we don't have to. But make sure they get the message loud and clear."

"I'll get it done."

"Good," Hollingsly said, ending the call and flipping the phone back onto the table. "Damn," he muttered, reaching for the bottle of Jim Beam.

CHAPTER 17

"This is where the body was found," said Jeff.

Forty years later, there was no evidence that the drainage ditch alongside the narrow, winding county road had been the scene of a brutal murder. No plaque marked the site to educate any curious passersby. No flowers from friends or relatives reminded travelers that this quiet, pastoral vista once witnessed the vicious shotgun execution of a young man whose only crime had been trying to help others.

Jeff and Ella stood silently beside the ditch, each contemplating the night of the murder. After reviewing the police report of the shooting death—which, they were dismayed to find, consisted of barely two typewritten pages—they had decided to visit the scene themselves. Although they clearly never expected that their visit would yield any clues to the killing, they both shared some emotional need to stand on the spot where Elijah Hall's life had been cruelly extinguished.

After a moment, Jeff glanced around.

"Must've been awfully dark," he murmured.

"What?" asked Ella, who had been lost in her own thoughts.

Jeff turned toward her. "It must've been awfully dark out here that night. No streetlights, hardly any houses around—even now." He paused. "I wonder if he knew," he said softly.

"Knew what?" Ella asked.

"Knew that he was going to die. When they pulled him over, did he know that his life was about to end?"

Ella didn't answer.

Suddenly, they both noticed a car racing down the road toward them. The dark sedan skidded to a gravel-spewing stop just a few feet in front of them. The driver's door flew open and a mountainous, dark-suited black man sprang from the car. Shaved head shining in the afternoon sun, a scowl creased his square face.

"Who the hell taught you how to drive?" Jeff yelled.

"Shit," the man growled. "Even with my damn eyes shut, I'm a better driver than you."

Ella looked from one man to the other, puzzled. She felt a shred of fear creeping in, wondering who the big man was, and where this confrontation was heading.

The men stared at each other for a moment and then Jeff's face lit up in a smile.

"How you been, Terrell?"

"Been pretty good, Jeff. How 'bout you?" the big man said, his voice a deep, syrupy drawl, as he wrapped Jeff in a smothering hug.

"Been okay," Jeff managed to gasp as he freed himself from the big man's grasp.

"Man, I'm not so sure you gonna be okay for long if you really plan on tryin' to take down the next governor. What the hell you thinkin' 'bout, boy? Didn't I teach you better after all these years?"

Jeff shrugged. "So, how much do you know about all this?"

The big man stepped back and looked at Ella. "Man, ain't you got no manners? When you gonna introduce me to this pretty young lady?"

"Sorry," Jeff said somewhat sheepishly. "Ella Garrity, Terrell Jackson. Ella writes for the *New York Times*. Terrell and I go back a ways," he said, nodding toward Jackson.

"It is a pleasure, Miss Garrity," Jackson said, the down-home drawl suddenly replaced by a proper, professional delivery worthy of an accomplished thespian.

"Nice to meet you," Ella said, her hand disappearing inside the big man's grip as they shook hands. "So just how far back do you two go?"

"Shit, we known each other since we was babies," Jackson said, shifting back into his street mien. "And I was the one made him famous back in high school. Without me throwin' all those blocks for him, his skinny little white ass would've never made it into the end zone all those times."

Jeff chuckled. "Can't remember a time I didn't know this guy," he said to Ella. "Although there were some times growing up that I wish I *hadn't* known him."

"Now, now, Counselor. Some things are better off not bein' mentioned again. Plus, I'm pretty sure the statute of limitations has run on all that old shit, anyway."

"Be careful," Ella smiled at Jackson. "I'm a reporter. And we don't pay much attention to those legal niceties. Especially if it's a good story."

"What have I told you about talking to reporters?" Jeff said to Jackson.

"Yeah, I know," Jackson drawled. "But that don't apply to the pretty ones. Especially if they're on your side. Right, Miss Garrity?"

"Right, Terrell. And it's Ella. Especially if I'm on *your* side," she answered playfully.

"I'm likin' this girl already," Jackson laughed.

"Speaking of being on our side," Jeff said, his tone now serious, "just how much did the sheriff tell you about all this?" Jeff said.

"Well," Jackson said, matching Jeff's tone. "He told me enough to know we're playin' with fire and probably gonna get good an' burned."

"You sure you're okay with that? I don't want to get you into something that might hurt your career."

"Shit, man. I'm a cop. If Tillman Jessup—or anybody, for that matter—killed someone, he should go down for it. Don't matter who he is or who he killed. It's the right thing to do. And," he said, a twinkle in his eye, "this could end up being the biggest case of my career. Even if it ends it."

"Okay, then. Glad you're in this with us," Jeff said. "Always nice to know somebody you can trust has your back."

"Same as always," Jackson grinned.

"I feel like I'm in a scene from *Lethal Weapon* and you guys are doing your best Mel Gibson and Danny Glover impersonations," Ella said, rolling her eyes. "Anyway, now that we've got all that settled, where do we go from here?"

"I'm backtracking on the original investigation—if you can call it that—to see if there's anyone still around who could help," Jackson said. "Not much luck so far. The two guys from the Highway Patrol who found the body and wrote up the report been dead for a while. Planning on talkin' to Reverend Butler while I'm out this way."

"We talked to him the other day," Ella said.

Jackson raised an eyebrow. "Any help?"

"Afraid not," Ella answered. "At least, not in the sense that he knew anything more than we do about how it happened or who might have been involved."

"But he can offer some details that only someone who was there that night would know," Jeff added.

Jackson nodded thoughtfully. "Well, I guess that's better than nothin'."

"There is something else. It's a long shot, but worth trying," said Ella, looking at Jeff.

"What's that?" asked Jackson.

"Long shot's probably an understatement," Jeff answered. "Ricky Earl—my client—claims that he was visited by an investigator for the Mississippi Sovereignty Commission after the killing. Says the guy already knew all the details of the murder, including who was involved."

"What happened?" asked Jackson.

Jeff shrugged. "Ricky Earl says the guy scared the shit out of him, so he told him everything. The guy promised him the whole thing would just go away, but if he ever said anything about the killing, he'd end up dead, too."

"So he kept quiet for all these years?"

"Wouldn't you?" Jeff asked.

"Guess so," Jackson agreed. "Do we know who this investigator was?"

"Yup, we think so. Name's A. J. Hollingsly. And there's a chance that he might still be alive."

Jackson frowned. "From what I've heard about those guys, they were some pretty hard-ass racists. Did some nasty shit. What's the chance—if this guy is still alive—that he'd be willing to talk?"

"Realistically? Pretty slim. We've been asking around, trying to find him, but no luck so far. But if we could get any kind of confirmation from him, anything at all, it could go a long way toward building a decent case against Jessup."

"And who knows," Ella added, "maybe he's had a change of heart after all these years. Even George Wallace changed his mind on segregation."

Jackson shook his big head and grunted. "Yeah, but he had to go get hisself shot, first. Plus, Wallace was just a shitload of talk. He wasn't the serious bad-ass that some of those Sovereignty boys were."

"Guess we won't know for sure until we find him and ask," said Jeff.

"Might not be as easy as all that," said Jackson. "Not too many of those ol' boys left. Most of 'em died off by now. And the few that're still around don't seem to want to talk much."

"So?" Ella asked, concern heavy in her voice. "Do you think we shouldn't try to find him?"

"Shit, no," Jackson grinned. "Let's go track down the ol' redneck son of a bitch and have a little visit with him. Might be fun!"

CHAPTER 18

The blood-orange sun was sliding below the wooded horizon as Terrell Jackson roared off down the road to visit with Reverend Butler. Jeff and Ella lingered at the scene for a few more minutes before climbing into Jeff's old Jeep and heading back toward Oxford. They drove in silence, each haunted by their visions of the murder of Elijah Hall, visions made all the more real after standing in the area where he had been gunned down.

"How's your hotel?" Jeff asked, finally breaking the reflective quiet.

"It's fine. And the people there are really very nice."

"How about the food?"

Ella smiled ruefully. "Not quite as nice."

"Want to grab a quick dinner?"

Her smile grew brighter. "Love to. What've you got in mind?"

"Well," he said, "there's actually a really good diner just up the road."

"A diner?" Ella chuckled. "What kind of a dinner date is that?"

"I'm sorry," Jeff stammered, clearly flustered. "But . . . it's a *really good* diner. And I didn't mean to make it sound like . . ."

"Like a date?" Ella interrupted. "Don't get upset. I was only kidding. And your diner sounds lovely," she added soothingly.

"Okay." He paused a moment. "But, if you want, we could find a nicer place . . ."

"Jeff," she interrupted again, a wry smile turning up the corners of her mouth. "Relax. I'm kidding. Really. Besides, I like diners. I'm a Mississippi girl, remember?"

He shot her a smile and the awkwardness passed. After a few minutes, he pulled into the parking lot of the Rebel Roadhouse, an old-fashioned, chrome-sided dining car that looked like it had been parked in the same spot for decades, which, indeed, it had.

Inside, they dropped into a vinyl-upholstered booth, complete with an anachronistic miniature jukebox perched on the table between them. After briefly scanning the menu, they each ordered cheeseburgers and French fries. While they were waiting for their food, Ella seemed distracted and fidgety.

"You okay?" Jeff finally asked.

Ella was silent for a moment, then leaned forward and looked intently at Jeff.

"I haven't been completely honest with you," she said softly.

"About what?" Jeff asked.

"Remember when we first met and talked about the series I was writing? About Mississippi, then and now?"

"Sure."

"Well, there's a reason I wanted to do the story. It's not just journalism. It's also personal."

"How?"

Ella took a deep breath and exhaled slowly. "I've always felt more than a little guilty about everything that happened in Mississippi's past. The Klan, the lynchings, the burnings."

"I think we all—well, most of us, anyway—feel some of that."

"But I've got a good reason to feel that way. I told you I grew up here. It was a small town. Indianola, down in the Delta. My family had lived there for generations. My father ran a drugstore that had been started by my grandfather. My mother was a teacher."

"But why would you . . . ?" Jeff began.

Ella put her hand up. "Please, Jeff. Let me finish."

He nodded.

"When I was home from college one Christmas vacation, I was telling my father about a course I had taken at Yale that studied famous trials. One of the cases dealt with the murder of Emmett Till, right here in Mississippi back in the fifties."

"I know all about the case," Jeff said sadly.

"Well, then you know that the killers were found not guilty, despite a ton of evidence against them. And that the Klan probably had a lot to do with the verdict."

Jeff shook his head. "It was awful. The horrible torture and murder of a fourteen-year-old black boy visiting from Chicago. And a complete miscarriage of justice. A defense lawyer told the all-white jury that their ancestors would roll over in their graves if they ever convicted a white man for killing 'a colored.' The two guys even confessed to the kidnapping and killing after the trial—said they had to kill the boy because he was disrespectful to one of their wives—but were never charged with anything else. Got paid four thousand dollars for their story. And walked away free. Not one of our greatest judicial moments," he added.

"So," Ella continued, "after I told my father how uncomfortable I felt in the class when we discussed the case—I was the only Southerner in the room, and actually from Mississippi, for God's sake—he started acting really strange, trying to change the subject and not looking at me. Finally, I asked him what was the matter."

She paused a moment. Jeff could tell she was struggling with her emotions. Then, she took another deep breath and continued.

"My grandfather was in the Klan, Jeff. And not just a rank-and-file Klansman. He was the damn leader of the local *klavern*, or whatever they called it."

She paused again, searching Jeff's eyes for some kind of reaction. Now it was his turn to take a deep breath.

"You never knew anything about it?" he asked, his tone gentle.

"Not until then. My parents had never said anything about it. My grandfather died when I was about ten. But all my memories are of this big, gentle, kind old man who everybody in the town loved."

She paused to wipe away two small tears that had gathered in the corners of her eyes.

"My father said he had wanted to tell me but had never found the right time," she continued. "Until then. He tried to explain that back in the fifties and sixties things were different. He claimed that my grandfather was not a bad man, but that most of the men in the town back then—especially the town leaders—joined the Klan. That the men who owned the businesses were all *expected* to join. Anyway, when I asked if my grandfather had ever been involved with the bad stuff—cross burnings and beatings—my father said he didn't think so. But, Jeff," she said, leaning closer to him across the table, "I don't think he was telling the truth. There was just something about the way my father answered, how he avoided looking me in the eye. I don't believe him," she stated flatly.

"Wow," Jeff said softly. "Have you talked about it anymore?"

"Nope. He refuses to discuss it. Says it's ancient history and there's no reason to drag it all up again."

"Look, Ella. It's Mississippi. We all know what this place was like back then. I think it's a pretty safe bet," he said, with a tender smile, "that you're not the only child of the Delta with a grandparent who was in the Klan."

"I know that. And I keep telling myself that. But part of me just can't get past the fact that my grandfather was a leader of the KKK."

Just then, the waitress arrived with their food. She scattered the plates across the table, gave them a quick smile, and headed back to the kitchen.

"Anyway," she sighed, "I wanted you to know."

"I appreciate it, Ella. I really do. But it doesn't mean anything," Jeff said reassuringly. "It's not who you are. And it was a long time ago. So let's just enjoy the fine food at this lovely dining establishment."

"Our dinner date?"

"Yeah," he grinned. "Our dinner date."

Ella took a bite of her cheeseburger and then looked over at Jeff.

"That makes us a bit of an odd couple then, doesn't it?" she said, dabbing at her mouth with a napkin.

"How do you mean?"

"Well, you're the son of a great integration crusader and I'm the granddaughter of a Klan leader. And here we are trying to solve a forty-year-old civil rights murder together."

Jeff smiled and shrugged. "A little odd, maybe. But I think we're doing okay."

They finished off their cheeseburgers and split a piece of pecan pie, content for the moment to talk about anything except the murder of Elijah Hall. After Jeff paid the check, despite Ella's protestations that they should split it, they strolled out into the cool Mississippi night. As Ella walked around the front of Jeff's Jeep, she suddenly stopped.

"Jeff! Look!" she cried.

Jeff stopped and looked down. All four tires on his Jeep were flat. And each had a hunting knife protruding, like an arrow, from the sidewall.

At that moment, Jeff's cell phone rang. He pulled it from his pocket and answered, still staring at the knives in his tires.

"Hello?"

"You been lookin' for a man that don't wanna be found," a deep voice drawled.

"Who is this?" Jeff said.

"No matter who it is. Only thing matters is you stop diggin' around where you don't belong. Before y'all get yourselves hurt. This here's your last warning. Next time'll be more than just your damn tires. You got it?"

Jeff pulled Ella next to him as his eyes darted about, looking for anyone who could be watching them.

"Wait!" Jeff said. "Who the hell are you? And where . . . ?"

The phone went dead.

CHAPTER 19

"What?" Tillman Jessup exploded. "Is he fucking crazy?"

Jessup was seated behind the desk in his office in the State Capitol building located in downtown Jackson. Across from him, perched uncomfortably on the edge of his chair, sat Royce Henning, his chief of staff. Henning, slim and stylishly dressed, his thinning blond hair receding slightly, had worked for Jessup for ten years. He was smart, charming, ruthless, and fanatically loyal to the man he believed would soon be Mississippi's governor and—possibly down the road—the president of the United States. Usually a model of self-composure, his elegant, angular, patrician features were now twisted and tortured by concern over the news he had just passed on to his boss.

"It makes no sense," said Henning, shaking his head. "I tried to get through to Haynes, but he's been ducking my calls."

"So how do you know it's true?" asked Jessup angrily.

"My source is solid and he . . ."

"Who told you?" Jessup interrupted. "And how does he know?"

Henning shook his head again. "You're better off not knowing. Trust me—he's very close to all of this. And he told me that Haynes is definitely moving forward with an investigation."

"An investigation! Jesus fucking Christ! Just the rumor of an investigation could fucking destroy us! Where the hell's all this coming from?"

"Not sure yet. But I'm working on it." Henning paused a moment, then leaned forward.

"Senator," he said delicately. "Is there anything here—anything at all—that I should know about?"

Jessup glared at him. "I can't believe you're actually asking me that question."

"I'm sorry, sir," Henning said hastily. "But if I'm going to make all this nonsense go away, I've got to know everything."

"No, goddamn it! I didn't kill any fucking black preacher forty *fucking* years ago! Does that satisfy you?" Jessup snarled.

"Yes, sir. Of course it does. But I'm sure you understand why I had to ask."

Jessup waved his hand dismissively. "Never mind. The important thing is how do we put a lid on this bullshit and make it disappear before we get buried by it?"

"Well," said Henning thoughtfully. "I'll try to talk to Haynes right away. I'll camp out in front of his office if I have to. What's your relationship with him?"

Jessup shrugged. "Never been real close. He's never asked me for any help and I've never offered any. But I never thought he'd come at me like this. Especially for something this absurd."

"It just makes no sense," Henning repeated. "Why would Haynes put himself in this position? He's got to know that we won't let this happen. And that he'll pay the price."

"Where the hell is all this coming from?" Jessup mused angrily.

"I don't know yet. But I promise I'll find out soon, sir. And then we'll do whatever we have to do to make it go away quickly and quietly."

CHAPTER 20

"No prints. No nothin'," said Terrell Jackson.

"How about the knives?" asked Jeff.

Jackson shrugged. "Typical hunting knives. Can buy them anywhere."

Jeff and Jackson were sitting at a long table in the district attorney's private conference room. District Attorney Gibb Haynes sat at the end of the table, deep in a quiet conversation with Sheriff Clayton Poole. The men were waiting for Ricky Earl Graves, who had been transferred from Parchman State Prison to the Lafayette County Jail.

"You had any luck tracking Hollingsly down?" asked Jeff.

"Nope. Don't suspect I will. Getting any of these ol' rednecks to give up a brother to a lawman—especially one my color—ain't likely to happen," answered Jackson. "But I'll keep on it. How 'bout you? You backin' off after your tires got decorated by them knives?"

Jeff shook his head. "Not after we got his attention. I talked to a friend of my father, an old-timer who was on the road for thirty years with the Highway Patrol. Said he knew Hollingsly from the old days and thinks he might be able to help. And Ella's become a bulldog about finding him. She's checking with a source at Social Security and also trying to run down an address from the Mississippi pension system."

"Just be careful, y'hear," said Jackson. "These boys don't play real fair."

Just then, there was a knock and the door swung open. Graves was escorted into the room, dressed in a prison jumpsuit and a hooded sweatshirt, his hands shackled in front of him. Jeff stood and motioned to the two guards to seat Graves in the chair at the far end of the table.

"Gentlemen," said Jeff, nodding toward his client, "this here is Ricky Earl Graves. Ricky Earl, this is District Attorney Haynes, Sheriff Poole, and Investigator Jackson."

Jeff took his seat and looked toward Ricky Earl. "So, here's the plan. You're going to tell these gentlemen your story, start to finish, just the way you told it to me. Don't leave anything out. And then they'll ask you any questions they might have."

Jeff nodded toward Haynes. "The district attorney has agreed that this conversation is completely off-the-record. Nothing you say here can ever be used against you if they decide not to make a deal with us. After this meeting, Mr. Haynes and I will decide if we have a deal and then we'll move forward from there. Agreed?"

Haynes looked hard at Ricky Earl for a moment, and then nodded.

"Good," Jeff said, leaning back in his chair. "Okay, Ricky Earl, you're on. Let's start at the beginning."

Ricky Earl looked around the table at his audience, placed his manacled hands on the table in front of him, and offered up a wolf-like grin.

"Seems pretty clear to me that y'all ain't thrilled to be spendin' time with the likes of me. Especially you, Mister Jackson," he said, looking directly at Terrell. "And, tell you the truth, I ain't so happy to be hangin' out with all y'all either. But this is just business, fellas, so let's get on with it." And, with that, he began to tell his story.

The men at the table listened carefully, each taking extensive notes, as Ricky Earl described the events that led to the murder of Elijah

Hall. Jeff was pleased that the details never wavered from the previous versions that Ricky Earl had provided. When Ricky Earl finished his narrative, Haynes began a decidedly unfriendly cross-examination. In rapid-fire fashion, Haynes questioned Ricky Earl's story, probing for inconsistencies, challenging his memory and his motives, seeking any signs of weakness in either the witness or his testimony. Occasionally, the district attorney would pause and huddle with Poole and Jackson before leaning across the table, pointing his finger at Ricky Earl, and continuing his barrage. Despite the open hostility, Ricky Earl kept his composure and was quick to provide all the answers, including an intense discussion of the particulars concerning the actual shooting and the location of the body afterward.

After more than two hours of questioning, Haynes tossed his pen onto the conference table and turned his attention away from Ricky Earl and toward Jeff.

"I think we've heard all we need from Mr. Graves. I'm going to send him back to the jail while we all talk a bit," Haynes said, pressing a button on his phone console which immediately brought the two prison guards back into the conference room.

Ricky Earl stood, a guard on each arm, and nodded sullenly to the men around the table. "Look, I know y'all don't like me none and I get that. But in the end, the truth is the truth. No matter who's tellin' it." He grinned. "Been a real pleasure, fellas. Hope we can meet up again real soon."

"I'll be over to talk with you as soon as we're finished here," Jeff said to Ricky Earl as he was escorted out of the room.

When the guards and their prisoner had left, Jeff looked at each of the men around the table.

"Well? What do you think?"

The district attorney was the first to speak. "He's a sleazy old bastard," he said thoughtfully. "But, God help me, I think I believe him. What about you, Clay?"

Sheriff Poole had remained quiet throughout the cross-examination, content to pass a number of notes to Haynes, which usually prompted a series of follow-up questions.

"Well," Poole began, shaking his head ruefully, "I sure as hell didn't want to believe that this redneck son of a bitch could be telling the truth. But I got to admit, after listening to him—especially when he talked about where the body ended up—well, goddamn it, I think I believe him, too."

Jeff looked at Poole, puzzled. "Why was the location of the body so significant?"

Poole shot a glance at Haynes, who nodded that he could go ahead and answer.

"Well, you saw how skimpy the file was, right?" Poole asked.

Jeff shook his head. "Couldn't believe it. Even for back then, I figured that there would be more than just two pages of police reports."

"Turns out, there was. We found a supplemental file locked away in an old evidence safe. Didn't look as if it'd been touched since the killing. Guess no one had any occasion to go looking for it until now. Inside were an autopsy report and some police photos of the crime scene that showed the body before the coroner got there. Don't know why they weren't ever placed in the main case file. We did some checking up and, apparently, the photos were never made public. Never even showed up in the newspapers. Just kinda disappeared. Just like the so-called investigation," he added sarcastically. "Guess the authorities really wanted the whole thing to go away as quickly and quietly as possible."

"So?" Jeff asked, turning toward Haynes.

Haynes took a deep breath and slowly exhaled. "So, you know how your client knew exactly what song they sang inside the church that night? And, since the pastor doesn't recall ever telling that to anyone, you argued that means he was actually there?"

"That made sense to me," Jeff said. "Plus, he passed the polygraph with flying colors. I know that's not admissible in court, but to me it means he's telling the truth."

"Could be," Haynes agreed. "Also, the report had the names of a couple who were out walking their dog that night. Heard what sounded like a gunshot and then saw a car and a truck speeding away. Both matched your boy's description. Woman's still alive and can testify. We checked motor vehicle records from back then and a 1960 Buick LeSabre was registered to Jessup's father. So, that gives us some corroboration." He paused. "But here's the clincher for me. Nobody's ever talked about the shotgun wounds to the back and how the body was found, with the head in the ditch, arms all spread out. It's not in the police reports or the newspapers, and, as far as we can tell, nobody ever saw the photos. So, the question is—how does your boy know all those details?"

"Because he was, in fact, there," Jeff said softly. "And it happened just the way he said."

"Right," said Haynes. "So now it seems like we got ourselves a murder and a witness."

"And a killer," added Jeff.

"Sure looks that way to me," answered the district attorney.

The men sat quietly for a few moments, each mulling the significance of Haynes's conclusion, before Haynes broke the silence.

"So, what kind of deal you lookin' for?"

"We'll plead to a conspiracy count. Sentence will be concurrent to the time he's doing now. We arrange for him to come up for parole in about a year. When he does, you go to bat for him. Big time. In the meantime, while he's waiting, he gets transferred to a minimum-security facility, with some serious protection." Jeff paused, looking carefully at Haynes. "Deal?"

Haynes sat with his hands folded in front of his face, his features contorted as he wrestled with his next step, a step that he knew could have enormous consequences—one way or the other—for him, both personally and professionally.

"Deal," Haynes said finally. He then looked around the table. "Gentlemen, I think it's time that we present what we've got to a grand jury and let the good citizens of this county decide if we try the next governor of Mississippi for murder."

CHAPTER 21

"A grand jury? You can't be serious," exclaimed Royce Henning when the district attorney had filled him in on what was about to happen to his boss.

"Afraid so," said Gibb Haynes, rocking gently in the big armchair behind his desk.

"Look, Gibb," said Henning, softening his tone as he leaned forward, his palms on the top of the gleaming desk. "We understand that you can't just ignore everyone who wanders into your office with a story to tell, no matter how crazy that story may sound. But you've got to realize . . ."

"You see," Haynes interrupted, in his deepest good ol' boy drawl, "that's the problem."

Henning cocked his head, puzzled. "What do you mean?"

"Well, turns out this here story's not so crazy after all," Haynes continued. "I'll admit I was more than just a little skeptical at first. But after we did some diggin', turns out this witness just might be tellin' the truth."

"Telling the truth?" Henning echoed, clearly exasperated. "You can't possibly believe that Tillman Jessup would ever have been involved in something like this—much less actually be the killer."

"Why not?"

Henning was taken aback. "Why not?" he repeated. "For God's sake, this is a revered public figure we're talking about. His family's been leaders of this state for generations. He's spent twenty years in the state senate, out in front on every major social issue. Jesus Christ, Gibb, just last year he was honored by the NAACP for his work improving the schools. And this is the guy you want to prosecute for a forty-year-old civil rights murder?"

"This ain't personal for me, Mr. Henning. Believe me, I wish Ricky Earl Graves had never showed up in my office. But, once he did, I can't ignore his story and just make him go away. Can't do that," he said, shaking his head. "Not for Senator Jessup, not for you, not for anybody."

"But don't you understand the damage that this whole thing will do? Just the fact that you're actually investigating this preposterous allegation . . . when that gets out it'll be impossible to stop the flow of rumor and innuendo. You're talking about the slanderous destruction of a sterling reputation that's taken a lifetime to build—and you're prepared to demolish all of that, everything Senator Jessup's done for this state, based on the word of a career criminal?"

Haynes stopped rocking and leaned forward. "First of all, it's not my call. That's why we have grand juries, so no prosecutor has that kind of unbridled power. The citizens of this county will decide if senator Jessup should be charged, the same way it works for anybody else. Second, we're not just relying on his word. Give us a little credit for doing our job. We've spent a lot of time investigating this case and, unfortunately for the Senator, we've been able to corroborate much of what Graves told us. Does that mean that Senator Jessup's guilty? Don't know that for sure yet, but we're still looking. In the meantime, I'll just do my job and we'll let a grand jury make the call."

"So that's it?" said Henning, anger creeping into his voice. "You're actually going ahead with this nonsense?"

"Looks that way," Haynes answered calmly. He paused a beat. "But if the senator's got anything he'd like to talk to me about, well, I'd be happy to listen. Maybe he'd like to be run on a polygraph, like Ricky Earl Graves was, to get his side of the story out there?"

"Don't be ridiculous!" Henning exploded. "There's no 'his side of the story' to be told. There's no damn story at all. Just this lowlife's lies. And you're falling for them!"

"Sorry you feel that way," Haynes said smoothly, standing to signal that their conversation was over. "But I appreciate you taking the time to talk with me."

Henning glared at the district attorney, then stood and walked to the door. He stopped and turned.

"This isn't a battle you want to fight, Gibb," he hissed. "Because when this is over and you've lost—that's when the damn war will really start. And I promise you, there's no way you'll survive that war!"

Haynes smiled. "You're not threatening me, are you, Mr. Henning?"

Henning was silent, merely offering a malevolent smile in return before slamming the door behind him.

CHAPTER 22

The media explosion was seismic. Ella broke the story of the investigation, and the fact that Jessup was the target, in a *New York Times* exclusive a few days before the grand jury was scheduled to take up the case. The local news outlets were not far behind. For days, the story garnered wall-to-wall coverage and captured the attention of television viewers and newspaper readers across the country. The scoop rocketed Ella into the journalism stratosphere, bestowing instant celebrity status, and made her the go-to person for the onslaught of reporters descending upon the town.

The intersection of the mystery of an unsolved civil rights-era murder with the ascending arc of a popular New South politician provided a delectable recipe for the insatiable appetites of the media hordes—especially the cable news channels. Each night, the cable shout fests would focus on the drama unfolding in Mississippi. Former prosecutors would solemnly, yet loudly, proclaim Tillman Jessup's guilt and celebrate the triumph of justice delayed, while defense attorneys would stridently bemoan the depravity of relying on the testimony of a career criminal to tarnish the reputation of an outstanding civil servant. In the meantime, political pundits offered wildly differing views of the political future of the "rising star" of Southern politics. As a result of her newly conferred "star journalist" rank, Ella was a frequent guest on the television shows. Although her appearances were a huge boost for the *Times* and her own career, she struggled in the arena of name-calling and premature conclusions, steadfastly refusing to take sides.

Tillman Jessup, following his bulldog instincts and ignoring the advice of his team of lawyers and advisors, decided to wage a pitched media battle against the district attorney's office. His crusade took him to every reporter with a microphone, computer, or pencil. No media outlet or Internet site was too small for his attention. And, in each interview, the theme was the same. "This is an outrageous and illegal attack on me, fueled by my political adversaries and driven by a reckless prosecutor," he would exclaim. "If these political opportunists can do this to me," he would shout, like a Sunday evangelist rousing a tentful of worshipers, "then nobody is safe from this type of wild and irresponsible personal assassination. First me, and then they'll come after you!"

District Attorney Haynes, on the other hand, remained uncharacteristically quiet. When asked about the case, he would simply declare that he would have no comment until the case was presented to a grand jury. Desperate for any hard facts, reporters camped outside the district attorney's office and peppered any and all employees with a futile barrage of questions. But Haynes had made it clear that he wanted absolutely no information to be leaked and that a violation of his edict would be a firing offense.

The day before the grand jury was scheduled to meet to consider the case, Tillman Jessup conducted what was billed as a press conference, but what was, in reality, a pep rally. In a fairly heavy-handed act of symbolism, Jessup invited the members of the media to join him behind the Lyceum, next to the James Meredith memorial, on the Ole Miss campus.

Flanked by his wife, who appeared both distracted and distressed by the turmoil, Jessup provided, in response to a few softball questions, a fiery and confrontational attack upon what he termed "this rogue and irresponsible prosecutor." When he was asked, specifically, if he had any involvement in the killing of Elijah Hall, he offered a dramatic pause and then launched into a barely-controlled tirade.

"How do you prove that you're innocent of an outlandish charge of a murder that occurred more than forty years ago?" he boomed, staring down the questioner. "Could you tell me where you were on a particular day, even ten years ago? Of course not! Nobody can! And yet, despite all I've done as a dedicated public servant of this state—despite all that my *family* has done over the years—despite all that, this rogue prosecutor, relying on only the statements of some despicable career criminal, is attempting to destroy me. And that, ladies and gentlemen, should frighten all of you. Because if he can attempt to do this to me, what protection would any of you ever have? The answer is—*none!*"

With the cameras still rolling and the audience now mesmerized by his performance, Jessup smoothly shifted gears from outrage to what appeared to be deep and passionate sincerity.

"Anyone who knows me, who has spent even a small amount of time with me, will know that I could never, ever, commit any crime, much less the brutal murder involved here. To think that I could be the kind of racist killer . . ." Jessup choked up a moment, wiping at his eyes, and struggled to gain control of his emotions. "Well, I'd just tell you to ask any of the thousands of constituents—black and white— who I've helped over the years. Go ahead," he said, ratcheting his voice up again in anger. "Go ahead and ask them! And when you do, you'll hear what they all have to say about me!"

He looked out defiantly over the crowd. "I will win this fight! I guarantee it! Because I am an innocent man and, as a great man told us decades ago, the truth will, indeed, set you free!"

With that, Jessup turned, took his wife by the arm and, followed by his entourage and a wave of applause, stormed off.

CHAPTER 23

Television satellite trucks had been parked in the Oxford Square since dawn. Reporters had quickly staked out territory for their stand-up shots, jockeying for the most impressive courthouse backdrops. The grand jury was scheduled to hear testimony that morning about the killing of Elijah Hall, and each of the media members was hell-bent on being the first to disclose to the anxiously waiting world whether Tillman Jessup would actually be charged with murder.

Inside the district attorney's office, the sense of expectation hung like the lingering moment between a jagged lightning slash and the subsequent crash of thunder. Gibb Haynes had decided that he would handle this case, from start to whatever finish might be involved, by himself. Although he claimed that he didn't want any members of his staff left "to hang and twist in the wind" in the event that the grand jury refused to indict Jessup, who would surely come looking for revenge, most were certain that "the old man" was really looking for his own personal Armageddon—his last great battle between good and evil before he rode off into the Mississippi retirement sunset.

Jeff, having navigated his way through the roiling sea of media outside, now sat beside Travis Murray in a room with a clearly nervous Ricky Earl Graves, who had swapped his jail jumpsuit for a pair of khaki pants and a blue button-down shirt. Ricky Earl's nicotine-stained fingers fiddled with his handcuffs as his eyes darted about.

"You sure I can't have just one quick smoke?" he pleaded.

"Nope," said Jeff, leafing through his notes. "No smoking anymore in government buildings."

"Whole damn country's gone to hell when a man can't even grab a smoke when he wants," Ricky Earl grumbled.

"So, how're the accommodations over in the jail?" asked Murray.

"Shitload better'n up in Parchman," Ricky Earl answered, referring to the infamous Mississippi state prison.

"If Jessup gets indicted, the DA said he'll keep you here until the trial. Safer for you and easier for them," Murray said.

"Suits me fine."

"Let's go over this whole thing one more time, okay?" Jeff said.

"Sure," said Ricky Earl. "Ain't got nothin' better to do."

"So, remember, this isn't the same as testifying at a trial. It's just you and the DA in a room full of grand jurors. Couple dozen people. No defense attorneys, no cross-examination, and no Jessup. The DA will take you through your testimony. Answer him carefully and make sure you *just* answer the question he asks. Don't go rambling on. If he wants more from you, he'll ask you. When he's finished, if some of the grand jurors have questions, just answer what they ask. Don't go offering anything more. Got it?"

"Yup. No problem."

"You'll be the second witness. Reverend Butler will go in before you to testify about everything that happened that night before the killing. Then you. Then Investigator Jackson will wrap it up with all of the investigation details."

Ricky Earl nodded, still fidgeting with his handcuffs.

"I still don't think it's such a good idea for the DA to put all three of them in front of the grand jury," said Murray. "Why not just do it the usual way and let Terrell Jackson testify about everything? Why make it such a big production and put Ricky Earl in there?"

"That was my thought too, at first," said Jeff, "but the DA feels like he's got to be completely up front about everything in this case. Especially if Jessup gets indicted. This way, he can say that Jessup got a better shot than most suspects, because he gave the grand jury the chance to assess Ricky Earl's credibility rather than just relying on a cop's testimony. Makes sense, I guess. This way, Jessup can't claim he was railroaded."

"So, we'll know today if he's gonna be charged?" asked Ricky Earl.

"Probably," said Jeff. "Once the grand jury's heard all the testimony, they'll vote. If at least twelve of them say yes, he gets indicted."

"What's the chance of that happenin'?"

"Don't know," said Jeff. "But I guess we'll find out soon."

Ricky Earl looked at Jeff and cocked his head. "You believe me, Mr. Trannon?"

Jeff locked eyes with him. "Yeah, I believe you," he said softly. "But let's get something straight. I don't think you're any kind of hero for doing this."

Ricky Earl nodded his head slowly. "That's okay. Ain't tryin' to be anyone's hero. Just tryin' to get outta jail." He paused and thought a moment. "And maybe do the right thing. For once in my life. But that's okay. I don't think I'm no hero, neither."

There was a knock on the door and a jail guard stepped inside. "They want him over there now," he said.

"Okay, then," Jeff said, slapping his palm on the table. "Let's go do the right thing."

CHAPTER 24

Jeff and Ella sat on a bench on the Square across from the courthouse. Two hours earlier, the district attorney had announced that a Lafayette County grand jury had voted to indict State Senator Tillman Jessup for the murder of Reverend Elijah Hall. All hell had broken loose. Reporters had scrambled for their phones and their cameras to break the news, and then they had assembled for a raucous press conference on the steps of the old courthouse.

Gibb Haynes had begun the conference by reading a brief statement, indicating that he had been in contact with Jessup's attorneys, had advised them of the grand jury's action, and had agreed that the senator would be arraigned the next day. In response to shouted questions, he had refused to disclose what the vote of the grand jurors had been and exactly who had testified, citing laws about grand jury secrecy.

"I want to be completely clear about this, so listen up," Haynes had said, when asked how the grand jurors had reacted to the case. "These good citizens took their responsibility very seriously. They knew how important this case was to everyone—and that includes both the defendant, Senator Jessup, and the State of Mississippi. My office has been more than fair to the defendant and his attorneys. So I don't want to hear any nonsense about this being some kind of political witch hunt. Never happened. Now we'll all just let a jury decide, the same way it's always been done around here. No special treatment asked for, and none given."

When asked if the prosecution would seek the death penalty in the event of a conviction, Haynes had been silent for a moment. "Haven't decided yet. But we'll have an answer for the court at the time of the arraignment."

Finally, a young reporter from the rear of the boisterous throng had jostled his way to the front and bellowed, "How can you justify to the people of Mississippi the act of indicting a respected public figure based on the testimony of a lifelong criminal?"

Haynes had raised his hands, signaling for quiet, and glowered at the questioner.

"I'm going to assume, sir," he replied sternly, "that you're not from around here. Because if you were, you'd know that I've been in this job for about as long as you've been alive, and during all that time I've always done what was *right*. Not what was popular. Not what was politically expedient. Just what was right. Understand something, all y'all," he said, shifting his gaze away from the questioner and taking in the entire gathering. "I take no pleasure in this. I've known Senator Jessup and his family for a long time and I realize that a lot of people are going to be very angry about this indictment. But our justice system is bigger than a senator and bigger than a district attorney. The grand jury has spoken, and now it's my job to present this case to a trial jury. And those good citizens," he said, shooting one last glare at the questioner, "will decide Senator Jessup's fate, sir, not me."

With that, declaring that there would be no further statements from his office until they arrived in court the next day for the arraignment, Haynes had swept off the courthouse steps and retreated to his office.

After that, the media circus had, except for a few stragglers, withdrawn until the following day's court date, leaving the Square cast in a sudden and overwhelming silence. After Ella had filed her sotry, she sought out Jeff, who had just met with Ricky Earl to break the news about the indictment.

"So," she said, "how'd Ricky Earl react to the news?"

"It's funny," Jeff said thoughtfully, "it wasn't what I expected."

"Why?"

"Well, I thought he'd be excited, but he actually seemed a little sad. Maybe not sad, exactly." He paused a moment. "But certainly not happy. I think the thing he was most pleased about was that he was going to be staying here for a while and not sent back to Parchman. Anyway, I imagine the folks up at the *Times* are happy."

She nodded. "This story's really got legs now. At first, it just looked to the national media like some Southern curiosity, a bizarre allegation that had flared up but would probably die down just as quickly. But now it's become a drama worthy of Faulkner, a story of race, politics, and murder. Pretty powerful recipe."

Jeff sighed. "We surely do know how to do drama down here."

They were both quiet for a few minutes.

"So?" she asked.

"So . . . what?"

"So, what do you think? Are you happy that he's been indicted?"

"Honestly? No. I mean, I'm certainly pleased as Ricky Earl's lawyer. That's my job. And I do believe Jessup killed Elijah Hall. But there's a part of me that wishes that it wasn't true. This trial's going to tear this place apart. Not just Oxford," he said, gesturing around the Square, "but this whole state. And I'm just not sure what's going to come from it."

After a moment, Ella said softly, "I think he'd be proud of you."

"What?" asked Jeff, puzzled. "Who?"

"Your father." She paused a moment, then continued. "I know about the Alzheimer's. But if he was still well, still himself, I think he'd be proud of you. Of what you're doing here."

"Maybe. I don't know. The funny thing is we never really used to talk much about the law and his cases. Talked a lot about sports, but not so much about other things."

"Too bad you can't talk to him about this case."

Jeff turned and looked at her directly. "Remember at the diner the other night? When you told me that you hadn't been completely honest with me?"

"Of course. Why?"

"Well, I haven't been completely honest with you, either."

"About what?"

"About me and my father."

"What do you mean?"

"When we first met, you asked me about being William Trannon's son and trying to follow in his footsteps. And I told you that it wasn't that bad and that, in some ways, it was helpful."

"I remember," she nodded.

"That wasn't really the truth. At least, not the whole truth." He looked off into the distance and was silent for a time.

"The truth is," he said, turning back to her, "it was never easy. You can't begin to imagine how big a star he is. Or was. The greatest football player ever. The greatest lawyer ever. The greatest judge ever. I mean, I was always proud of him and proud to be his son." He sighed. "But I could just never be him, you know what I mean? I was a good football player, but I'd never be 'Fast Willie.' I knew it and everybody in the stadium knew it. And I was a pretty good lawyer, but whenever I walked into a courtroom I was always 'Justice Trannon's son.' I tried to fight it—to make a name for myself. I stayed here at Ole Miss to play football and to go to law school, and I did pretty well. Then I became a prosecutor, and a good one, too. But finally," he said, his voice etched in deep sadness, "I realized that things were never going to change. That no matter what I ever did, I was always going to be 'William Trannon's son.'" His voice trailed off.

"I still think he'd be proud of you," Ella said. "From what I've learned, his life was all about justice. And that's what this is all about, too." She placed her hand over his. "He'd be proud that you are his son."

"Maybe," he said wistfully. "I guess I'll never know."

CHAPTER 25

On the day of the arraignment, Jeff felt like a salmon swimming upstream as he picked his way through the crowds milling about in the Square. A large group of spectators was camped out early near the courthouse entrance, hoping to catch a glimpse of the famous defendant as he made his first court appearance. Marveling at the collection of television satellite trucks circling the Square, Jeff had chuckled to himself, reminded of old lithographs of Western frontier prairie schooners circling a campsite.

Inside, every seat had been claimed hours before the hearing was scheduled to start. The grand old courtroom was an architectural marvel. After entering the courthouse on the ground floor, a gracefully turned staircase led to the second-floor main chamber. Two colossal wooden doors provided passage into the room. Inside, eight gently curving rows of benches afforded seating for the press and public, while large conference tables inside the railing housed two small armies of lawyers, each armed with arsenals of thick files, scores of law books, and piles of notepads.

Above, a quaint balcony, reached by a small back staircase, held the overflow crowd. The panoramic view from this vantage point was striking. Beneath the soaring ceiling dotted with six strikingly elegant chandeliers, each side wall was marked by a set of exquisite double doors that opened onto small columned balconies, together with two towering windows in each corner, all offering any visitors expansive views of the Square and North and South Lamar Boulevards. The walls were painted a soothingly elegant pale blue, setting off the precise architectural details of the stylish white ceiling moldings. Along the right wall was the jury box, holding fourteen soft-leather swivel chairs, walled off from the rest of the courtroom by a waist-high wooden balustrade. Behind the jury box was a single door that opened into the jury deliberation room. Standing sentinel in the front of the chamber was an impressive, raised, ornately carved wooden bench, home to the judge who would preside over the trial.

Jeff, Ella, and Travis Murray were seated in the first row on the right side, directly behind the prosecution table. Across the aisle, in the first row behind the defense table, sat Kendra Leigh Jessup, flanked by a score of political aides and supporters.

While scribbling observations in her notebook, Ella alternated curious glances between Senator Jessup, deep in huddled conversation with his legal team, and Kendra Leigh. The former beauty queen sat silent and stoic, appearing pale and drawn, dressed in a severe black skirt and jacket, her attention seemingly fixed on the emblazoned seal of the state of Mississippi on the wall high above the judge's bench.

"Wonder what she's thinking," she murmured to Jeff.

"Who?" said Jeff, who had been staring intently at the defense assembly.

"Mrs. Jessup," answered Ella, nodding toward the group across the aisle. "I wonder what she's thinking about. Her perfect life on the verge of collapsing. I kind of feel sorry for her."

"Don't know," said Jeff. "But I don't think I'd want to be one of Jessup's lawyers. Just look at him, bossing them around. Not your typical client, I guess."

"Who's the new guy?" Ella asked, nodding toward one of the lawyers, who had detached himself from Jessup and the sycophantic cluster and was standing to the side, reviewing some notes.

"Channing Wallace," answered Jeff, shifting his gaze toward the new lawyer. He was a tall, graceful man, with carefully styled, swept-back silvery hair, a narrow, handsome face marked by a long aquiline nose and dark, intense eyes. Dressed in an impeccable English vested pinstriped suit, his patrician bearing and easy confidence made it clear that he was accustomed to being in charge.

"Something of a legend here in Mississippi," Jeff continued. "Big-time trial lawyer from up in Jackson. Made a fortune suing the tobacco companies a few years back. Now just picks and chooses some high-profile cases to handle when he's not hanging out with politicians and Hollywood types."

"Is he as good as he looks?" Ella asked, obviously impressed by the man's appearance.

"Yep. He's definitely a heavyweight. But don't worry," Jeff said, shooting her a grin. "Gibb Haynes can handle him. Wallace is smooth, all right, and smart. But Old Gibb can charm the rattles off a rattlesnake. The jurors around here just love him." Before Ella could respond, there was a rustling in the courtroom as the clerk took her seat in front of the bench indicating that the court session was about to begin. People scrambled for their seats and, a moment later, the door behind the bench opened and Circuit Court Judge Rogers Langston entered the chamber to a call of "All rise!" from the bailiff.

Quickly taking his seat, Judge Langston took a moment to carefully arrange a collection of files and law books on his desk, then looked up and, with a slight, imperious wave of his hand, indicated that all should be seated. When everyone had settled into their seats, he adjusted the wire-rim glasses perched on the end of his nose and looked out over the audience.

Judge Rogers Langston was most at home in his courtroom. A careful and studious man, a graduate of Ole Miss and Harvard Law School, he had a well-earned reputation as a demanding and precise jurist, with the capacity to be charming at one moment and excoriating the next. Despite his occasionally harsh treatment of lawyers who failed to adhere to his lofty standards, he was unfailingly courteous to his jurors, all of whom tended to leave his presence with a deep respect for him and how he ran his courtroom. A slender, wiry man in his early sixties, with a wispy, receding hairline, an oval face with sharp features and deep-set, intelligent eyes, he rarely raised his voice, since his reputation was so profound that he was capable of controlling unruly lawyers and reluctant witnesses with just a single steely glare. Yet, despite his training and demeanor, he was something of a maverick in court—given to deciding cases based not so much on the letter of the law but rather on what he believed was the right thing to do. As the lawyers who appeared before him often said, you were never entirely sure what result you would get in Judge Langston's court, but you were always sure that you would get what he felt was justice.

"Ladies and gentlemen," he said in a deep, honeyed, Mississippi-native drawl, "I realize that this case has garnered a great deal of attention," he nodded pointedly toward the collection of reporters crammed into the first three rows, "but I want you to be assured that this case will be handled no differently from any other. And I also want all y'all to be equally assured that I will tolerate no outbursts whatsoever in my courtroom. Do I make myself clear?"

He took a moment to let his admonition sink in and then turned his attention to the squads of lawyers now spread out along the two vast counsel tables. District Attorney Gibb Haynes sat in the first seat, nearest to the center podium, flanked by two assistants, with Sheriff Clayton Poole and Investigator Terrell Jackson located in chairs directly behind him. At the adjoining table, Channing Wallace was in the first chair, Senator Jessup parked very closely next to him, with his chief of staff, Royce Henning, directly behind him, and a phalanx of assistants, young and old, male and female, stretched out along the perimeter of the defense table.

"And you, ladies and gentlemen, are certainly welcome to my courtroom," Judge Langston said in his most courtly tone. "I must say," he added with a twinkle in his eyes, "that I can't seem to ever recollect such an impressive array of legal minds gathering for a simple arraignment. Be that as it may, let's all get down to business, shall we? Mr. District Attorney, will you be handling this matter?"

"I will, Your Honor," Haynes answered, rising from his seat and moving to the podium.

"Please proceed, then."

"Thank you, Your Honor." Haynes cleared his throat dramatically. "This is the matter of the State of Mississippi versus Tillman Jessup," he continued, his voice now booming throughout the recesses of the grand courtroom. "A grand jury of this county has charged Mr. Jessup with the crime of murder and he is here now, with counsel, to be arraigned."

"Thank you, Mr. Haynes," Judge Langston said, shifting his gaze to the defense table. "Mr. Wallace, will you be acting as lead counsel for the defendant?" he asked.

Channing Wallace rose majestically from his seat. "I will, Your Honor. And it's nice to see you again, sir."

"Always a pleasure to have you come visit with us," the judge said smoothly. "So then, how does your client plead to the charge?"

Wallace nodded to Jessup, who also rose from his seat and looked directly at the judge.

"Your Honor," Wallace answered, his voice rising, "my client, Senator Tillman Jessup, is absolutely and unequivocally innocent of this scandalous charge and, as a result, will of course plead not guilty."

"Your Honor," Haynes said angrily, "perhaps Mr. Wallace could save his speeches for the jury and simply enter a plea—"

"I am entering a plea," Wallace exploded. "I'm entering a plea on behalf of an innocent man who's been unfairly subjected—"

"That will do, gentlemen," interrupted the judge. "Thank you, Mr. Wallace." He turned back to the district attorney. "Mr. Haynes, before I consider the question of bail, I need to know the prosecution's position on possible sentences. Although this case is more than forty years old, it qualifies as a capital case, given the state of the law at the time, which could bring into question the death penalty. Have you made a decision whether, in the event of a conviction, you would seek the death penalty?"

"Your Honor," Haynes said in his most prosecutorial tone, "I have advised counsel for the defendant this morning that, after careful consideration, we will *not* be seeking the death penalty if the jury returns a conviction."

There was a murmur throughout the courtroom which Judge Langston silenced with a swift glance.

"All right, then, since this will not be a capital case, I'll consider the question of bail. What's your pleasure, Mr. Haynes?"

"The prosecution would ask, Your Honor, that bail be set in the amount of one million dollars."

"Mr. Wallace?"

"Well, Your Honor," Wallace began, shaking his head sadly, "I can certainly understand why the district attorney should decline to seek the death penalty—especially in this case—but I most certainly can't understand why he'd be looking for bail in that amount—"

"Mr. Wallace," the judge interrupted once again, "this is, after all, a murder case. And, although I appreciate your able protestations on behalf of your client, you don't really expect me not to require some type of bail in a murder case, do you?"

"Your Honor," Wallace answered, his tone of indignation rising, "my client is not some hardened criminal with no roots in this community. I'm sure that the court will recognize Senator Jessup's long and distinguished service on behalf of this state, together with his family's extensive historical role in the cultural and charitable well-being of this society. If this entire episode was not such a travesty of justice, it might actually be humorous to have the district attorney seeking one million dollars in bail to guarantee that Senator Jessup will, in fact, appear at trial." He turned theatrically toward Haynes. "I'm rather curious about where the district attorney thinks the senator might be going?"

"Your Honor," Haynes replied, "of course we recognize the defendant's roots in the community and no one is suggesting he should be treated like a career criminal. But the fact remains that this is, nevertheless, a murder charge and some reasonable bail should be required."

"But, Your Honor," a now even angrier Wallace blurted, "to even suggest—"

Judge Langston raised both hands to silence the lawyers.

"Gentlemen, I understand your positions. Here's what I'm going to do. Mr. Wallace, although I don't have any great fear that your client will abscond before trial, this is, after all, a murder charge, so I'm going to set bail at five hundred thousand dollars. However, I will order that your client may post property to satisfy the bail. I'm also going to require that your client surrender his passport while this case is pending. Now," the judge said, scribbling some notes on the case file, "let's talk about scheduling."

"Your Honor, the defense, relying on our right to a speedy trial, will insist that this matter be brought to trial immediately," Wallace trumpeted. "Senator Jessup has been forced to unfairly live his life under the cloud of these despicable lies for too long now, and we are adamant about having our day in court as soon as possible so that the good jurors of this county can restore his name and reputation."

Judge Langston cocked an eyebrow quizzically. "Are you sure that's your preference? To go to trial immediately?"

"Absolutely, Your Honor."

The judge turned toward Haynes. "Mr. District Attorney? Are you prepared to proceed quickly?"

"We are, Your Honor. If that's the request of the defense, we're prepared to accommodate them."

"Well, then," the judge said, slightly perplexed. "I must say that I'm somewhat taken aback. Usually, I'm besieged by requests for more time before trial. And often from both sides. But I certainly understand your position, Mr. Wallace, and given these circumstances, I will agree to your demand."

He motioned for his clerk to approach the bench and engaged in a whispered discussion while she paged through a calendar. Finally, he nodded his agreement to the clerk and directed his attention back to the lawyers.

"All right, gentlemen. Get your witnesses ready. We'll begin picking our jury two weeks from today. Agreed?"

There was a chorus of "Yes, Your Honor" from both sides, as Wallace placed a reassuring hand on the shoulder of a smiling Senator Jessup.

"I would like to meet with the lawyers in my chambers in fifteen minutes so that we can set an expedited schedule for any pre-trial issues, including any jury selection questions. Anything else?" Both Haynes and Wallace shook their heads. "In that case, we are adjourned."

As soon as Judge Langston had left the bench, there was a rush of media to the rail, all shouting questions at once. Haynes waved his arms and firmly declared, "We'll have no further comment until the trial begins," as he packed up his bags and worked his way through the crowd, followed by his team.

On the other side of the courtroom, Wallace and Senator Jessup, both smiling broadly, began to patiently answer every question offered by the press, as the ever-present Royce Henning hovered, eagle-eyed, on the fringe of the gathering.

Jeff and Travis Murray stood in the back of the courtroom, while Ella waded into the media scrum, her notebook and pen in hand.

"This isn't going to be easy, Jeff," Murray said glumly.

"Nobody ever said it would be."

CHAPTER 26

The whip-like slap sent Kendra Leigh Jessup stumbling backwards over a coffee table and sprawling across the floor. Her husband kicked the table to the side and stood menacingly over her as she tried to scramble away on her hands and knees.

"If you ever question me like that again, you'll be damn-sure black and blue for a month! You hear me?" Tillman Jessup screamed.

She backed herself, cowering, into the nearest corner of the room. "I only meant . . ."

"I don't give a good goddamn what you meant," he hissed, his lowered voice even more threatening than his screams had been. "It's enough that I got to answer questions about that damn preacher's death to the fucking press. I'm sure as hell not going to answer to you, too!"

"I'm your wife, for God's sake," she sobbed, her hand to her face where her right eye was already red and swollen. "I have a right to ask . . ."

"You don't have a right to ask *shit*," he snarled. "Only right you got is to do what I tell you. Just go to your little parties and wear your pretty clothes, and keep your damn mouth shut. Unless I tell you to open it. You got that?"

She glared at him, her fear changing to flaring anger. "Why can't you just look me in the eye, one time, and tell me that you had nothing to do with that man's murder? Why won't you just say that?"

"'Cause I don't have to answer to you, goddamn it!" he said, balling his fist as he stepped closer to her huddled figure.

"Go ahead, hit me again," she taunted him. "And then just how're you going to explain to your adoring fans—and the damn press—why your wife's all beat up?"

Jessup stopped and glowered at her. Finally, he backed away. "Why don't you just take a handful of your pills and your damn vodka bottle and get the fuck outta my sight."

Kendra Leigh struggled to her feet and, still slightly wobbly, started to walk past him toward the door. Jessup stepped back to let her pass.

"And make sure you're sober by next Monday. We got to pick a jury and it wouldn't do for the public to catch a glimpse of the real you. The drunken, pill-popping, pathetic former homecoming queen."

"Fuck you," she muttered as she stumbled out of the room.

CHAPTER 27

"Any luck?" Jeff asked.

"Nope," said Terrell Jackson.

Jeff, Jackson, and Ella were gathered around a conference table in the district attorney's office, comparing notes on their quest to locate A. J. Hollingsly.

"Came up empty on any gas, electric, or telephone accounts. Only one bank account and it was opened up with a post office box as an address. This guy's buried himself real deep and apparently don't want to be found. Ever. How 'bout you?"

"I was able to track his pension payments," Ella said. "Not much money involved. It's a direct deposit into an account at a Jackson bank. No activity at all on the account other than some occasional cash withdrawals—but always from different branches and always from ATM machines. And the address they have for him also turned out to be a post office box. Somebody pays cash for the box and renews it each year. No phone number or address."

"I might have something," Jeff said. "Just got a call this morning from an old friend who worked for years on the Highway Patrol. Didn't have anything definite, but had heard from a couple of contacts that Hollingsly was living up northeast in the hill country."

"Any address?" asked Jackson.

Jeff shook his head. "Just the general area. Thought he'd become something of a hermit, hiding out and avoiding any contact with just about anyone. Here's the interesting part: It seems that he's become a kind of cult figure up there, a hero to the small lunatic fringe that're still fighting for the Old South and segregation. Apparently, they're very protective of him and his privacy."

"So what's our next step?" asked Ella.

"I think I need to take a ride up there," said Jeff.

"You mean *we* need to take a ride up there," Ella said.

Jeff shook his head. "Listen, after what happened—"

"No, *you* listen," Ella said firmly. "This is my story, maybe the biggest damn story I'll ever work on. It's got Pulitzer Prize written all over it! So, don't go talking about it being dangerous. I'm a big girl. I know what I'm doing. And I'm coming with you."

Jeff was quiet for a moment and then nodded. "Okay."

"You plannin' on sending him an invitation to join you for tea?" asked Jackson, rolling his eyes.

Jeff smiled. "Don't think that would work. I just figure if we rattle his cage a little bit, show up and start asking around, maybe we'll get lucky and get to talk with him. Even if it's just for him to tell us to get lost. At least we'd get face-to-face to make our pitch to him."

Jackson shrugged his massive shoulders. "I think that plan's a little bit crazy, but I ain't got any other suggestions, so go ahead and give it a try."

"You riding with us?" Jeff asked.

"Would love to, but the DA's got me runnin' around gettin' witnesses ready for the trial. Can you wait a day or two?"

Jeff shook his head. "Don't think so. The sooner we take a shot at him the better. Especially with jury selection starting next week. Probably just as well that we go alone. Don't take this personally, but I don't think having a big ol' black man along would really help us get an audience with Mr. Hollingsly."

Jackson grinned. "Okay, but be careful. You know how ornery those old rednecks can be." He turned serious. "Make sure you call me right away if there's any problem."

"Will do. But hopefully there won't be any more trouble. Why don't you grab a subpoena for me to give to him if we find him? That way, even if he refuses to talk to us, we can at least jerk him around a little bit, arrest him if he refuses to show up. Maybe put some pressure on him, convince him to tell his story. Who knows?"

"Good idea. I'll go get a subpoena issued," Jackson said, raising his big frame out of the chair and heading for the door. He stopped in the doorway. "Jeff," he said, raising an eyebrow. "No kiddin' around, man. You be careful."

CHAPTER 28

Three hours later, Jeff and Ella were driving through the gently rolling hills and pine forests of northeast Mississippi, armed with a subpoena and nothing more than a vague idea of where they were heading.

"So, what's the plan?" Ella asked, dressed in jeans and a sweater, her flowing hair pulled back in a thick ponytail.

"Good question," Jeff said. "I thought maybe we'd look for a place where the local folks hang out—maybe a gas station, grocery store, or a bar—and start asking around for our boy."

"That's it? That's the plan?"

"Yep. That's pretty much it. Unless you've got a better idea?"

Ella smiled and shrugged. "I guess that's as good as any. Might as well give it a shot."

It was a pleasant drive. They spent the time talking easily about their childhoods, their college experiences, and their families. Jeff found himself looking forward more and more to the time they were spending together. Ella was smart and clever. And Lord knows she was easy on the eyes. His last romantic involvement had ended badly. After a turbulent three-year relationship with a gorgeous but needy, self-absorbed, drama queen of a girlfriend, he hadn't been terribly interested in starting up another one any time soon. But Ella seemed different. Independent and self-confident, with a sense of humor, she had a grand life goal and precise plans on how to get there, and Jeff felt himself being inextricably pulled into her orbit. And he enjoyed the feeling.

"There!" Ella exclaimed, pointing at a building up ahead. "Stop there!"

Peering through the Jeep's dusty windshield, Jeff saw the roadside sign for "Ike's Hunting & Fishing." He quickly yanked on the wheel and turned into the dirt and gravel parking lot. The store was a one-story wood and shingle structure with a sagging corrugated steel roof and a porch that ran the length of the front of the building.

"Looks like as good a place to start as any," said Jeff.

"You stay here. I'll go in and ask around."

Jeff shot her a questioning glance. "Why you?"

"I just think they might be more inclined to talk to a woman, that's all. Don't take it personally," she added, with a small, apologetic smile.

"Okay," he said, not entirely convinced. "Let's see if you have any luck. I'll be right here if you need me."

Ella tugged on a baseball cap, her ponytail popping out of the back, climbed out of the Jeep, and entered the store. It appeared empty except for a thin, middle-aged man perched on a stool at the register reading a newspaper. He was dressed in worn overalls and a camouflage hunting shirt with a "Bassmaster" cap tilted back on the crown of his head.

"Yes, ma'am," he drawled amiably, obviously happy to have his boredom interrupted by such an attractive woman. "What can I do for you?"

"Well," Ella said, flashing a megawatt smile. "I'm not from these parts. From down in the Delta, actually. And I'm trying to find someone who I believe lives around here."

"Maybe I can help," he said, returning her smile.

"You see, I'm a writer—name is Ella Garrity—and I'm researching a story on Mississippi's past. You know," she said, lowering her voice conspiratorially, "the good old days, before everything changed. If you know what I mean."

"Yes, ma'am. I surely do," he said, nodding earnestly.

"Good. Well then, maybe you can help me. The man I'm looking for is kind of an old-fashioned patriot and I'd love to talk to him about how things have changed." She smiled again. "I believe his name is A. J. Hollingsly. Do you know him, by any chance?"

A shadow passed swiftly across the man's face, replaced by another smile, this one seeming more forced and less warm. "Don't think I do," he said, shaking his head. "Nope, doesn't sound familiar. Sorry."

"That's okay," said Ella pleasantly. "I'll just ask around some other places and see if I have any luck. Thanks anyway."

"Okay, then. Nice talking to you," he said, as she turned and left the store.

"How'd it go?" asked Jeff as she climbed back into the Jeep.

"Claims he never heard of Hollingsly. But I'm pretty sure he wasn't telling the truth. Or at least he knows something about him. His whole attitude changed when I mentioned the name."

"Not a surprise. Didn't figure anybody would actually jump to help us."

"So, let's head up the road a bit and see if we can find some other good folks who can help us rattle his cage a little more," she said with a grin.

"You're actually having fun, aren't you?" Jeff said.

"Beats doing research in a library. I'm starting to feel like Brenda Starr." She arched an eyebrow. "You do know who Brenda Starr is, right?"

"You think I'm a cultural illiterate?" he asked, feigning hurt feelings. "Famous comic-strip reporter, always getting in and out of trouble. And quite a babe, by the way."

"Okay, you passed that test. So let's go see if we can find our redneck friend."

CHAPTER 29

Jeff and Ella sat in a booth at the rear of an old roadhouse tavern, finishing up their dinner of cheeseburgers and French fries. They had spent the better part of three hours driving up and down the narrow county road, stopping at every gas station, convenience store, and bar they found. At each, Ella reprised her role, first charming the men she came across, and then trolling for any information about Hollingsly. Although most of the men questioned seemed genuine when they denied recognizing the name, two—a man at a gas station and another at a liquor store—offered claims of ignorance that seemed suspect. Both had reactions similar to the first man she had confronted—a cheerfulness that altered abruptly once Hollingsly's name came up, swiftly morphing into suspicion masked by the stiff semblance of a smile. Finally, they decided that they had scattered all of the bait that they could. Now, they needed to wait to see if they got any nibbles.

"I think we've fallen into a rut in this relationship," Ella said, popping the last of the French fries into her mouth.

"Excuse me?" Jeff said, puzzled.

She waved her hand across the table. "Cheeseburgers and fries. Sound familiar?"

Jeff grinned sheepishly. "I see what you mean. You're right. Guess I haven't really offered you many culinary delights. How about this?

How about tomorrow night, back in Oxford, we do a real out-for-dinner? And no burgers allowed."

"That sounds suspiciously like a date."

Jeff nodded. "It does, doesn't it? So, how about we call it a date?" he asked, holding her gaze.

"I'd like that," she smiled.

"Great." He returned her smile. "A date it is."

A few minutes later, they paid the check—Ella insisted that they split it this time—and then strolled outside to the parking lot. As they approached Jeff's car, two men stepped out of the shadows and blocked their path. One was tall, lean, and bearded, while the second was short and stocky. Both wore jeans, work boots, leather jackets, and baseball caps and appeared to be in their late twenties. Neither was smiling.

"The man you been lookin' for would like to have a chat with you," said the taller man.

"That's fine," said Jeff, forcing a smile as he shuffled over toward Ella. "We were hoping we'd get a chance to meet him."

"Let's go," the tall man said, nodding toward a big, dark SUV parked about twenty feet away. "Get in."

"Where are we going?" asked Ella.

"You'll know when we get there," the shorter man grunted. "Now get in."

"Wait a second," Jeff said, raising his hands. "We're not going anywhere until—"

"We ain't *askin'* you," the tall man hissed, a revolver suddenly appearing in his hand. "We're tellin' you. Get in the damn car! Now!"

Jeff took Ella's hand as they were prodded by the two men toward the SUV. He looked around quickly, hoping that someone else was in the parking lot and could help. But the lot was empty.

They were shoved into the back seat and the short man climbed in next to them. "Here. Put these on," he said gruffly, throwing two black hoods at them. "And give me your cell phones."

Jeff nodded to Ella who, despite the fear in her eyes, remained calm. They handed him their phones, which he dropped into his jacket pocket, and then pulled the hoods over their heads. Jeff grabbed her hand and held it tightly. As Jeff leaned over to whisper to her, the short man yanked him back.

"Shut the fuck up! No talking!"

The SUV roared out of the parking lot and picked up speed on the highway. Jeff tried to follow their route in his mind but the driver seemed to be making an inordinate number of turns, obviously trying to confuse his passengers. After what seemed to Jeff to be about fifteen minutes, the SUV pulled off the highway and headed along what felt like a twisting dirt road. A few minutes later, the SUV braked to an abrupt stop.

The doors opened and they were pulled roughly from the back seat. Jeff and Ella stumbled as they were shoved forward and through the door of a building. Once inside, the two men pulled the hoods off and steered their captives to the middle of the room, pushing them into two wobbly, warped cane chairs. They squinted into the darkness, blinking rapidly, trying to figure out where they were. It looked like an old, dirt-floored barn with rusted tools, a few pieces of broken furniture, and withered hay scattered about. The only illumination came from the flickering light of an oil lantern perched on top of a small bench next to their chairs, which sent shimmering shadows dancing along the cracked and weather-beaten wooden walls.

"You guys have any idea how many laws you just broke?" Jeff said, hoping that the anger in his voice might mask his fear.

"Shut the fuck up!" the tall man yelled. "You ain't the one in charge here."

He beckoned to the other man, who had been staring at Ella. They went off into the corner of the barn where the tall man whispered something, and then punched in a number on his cell phone. After a moment, they heard him say "They're here." Then he hung up. The two men stayed in the corner, whispering, the short one occasionally shooting a leering glance at Ella, until they heard the sound of a car pulling up outside just a few minutes later.

The door to the barn opened and A. J. Hollingsly walked in. Dressed in khaki pants and a short-sleeved plaid shirt, nearly bald except for tufts of gray hair above his ears, from a distance he looked like just about anyone's grandfather. He spoke briefly in a hushed voice to the two men, and then ambled over to Jeff and Ella. As he came closer, the kindly grandfather image quickly evaporated. Despite his age, his wiry frame was still trim and he moved easily. Behind his thick, black-framed glasses, he had the face of a barroom brawler, with a nose that had been broken repeatedly and thick scar tissue running in so many directions across his face that it looked like a relief map of the Appalachian mountain country. He stopped in front of the chairs, hands on his hips, and glared at Jeff and Ella.

"Seems like y'all just can't take a hint," he growled in a deep, gravelly drawl. "Thought that carvin' a chunk outta your car tires might've convinced you to leave me alone. Guess not."

"We were just hoping that we could talk to you for a few minutes," Jeff said, as conversationally as he possibly could. "We certainly don't want to impose on your privacy and we wouldn't bother you unless it was something very important."

"Somehow, I reckon that your idea of what's important and my idea are pretty different." He looked at Ella. "I know who *he* is but who're you?"

Ella gathered up all the bravado that she certainly didn't feel at the moment. "Ella Garrity," she answered. "From the *New York Times*. And if I'm not mistaken, your boys here don't seem to know the difference between kidnapping and an invitation to talk. Do you?"

"Well, Miss Garrity, we ain't up in New York right now. And if I was you, I might consider bein' a little more polite. And y'all might also want to let me do the questionin' here."

"Look, Mr. Hollingsly, we're not looking for any trouble," Jeff said soothingly. "We just wanted to ask you some questions about a case you investigated back when you worked for the Sovereignty Commission."

Hollingsly raised an eyebrow and cocked his head to one side. "And what makes you think I'd have any interest in talkin' to y'all about anything?"

"You were a law enforcement officer once," Ella chimed in. "We thought you'd still have an interest in making sure justice was done."

"Justice?" Hollingsly laughed. "What the hell do y'all know about me and justice?"

"We know that you investigated the killing of Elijah Hall back in 1960," Jeff said. "We know that you talked to Ricky Earl Graves about the shooting right after it happened. And we know that you found out all the details, including who was there and who pulled the trigger."

"So that's what this is all about," Hollingsly said, looking hard at Jeff. "Shoulda known. So why do y'all think I was involved?"

"Because Ricky Earl is my client," Jeff said softly. "And because he told us all about your conversation back then."

Hollingsly was quiet for a moment. "So you're the one behind Tillman Jessup's prosecution?"

Jeff nodded.

"Boy, you got no fuckin' idea what you got yourself into," he said, his voice dropping deeper in anger. "Do you really think I'm gonna help you? I was glad those boys blew that damn nigger preacher away. Woulda done it myself if I thought I coulda got away with it. And I thought all these years that them there boys were in the clear. Until you and your New York bleedin' heart, nigger-lovin' friend here," he tilted his head toward Ella, "decided to butt in where you don't belong."

"Listen, Mr. Hollingsly," Jeff said, "the only—"

"No, you listen, you self-righteous little bastard," Hollingsly said menacingly, stepping closer to Jeff. "It's because of people like you—and your damn father—that our whole way of life disappeared. It's because of you that we got nigger judges and nigger congressmen and nigger cops and niggers takin' good payin' jobs from people like me. I was happy to help cover up that nigger's killin' and I sure as hell ain't gonna do nothin' to help convict anybody now." He glared at Jeff, then Ella.

"All right," Ella said softly, trying to diffuse his anger. "We got our answer. Like we said, we didn't want to impose. We just felt we had to ask."

"One last question," Jeff said defiantly. "Did Tillman Jessup pull the trigger?"

Hollingsly smirked. "What do you think, boy?"

"I think he did. And I think you've been protecting him all these years."

Now Hollingsly laughed out loud. "You're damn right he did. He's the only one of them punks had the balls to do somethin' about them outside nigger agitators. That's why he's gonna make us a great governor."

Jeff looked at Ella. She shot him a look that said *let's get out of here, this guy's crazy.* He nodded.

"Okay, Mr. Hollingsly," Jeff said respectfully. "We apologize for taking up your time. I'm sure you understand that we needed to ask you. Now that we have your answer, if you'd just have your men take us back to my car, we won't bother you again."

Hollingsly didn't seem to have heard Jeff. He was staring off into the distance.

"Mr. Hollingsly?" Jeff said.

Hollingsly turned back toward Jeff and glowered at him, his eyes hard.

"Afraid it ain't so simple anymore," Hollingsly said, shaking his head sadly. "You were warned, boy. But you just had to go bargin' in where you don't belong. And you had to bring this pretty little thing along with you."

"If anything happens to us, plenty of people know we came here looking for you. And they'll come after you hard," Jeff said angrily.

"So what? I got four people will swear I been playin' poker with 'em all night," he sneered. Turning, he gestured toward the short man. "Keep an eye on 'em."

The short man pulled a revolver from his waistband and pointed it at Jeff and Ella. Hollingsly pulled the taller man into the corner of the barn where they engaged in a hushed but animated discussion.

Jeff leaned toward Ella. "I don't like this. We need to get out of here. And soon."

"Okay," Ella whispered. "How?"

Before Jeff could answer, Hollingsly turned and walked toward the door. He stopped in the doorway and looked back at the tall man.

"I don't care what you do with 'em," he said in a low and threatening tone. "And I don't want to know. Just make damn sure it looks like an accident."

Hollingsly left the barn, slamming the rickety wooden door behind him.

CHAPTER 30

As soon as Hollingsly left the barn, the two men huddled near the doorway. The short man kept looking over at Ella and smirking, while the taller man, who had grabbed a length of rope from a hook on the wall, seemed upset and repeatedly shook his head.

Jeff leaned over toward Ella. "We can't let them tie us up," he whispered. "We've got to get out. Now."

Ella nodded, her eyes wide, trying hard to maintain her composure.

"Here's what we'll do," Jeff said, holding her frightened gaze and trying to sound much more confident than he felt. "I'll take down whoever gets closest to me. But I need you to keep the other one busy. Just for a moment, before I can get to him, too. Do whatever you can—grab him, kick him, jump on his back, whatever. Just try to keep him off me. Understand?"

Ella nodded.

"When they start to head over here, act real scared. Make them think we'll go along quietly."

"Shouldn't be too hard to do," she said, peeking over at the two men still arguing near the door.

"Hey. Listen to me. We'll get out of this," he said, reaching for her hand and squeezing it tightly. "I promise."

The men broke their huddle. The tall man, still holding the rope, walked toward Jeff while the other one, grinning lasciviously, made his way toward Ella.

"Please," Jeff begged, his voice quavering. "You don't want to do this. Just let us go. We won't tell anybody. I promise!"

Next to him, Ella began whimpering. "Please don't hurt us. Please!"

The short man laughed, leering at Ella. "Well, maybe we'll have a little fun with you first," he leered at Ella. "Then, depending on how friendly you are, maybe we won't hurt you so much. Up to you, pretty lady."

"Gimme your hands!" the tall man barked as he stopped in front of Jeff.

Sliding fearfully back in his chair, Jeff slowly held his hands out in front of him. As the man bent over to grab them, Jeff suddenly rocked forward, slamming his forehead into the bridge of the man's nose, splintering bone and cartilage. The man howled from the piercing pain as blood spurted from his shattered face.

Before the short man could react, Ella drove her foot up and into his groin, sending a thunderbolt of pain through his body. As he fell to his knees in agony, she jumped up, grabbed the flimsy cane chair, and brought it crashing down on his head. He toppled over on his side, groaning, and curled into a fetal position.

Meanwhile, the tall man had staggered backward, hands over his face, trying to clear the blood from his eyes. Jeff leaped at him, driving his fist deep into the man's solar plexus, and then landed a fast uppercut to his chin. The man slammed against the wall and collapsed to the floor.

Jeff turned quickly toward Ella and, seeing that the other man was down, grabbed her by the arm.

"Let's go! Now!" he yelled.

They took two steps toward the door when she abruptly stopped, pulled away, and turned back toward the short man, who was still writhing in pain on the ground.

"What're you doing?" Jeff shouted.

"Our phones! He's got them!"

She reached down and grabbed their phones out of his coat pocket. As she straightened up, she delivered a swift kick to the man's ribs.

"How's that for being 'friendly,' asshole?" she said, sneering.

Turning back toward Jeff, she looked over his shoulder and screamed.

"Jeff! Behind you!"

Whirling around, Jeff saw the tall man rushing at him, an ax handle held high over his head. Jeff hunched down and drove his shoulder into the man's mid-section, pile-driving him back against the wall. The two of them crashed to the ground. Jeff quickly rolled away, looking for anything he could use as a weapon. He spotted an old, rusty shovel on the ground, grabbed it, spun around, and swung it with all his strength as the man came charging at him. The blade of the shovel caught him flush on the side of his head. There was a crack that sounded like a fastball rocketing off a metal bat. The man flopped backward, his eyes rolling back in his head, and lay still.

Jeff dropped the shovel, grabbing Ella's arm, and they both dashed toward the door. As he pushed the door open, there was the crack of a gunshot from behind them and the doorframe above their heads blew out, splintering into shards of flying wood. They ducked and scrambled through the door.

CHAPTER 31

The moon slid between the clouds, casting the woods surrounding the barn in shades of flickering darkness. Jeff and Ella burst out of the building and, as another gunshot rang out, they scrambled around the corner toward the dirt road. As they ran past the parked SUV, Jeff slid to a stop, quickly reached through the open driver's side window, yanked the keys out of the ignition, and hurled them into the woods. A bullet pinged off of the roof of the SUV. Grabbing each other's hands, they sprinted down the road and were quickly swallowed up by the dark canopy of trees.

Racing along, carefully skirting the deepest ruts in the twisting path, they soon came to a paved road. Bent over, gulping air, they peered both ways, hoping to see the headlights of a vehicle that could carry them to safety. Nothing but darkness both ways.

"I've got . . . an idea," Jeff gasped. "They'll be searching for us out on the road . . . betting we took off looking for a ride."

"Isn't that what we should do?" Ella wheezed, looking around frantically.

"But if we try to flag down a set of headlights, how'll we know it isn't them—or their buddies—out looking for us?"

"Okay. So what's your plan?"

"We stay right here."

"What?"

"Not right here, out in the open." He gestured back into the woods. "Back in there. Far enough off the road that nobody'll see us. But close enough to look for help when it gets light out. They'll expect us to run, so we'll stay right here."

"Sounds good to me. Let's go."

They picked their way back into the deep woods, careful not to leave a trail by tearing up the foliage. Finding a thick stand of trees ringed by heavy undergrowth, they dropped to the ground, parked themselves behind an enormous oak, and listened.

After a few minutes of resounding silence, Jeff whispered to Ella. "The phones?"

"Got them here," she whispered back, pointing to her coat pocket.

"Good thinking to grab them."

"Thanks."

"Give me mine. As soon as it's clear I'll call Terrell and get help out here."

She slipped the phone into his hand and leaned back against him.

"Sorry about getting you into this," he said softly, wrapping his arm around her. "Kinda steep price to pay, even for a big story."

"Not your fault. I knew what I was signing up for."

"Yeah, but we didn't know we'd be dealing with a bunch of killer rednecks."

She turned her face to his. "They *were* going to kill us, weren't they?"

He nodded.

She was quiet for a moment. "Nice work in there. Where'd you learn to fight like that?"

He shrugged. "Worked as a bouncer in college. It got rowdy sometimes." He looked down at her. "What about you? You kicked that guy's ass."

She grinned. "Two older brothers. And a self-defense class when I moved to New York. Got my nose broken, but I guess it finally came in handy."

"Guess so." He gave her shoulder a soft squeeze. "I think it's safe to call now."

Jeff held his hand over the face of his phone to shield the light and punched in Terrell Jackson's number. After a few rings, he whispered quietly, his head bent over and the phone held close to his mouth. He quickly explained what had happened and that he had just a general idea where they were. After listening for a minute, he answered softly, "Will do, but make it fast," and ended the call.

Ella looked up at him. "Well?"

"He said for us to lay low and keep my phone on vibrate. They'd triangulate with the cell towers, get a bead on us, and call when they're close. He said he's sending the cavalry so we should hold on." He smiled at her. "He'll get us out of here."

She nodded and tucked herself closer into him. She began to shake and he held her tightly until the shivering stopped, then leaned over and gently kissed the top of her head.

"Nice work, Brenda Starr," he whispered.

CHAPTER 32

The first light of dawn etched a soft purple ribbon along the edge of the dark sky. Jeff and Ella had spent the time huddled together, seeking some warmth against the cool night air. They had not spoken much while they waited, content to simply hold on tightly, savoring their escape, each thankful for the presence of the other. Twice they had heard the growl of vehicles on the dirt road but were unable to see anything from their hiding place in the woods. As the curtain on the day rose and the darkness grudgingly gave way to streaks of pewter daylight, they began to stir, anxious for some sights or sounds of rescue. Finally, Jeff's phone began to vibrate.

"Yeah?" he whispered into the phone.

"We're close," said Terrell Jackson, on the other end. "You okay?"

"We're good. Don't think anyone's still around."

"We'll pop the siren and the lights. Y'all c'mon out to the road when you hear us."

A moment later, Jeff and Ella heard the wailing of the sirens as two Mississippi Highway Patrol cars, together with Jackson's unmarked cruiser, came barreling down the roadway. They thrashed their way out of the underbrush and started waving their arms at the approaching vehicles. Terrell Jackson pulled up next to them while the two Highway Patrol cars wheeled into the dirt road and roared off toward the old barn.

Jackson sprang out of his car, gun in hand, his eyes darting about as he rushed to them.

"Man, I thought I told you to be careful," he said, the concern seeping through the feigned anger in his voice.

"We *were* careful," Jeff replied. "But then these guys decided not to play nice."

Jackson went straight to Ella and wrapped his big arm around her shoulder.

"How 'bout you? You okay?" he asked her gently.

"I'm fine, Terrell. Thanks," she smiled weakly.

Jackson looked around again, his weapon still drawn.

"Once we got a general idea where you were, one of the Highway Patrol boys thought he remembered an old barn out this way. Helped us get here a little quicker." He nodded toward the dirt road. "They're checkin' it out now." He turned back toward his car. "Jump in. Let's go see if they found anythin'."

As they drove down the dirt road, Jeff quickly filled Jackson in on the details of their capture and escape. When he finished the story, Jackson smiled approvingly at Ella.

"So this pretty little thing kicked the ever-lovin' shit outta one a them rednecks? Good for you, little girl! You can play on my team anytime."

Ella shrugged and offered a small smile, obviously pleased at the compliment from the big man.

"So, what kinda shape you leave those boys in?" asked Jackson.

"Not sure about the one guy," Jeff said. "I tagged him pretty good with the shovel. But the other one wasn't too bad. He took some shots at us when we ran out. But nobody followed us, so my guess is they were banged up pretty good."

"How 'bout Hollingsly?"

"Once he left, we never saw him again. We heard some cars later but didn't see them. Don't know if he came back or not," answered Jeff. "These are some serious bad guys, Terrell."

"Damn right, they are. Warned you about these backwoods crackers. Some of 'em are worse than the old KKK," Jackson said, shaking his head. "At least now we can go after the two that roughed you up. Shouldn't be too hard to track 'em down. We'll drop kidnapping charges on 'em, squeeze 'em a bit, and see if we can get 'em to roll over and testify against Hollingsly. Then we lean on Hollingsly to give up Jessup."

"I don't know," Jeff said. "Hollingsly seemed like a tough old bastard."

"They all seem tough—until they're lookin' at spendin' the rest of their life in a cell in Parchman. Tends to soften 'em up a bit." Jackson chuckled. "May be that this little ol' adventure of yours was just what we needed to bust this case wide open."

They pulled to a stop next to the Highway Patrol cars in front of the barn. One of the patrolmen was standing in the doorway, talking on his radio.

"You two wait here," Jackson said, climbing out of the car. "Just gonna check on what they found inside."

As Jackson reached the doorway, the patrolman glanced quickly back at Jeff and Ella, whispered something to the detective, and followed him into the building.

"You really think we'll be able to track those guys down?" Ella asked.

"Maybe. We can give a pretty good description of them. Plus, they might need some medical care so we can check with any local hospitals and doctors."

Jackson came striding out of the barn, a grim look on his face. He leaned into the open car window and looked first at Ella and then at Jeff.

"Any sign of them?" Jeff asked.

"Yep," Jackson said solemnly. "Found 'em both inside."

"They're still there?" said Jeff, surprised.

"Yep, still there. Problem is they each got a bullet in the head."

CHAPTER 33

It was early afternoon before Jeff and Ella left the district attorney's office. Terrell Jackson had driven them back to Jeff's car and then escorted them on the drive back to Oxford. They told their story, from start to finish, at least three different times and, after providing a detailed description to a police sketch artist, they came up with a pretty good rendering of Hollingsly.

Jackson had been in and out of the conference room, coordinating the details of the new murder investigation. As Jeff and Ella were about to leave, Jackson stuck his head in the door.

"Got IDs on the two dead guys," he said.

"Anything helpful?" asked Jeff.

Jackson shook his head. "Not much. Both were ex-cons. Drifters. No immediate family around. Having trouble even findin' someone to claim the bodies."

"Hollingsly might be an old redneck bastard—but he's a smart old redneck bastard," Ella said. "No evidence to connect him with this. Just our word against him and his poker buddies. And no trail to follow."

"We'll find him," Jackson said, his jaw set in a hard line. "Now we got the son of a bitch in our sights. We'll get him. Now," he said, his voice softening, "you two got to get some rest. Been a hell of a night."

They stepped outside, squinting in the midday sunlight.

"C'mon," Jeff said, taking Ella's hand. "I'll walk you to your hotel. It's just a couple of blocks past my place."

They strolled quietly down the street toward the courthouse, both lost in their own thoughts. What had started out as a simple newspaper article had quickly escalated into a major story—and now had exploded into a multiple murder case. The speed of the journey, and the rising and plunging along the way, had been dizzying. They were both physically and emotionally exhausted.

"So, where do you live?" Ella asked.

Jeff nodded toward a condominium complex about a block ahead across the street. "Got a place in there."

"Looks nice."

"It's pretty new. Did a nice job on them. Used to be an old cotton warehouse. Somebody was smart enough not to knock it down and turned it into condos, instead."

They walked in silence until they were adjacent to the condo complex.

"Jeff," Ella said softly. "I'm still a little shaken up by last night. Not sure I want to be by myself in a hotel. Would you mind . . . ?"

Jeff squeezed her hand. "I was trying to figure out a way to ask if you'd rather stay at my place—without seeming like I was trying to hit on you at an awkward moment," Jeff said sheepishly.

Ella smiled. "So this is what I have to go through—get kidnapped, shot at, and nearly killed—to get you to hit on me?"

"Sorry. Afraid my social skills are a bit rusty. C'mon."

They turned in to the courtyard, climbed the stairs to the second floor, and entered the unit on the corner. Inside, the condo was big and airy, with exposed brick walls and floor-to-ceiling windows, salvaged and refurbished from the old warehouse, and a balcony that looked out over the Square. The interior decorating was spare. A leather couch and two large armchairs were grouped in front of a big-screen television in the living room, and a marble island separated the living space from a modern kitchen. There were a few generic prints on the walls. Books seemed to be scattered everywhere.

"Very nice," Ella said, glancing around. "Definitely a bachelor's place—but, still, very nice."

"You sound surprised," Jeff said.

"Actually, pleasantly surprised."

"What'd you expect?"

"Honestly?"

"Yeah."

"Well, I kind of thought your place would resemble a frat house," she said. "You know—ex-jock, single."

She shrugged apologetically.

"Glad you like it. Can I get you something to eat? Not sure what I've got," he said, turning toward the kitchen.

Ella grabbed his arm and turned him toward her.

"Boy, I guess you *are* a dumb jock."

He looked at her, an eyebrow raised, a smile creeping across his face.

"Not hungry?"

"Not right now."

"Well, then, maybe I should show you the rest of the place."

She smiled as he took her hand and led her into the bedroom. Inside, a king-size bed presided over a corner room punctuated by an armoire, a small writing desk, and a blizzard of clothes strewn haphazardly about.

"Definitely single, ex-jock décor," Ella chuckled.

Jeff turned her around to face him, wrapped his arms around her, and pulled her close to him.

"You okay?" he asked tenderly.

"I am now."

He leaned down and kissed her gently, first on her forehead, and then on her neck.

She tilted her head back, gazed into his eyes, and touched his face with her fingertips. Her lips touched his, first softly, searching, then they erupted with passion, their mouths hungrily probing, hands grasping.

They spent the rest of the afternoon alternately making love and collapsing in exhaustion. Their first time was explosive, as if all the fears and violence of the night before needed to be exorcised from their spirits. Afterward, their lovemaking was gentle and inquisitive, two new lovers seeking the enveloping ecstasy found in the intertwining of their bodies and souls.

They sat up for hours, eating reheated pizza and drinking cold beers, talking about Hollingsly and their near-death experience, about Jessup and the upcoming trial, about Mississippi and the parallels and differences in their lives. Finally, they made love once more and then slept soundly until the sun rose on a new day.

CHAPTER 34

"Well, if there was ever any doubt that Jessup was the killer," Jeff said, "we've certainly put that question to rest."

The entire prosecution team was seated around a conference table in the district attorney's office. Gibb Haynes sat at the head of the table, flanked by Sheriff Clayton Poole, Terrell Jackson, and two young assistant prosecutors. Jeff and Travis Murray were seated at the far end.

"We all sure as hell know that," the district attorney said, gesturing at those around the table. "Unfortunately, the jury'll never hear about your adventure and Hollingsly's statements about Jessup. Can't figure out, for the life of me, any way we could make that kind of testimony admissible without getting him on the stand."

Jeff nodded his agreement. "Anything new on the search for Hollingsly?"

"Nothing yet," answered Haynes.

"Now that he's the subject of an official murder investigation, I thought we might have some luck. But he's apparently gone to ground and ain't nobody talking," said Sheriff Poole.

"Well," said Haynes, "I think we just got to assume we're going to trial on Monday with what we got. In the meantime, we keep looking for Hollingsly and, if we find him, we squeeze the hell outta him to get him to testify. A murder charge might make him look at things a little differently. If not," Haynes looked directly at Jeff and Travis Murray, "it looks like ol' Ricky Earl's gonna be carryin' the ball for us all by himself. Can he handle it?"

"He'll be fine," Jeff said reassuringly. "Let's just hope we can find a jury that'll be willing to listen."

Terrell Jackson snorted. "Yeah, right. Like a jury from 'round here's gonna take some ol' nasty redneck convict's word over that of Tillman Jessup, with all his money and family name and army of expensive lawyers." He snorted again.

"Listen here," Gibb Haynes said. "I know we got an uphill battle. And I'm not stupid enough to bet the farm on this one. But I'm not willing to surrender, either. This is a whole different place from back when Elijah Hall was murdered. No more all-white racist juries. No more of the KKK and Sovereignty folks runnin' around interferin' with the justice system. Hell, who would've thought a Mississippi jury— whites and blacks—would finally convict Byron De La Beckwith of killing Medgar Evers back in '63? Took more than thirty years and two hung juries, but it finally happened. Lord knows it's not going to be easy. But, if I didn't think we had a shot, I wouldn't be sitting here with all y'all gettin' ready to go to trial."

"Yeah," Travis Murray smiled ruefully. "Except De La Beckwith left his rifle, fingerprints and all, at the murder scene. And he boasted over the years to a lot of people that he was the killer. Not quite our case. Too bad Jessup wasn't as accommodating."

"Look," Jeff said. "Gibb's right. It's not going to be easy. And we all knew that before we started. But, if nothing else, De La Beckwith's conviction made it clear we've turned the corner on these old civil rights cases and at least now they'll be taken seriously. So now it's our job to find us a jury that'll listen. Maybe we win and maybe we don't. But at least this murder—and this victim—will finally see the light of day. And that's a damn sight better than what happened here forty years ago."

The district attorney looked around the table. "Okay, then. So maybe we're the few Spartans taking on the Persian hordes at Thermopylae. But when this is over, they'll damn sure know they were in a battle."

"You do know the Spartans all died, right?" Jeff asked with a bemused grin.

The district attorney grinned back at all of them. "No need for y'all to get hung up on those little details." He pulled out a legal pad and tossed it on the desk in front of him. "Now, let's get to work deciding what our jury should look like."

CHAPTER 35

The defense team was gathered in the expansive library of Jessup's sprawling mansion. Located on a lake on the outskirts of Oxford, the house was a near replica of Scarlett O'Hara's Tara, all white columns, wrap-around porches, and symmetrical wings flanking the central three-story structure. The library—which had been transformed into the defense "war room"—looked out onto manicured gardens that sloped gently down to the shore of the lake. Inside, a large conference table was strewn with documents and law books. Two young lawyers were busily stuffing papers into various binders while Channing Wallace, Tillman Jessup, and Royce Henning huddled around a coffee table.

"The good news," Wallace was saying, "is that the jury selection procedure here in Mississippi gives us an awful lot of opportunity to get all our arguments out there to these people even before the final jury panel is chosen. So, hopefully, we'll be able to get a pretty good read on them before we have to start choosing."

"What about the prosecution?" asked Henning.

Wallace nodded. "They get the same chance to talk with them. But," he added, looking at Jessup, "we've got a more compelling story. And we've got a genuine folk hero sitting next to us at counsel table—while they've got to convince the jury to believe a man who's so scary that, if the jurors saw him on the street, they'd cross to the other side to avoid him. Not really a fair fight," he sniffed.

"So, how much of our defense do you tell them about before the jury's picked?" asked Henning.

"In this case? Everything," answered Wallace. "I'm essentially going to give them my opening statement when we're picking them. No sense holding anything back."

"How about the question of the senator testifying? How will you deal with that?"

Wallace seemed to bristle for a moment, and then assumed the attitude of a teacher trying to explain a complicated concept to a faltering student. "As I've tried to explain to you before, it's generally a bad idea to put a defendant on the stand to testify, unless you absolutely have to. Changes the whole dynamic of a trial. Practically—even if not strictly legally—it subtly shifts the burden of proof to the defense." He shook his head vigorously. "I'm not inclined to do it—and I'm certainly not going to talk about it to the jury beforehand. Don't want to promise something that we probably won't end up delivering."

"No," said Jessup, slamming his fist on the table.

Wallace turned toward him, puzzled. "No—what?"

"I'm testifying," he said, glaring at Wallace.

"Senator, we've discussed this . . ." Wallace began.

"I don't care what we discussed," Jessup interrupted. "I'm testifying!"

Wallace looked to Henning for help, but when it quickly became clear that Henning would not dare to contradict his boss, Wallace turned back to Jessup, his tone now more pleading than professorial.

"Senator, I can understand why you'd want to take the stand to deny all of this, but . . ."

Jessup again angrily interrupted. "No, you obviously *don't* understand. I'm not one of your sleazy banker clients who's only interested in hearing the words 'Not Guilty,' and who don't give a shit how they win their cases. Their only damn interest is getting back out on the street so they can continue rippin' off the poor sonsabitches they been rippin' off for years. I'm tryin' to win a goddamn election! It's not enough to have this jury say 'Not Guilty' because the prosecution didn't prove its case. 'He might've done it but we're just not sure' doesn't get me into the governor's mansion. I need this jury to say that I'm innocent and that this case has been an abuse of the justice system from the beginning. And the only way that happens is if I get on the damn witness stand to deny it all. Otherwise, it'll never go away. I'll be haunted by it until I die."

"You can't forget that we're trying to win an election here," Henning chimed in.

Wallace wheeled to face Henning, directing the anger at him that he didn't dare direct at Jessup. "I understand that you're trying to win an election. But you don't seem to understand that I'm trying to keep the senator from spending the rest of his life in prison. And if you'll just let me do my job, we'll win this case and you can then go ahead and do your job and get him elected."

Wallace and Henning glared at each other until Jessup, now calmer, broke the tension.

"Listen here, Channing," Jessup said soothingly. "We all know that you're lookin' out for my best interests the only way you know how. And I appreciate that. I really do. But you're just going to have to do it my way this time. There's a whole lot more at stake here." He reached over and patted Wallace reassuringly on the shoulder. "This is my decision and I take full responsibility for it. But I sure as hell know that you're gonna destroy this Ricky Earl Graves when he gets on the stand. And then I'll get up there and make sure that those twelve folks will finish up on our side. Not just 'Not Guilty' but absolutely goddamn 'Innocent.' So I want you to tell those jurors, from the get-go, that I'm an innocent man and an innocent man will damn sure get on that witness stand and testify."

Wallace leaned back in his chair, took a deep breath, released it slowly, and finally nodded.

"Fine, Senator. You're the client and, ultimately, it's your decision to make."

"Thank you, Channing. I appreciate your understanding. Now," he said, clapping his hands together. "What else do we need to talk about before we start on Monday?"

Looking down at a legal pad on the table, Wallace pursed his lips as he scanned his notes. "I think we seem to be ready to go." He looked up at Jessup. "The only thing left is for me to have a quick chat with Mrs. Jessup about what I'd like from her during the trial."

A shadow passed quickly across Jessup's face. "Afraid she's not feeling too well right now. But she'll be okay by Monday. And I'm sure she'll do just fine during the trial. She's a good soldier. Been the wife of a politician long enough to know how to handle just about anything," he said with a politician's smile. "Now, it's about time we had ourselves a little drink."

As he was making his way around the table to the elaborately stocked bar, his cell phone began to vibrate. Flipping the phone open, he stared for a moment at the "Restricted" notation on the incoming number screen. Frowning, he hit the talk button.

"Hello?"

"Senator Jessup?" the caller asked, in a deep, gravelly drawl.

"Yes? Who is this?"

"A voice from your past." A pause. "Name's Hollingsly."

CHAPTER 36

Jessup appeared puzzled for a split second, then blanched, and, turning his back to the others, lowered his voice.

"I'm sorry," he said brusquely. "I didn't catch your name."

"Are you alone?" the voice asked.

"Actually, no."

"Well, I think you're gonna wanna hear what I have to stay, so why don't y'all find a nice quiet place so we can talk. Only gonna take a minute of your time."

Jessup looked over at Wallace and Henning and gestured that he had to take this call. He opened a set of French doors and walked out into the gardens.

"I'm sorry," he said in a formal tone. "I don't think I understand what this is about."

"Let's us not waste each other's time, Senator," the voice said. "Y'all damn well know who I am and what this all's about. First of all, there ain't no taps on any of your phones. I had 'em all checked out. So you can relax. And you can be damn sure I ain't taping anything, either. No need for you to do any talkin'. You just listen, okay?"

"Okay," Jessup replied uncertainly, his mind racing.

"Bunch of folks been tryin' to track me down. They're real interested in my role investigatin' the killin' of a nigger preacher back in 1960.

Seem to think that I know somethin' about who did the killin'." He laughed, a dark, malevolent, mirthless sound. "Can't for the life of me figure out why they'd think *that*. Or why they'd think, even if I did know somethin', I'd ever want to talk with them about it. Or why your name keeps comin' up."

"And what did you say to these people?"

There was a long pause. For a moment, Jessup wondered if Hollingsly was still on the line. Finally, he heard more laughter.

"Hell, I made it clear—real clear—that I ain't got no interest in talkin' to them or anyone else about whoever did us all a favor and sent that damn nigger on his way to meet his maker. Then I decided to take myself on a nice, long vacation."

Jessup was quiet, unsure how he should respond.

"Like I said," Hollingsly rasped. "Ain't no need for you to do no talkin'. Just wanted you to know that I ain't gonna be any kind of problem for you. And, if things work out, neither will Ricky Earl Graves."

"I don't understand," Jessup whispered. "What . . ."

"Never mind. Nothin' for you to worry about. Just know that y'all still got some friends lookin' out for you. Now, why don't you just head back in the house and huddle up with your lawyers. No need for them to know anything about this here conversation."

Jessup looked around frantically.

"How do you know . . . ?" he stammered. "Where are you? Are you watching me?"

Hollingsly was gone.

CHAPTER 37

Jeff crossed the street, heading toward his apartment, lugging a bag of groceries. Ella, who was upstairs waiting for him, had suggested that they cook dinner at his place and then make it an early night. The Jessup trial was set to begin with jury selection in the morning.

As he entered the courtyard, he heard his name called.

"Mr. Trannon?"

Jeff turned, squinting into the shadows of the settling dusk. A man stepped off of the sidewalk and walked toward him, hand outstretched in greeting.

"Mr. Trannon, I'm Royce Henning and I was hoping to have a word with you." Henning was wearing a tweed blazer over a roll-neck sweater, and sharply creased jeans. Stylish, as always.

Jeff had initially taken a quick step backward, unsure of the stranger's identity. Once he recognized Henning, he stepped forward and, somewhat uncertainly, shook his hand.

"I'm Senator Jessup's chief of staff, and . . ." Henning began.

"I know who you are, Mr. Henning," Jeff said, his voice tinged with suspicion. "What can I do for you?"

Henning looked around and, satisfied that they seemed to be alone on the street, dropped his voice to a near whisper.

"I wondered if we could have a very private—and very candid—talk?"

"About?"

"About the trial."

Jeff looked at Henning deliberately for a moment. "What about the trial?"

"Well," Henning said smoothly, "you and I are both lawyers, and we've had many occasions over the years to settle cases. Some more difficult than others. But my experience has always been that, if both sides are reasonable, deals can usually be made. Deals that work for everyone."

Jeff nodded, not entirely sure where this conversation was going. "True, I guess. But why talk to me about the trial? I'm not a party."

"Technically, no, you're not. But," Henning said, an eyebrow slightly raised, "you do represent an important player in the trial."

Henning paused, waiting for some response. Jeff said nothing.

"And," Henning continued, "as this person's lawyer, I'm sure your primary interest is in his well-being. Correct?"

Jeff stepped closer, anger flaring. "Are you threatening . . . ?"

Henning raised his hands. "Please, Mr. Trannon. Of course I'm not threatening anything. You misunderstand me. I simply want to have a conversation about what would most certainly be in your client's best interest. And since your obligation, as his lawyer, is to protect his interests, I assumed you'd like to, at the very least, hear what I have to say?"

Jeff searched Henning's eyes, looking for some sign of where this conversation might be heading and wondering if he should even be talking to him. Finally, his curiosity prevailed.

"I'm listening," Jeff said coldly.

Henning offered an ingratiating smile. "Good. Well, then, here are my thoughts on the subject. Just thoughts, mind you. Your client is surely looking for some way to get out of jail. Understandable. And you, as his lawyer, are, of course, looking to help him. Because that's your job. Well, I have a suggestion—hypothetically—that your client might find attractive." He paused.

"Go on," Jeff said.

"Well, if we are correct, as I believe we are, that there is no way that any jury is ever going to convict Senator Jessup of this ridiculous charge . . ."

Jeff started to interrupt, but Henning held up his hand.

"Please, just listen to me, first. If we're correct, then your client will be left sitting in jail, with a big target on his back—the blacks will want to get at him because he's admitted to being a part of the preacher's killing, and the whites will be after him for snitching—and all he'll have to show for it are some vague promises about a possible parole. In the meantime, Senator Jessup will then be Governor Jessup—perhaps, paradoxically, more popular than ever after this trial—and guess who plays a major role in the granting of parole? And in the granting of pardons and the commutation of sentences?" Henning flashed his unctuous smile again. "That's right. The governor."

Jeff glared at Henning, the muscles in his jaw twitching as he tried to control his anger.

"So just what is it you're suggesting, Mr. Henning?"

"Suggesting?" Henning asked innocently. "Why, I'm not suggesting anything. This is just a hypothetical conversation, remember? But, if I'm right—and I'm certain that I am—then perhaps your client would be better off, and have a better chance of seeing the outside of the jail walls before he dies, if the next governor of Mississippi had some reason to consider his parole application, or even a commutation request, favorably. As opposed to, say, *un*favorably." He paused a moment. "Hypothetically speaking, of course. Just two lawyers mulling over possible resolutions of a complicated case."

Jeff took a deep breath and slowly released it, still glaring at Henning.

"Well, Mr. Trannon, I must be off. Busy day tomorrow. You, too, I imagine. Thanks for your time," he said, turning back toward the street and quickly striding away.

Jeff stood unmoving, rooted to the spot, for a full five minutes, thoughts about what had just taken place tumbling about in his mind. Finally, he trudged up the stairs to his apartment.

"Wow," exclaimed Ella, as he crossed the living room, his face contorted by anger, and tossed the grocery bag on the counter. "What's that look all about?"

Jeff turned to her. "You won't believe what just happened." Pacing back and forth across the living room, Jeff told her about the conversation with Henning. Ella listened carefully and silently to the story. When Jeff had finished, she looked at him intently, her head cocked slightly.

"So, what are you going to do?" she asked.

"I don't know," he said, exasperated. "I don't know. Knowing Henning, if I try to make an issue out of it, he'll just completely deny we ever had the conversation. Would be his word against mine. Plus," he added, still clearly wrestling with the implications, "even if he admitted it, he'd argue that it wasn't anything more than, as he said, 'two lawyers talking hypothetically about a case.' And he was smart enough to not actually make any offers, anything that could be viewed legally as a bribe attempt. Damn it!" he said, throwing himself down onto the couch.

"Are you going to tell Ricky Earl about it?"

Jeff rubbed his hands on both sides of his face. "I don't know," he repeated. "Henning's such a clever bastard. He's boxed me in. He kept mentioning my obligation to Ricky Earl to get him the best deal I can. Trying to play on my responsibility as his lawyer."

"But what he's offering is, at the very least, unethical. And maybe illegal. You can't tell Ricky Earl. Why would you?"

"Because he's my client," Jeff answered, an anguished look on his face. "My duty is to him. What if this really is his best chance at ever getting out of jail . . . ?" His voice trailed off.

"Jeff, you can't be serious. After all your talk about justice? About not letting somebody get away with murder, no matter how important that person is?"

Jeff looked at her, his eyes troubled and uncertain.

"Look," she said gently, sliding next to him and taking his hand in hers. "You don't have to do this right now. Let's have some dinner, try to relax, and sleep on it. We'll figure out what to do in the morning. Okay?"

Jeff sighed deeply and nodded.

"Damn it!" he whispered.

CHAPTER 38

"Shit, man! You're my lawyer—what do I do?" Ricky Earl pleaded.

Jeff and Ricky Earl were sitting in a conference room in the district attorney's office. It was early Monday morning and jury selection was scheduled to start in a few hours. Sheriff Clayton Poole had brought Ricky Earl over from the jail and was waiting outside the room. Inside, the tension was rising. Jeff had decided that he needed to share the Henning conversation from the previous night with his client. Ricky Earl's reaction had been predictable. At first, he seemed puzzled as Jeff described the conversation, then he became angry. Now, he was a combination of frustrated, frightened, and uncertain.

Squirming in his chair, his fingers twirling around a phantom cigarette, he leaned forward, his hand slapping the table.

"C'mon, man! Whatta we do?"

Jeff sat calmly, and looked him square in the eyes.

"We do exactly what we've planned on doing," Jeff said coolly. "You testify."

"But how do we know what he said ain't true? That if Jessup beats this and is the governor, that he ain't gonna come gunnin' for me? And make sure I never get the fuck out?" Ricky Earl said, his voice rising.

"We don't know. At least, not for sure. But what we do know— for damn sure—is, if you try to back out of your deal now and refuse to testify, you got nothing. Absolutely nothing. The DA certainly wouldn't go to bat for you in front of the parole board. Damn, who knows when you'd even *see* the parole board. And if you did, Haynes would probably object to any release."

"But what about Jessup? If I don't testify, he walks. And didn't his boy say he'd look out for me then?" Ricky Earl asked.

"Are you some kind of fuckin' idiot?" Jeff exploded. "Do you really believe that Jessup will help you out? That he'll do anything for you? How would that look? How would he explain why he's helping out the guy who first claimed he's a killer, then took a dive for him?" Jeff sat back, and forced himself to calm down. "And then what'll we do? Sue him if he doesn't help you? C'mon, man, you're smarter than that."

"I don't know," Ricky Earl said, shaking his head, his eyes wide and confused. "I'm just tryin' to figure out what the fuck's my best bet."

"Your best bet is to go with the guys we trust. We can trust the DA, whether we win this case or not. He'll keep his word. Does that absolutely guarantee you get out? No—but it gives us our best shot." He paused. "We got no shot if we're counting on Jessup. Just a prayer."

Ricky Earl leaned back and sighed. "Never been much of a prayin' man," he said softly. "Don't think anybody'd be listenin' given what I done with my life."

Jeff leaned forward, his eyes narrowed. "Are we good, then?"

"Yep. We're good." He shrugged. "Might as well sell my soul— whatever the hell's left of it—to the devil we know."

"Okay," Jeff said. He stood and knocked on the door. "We start picking the jury today. Not sure how long that'll take. Best guess is you'll be testifying at the end of the week."

The door swung open and Sheriff Poole stuck his head inside. He looked first to Jeff, and then to Ricky Earl.

"You still good to go?" he said, looking hard at Ricky Earl.

"Yeah, man. Good to go," Ricky Earl answered.

"Okay, then," the sheriff said, clapping him on the shoulder. "Wouldn't be a good idea for you to start fuckin' with us now."

"I'll stop back later today and let you know how the jury selection's going," Jeff said.

Ricky Earl gave him a nod as he and Sheriff Poole left the room.

A few minutes later, they arrived back at the jail. Entering the medical wing, a more secure area where Ricky Earl had been housed since he had been brought in from Parchman State Prison, Poole escorted him to his small private cell. Inside the six-by-nine-foot cubicle were a metal bunk attached to the wall, a metal toilet, and a small desk, also attached to a wall.

"You doin' okay?" the sheriff asked, not unkindly.

Ricky Earl shrugged. "Not too bad. Gettin' a little antsy now the trial's actually startin'."

"You'll be fine," Poole assured him. "Jeff's a good man. He'll look out for you. And the DA's a straight shooter." He glanced around and then stepped into the cell, closer to Ricky Earl. "Here." He pulled something out of his jacket pocket and placed it quickly into Ricky Earl's hands.

Ricky Earl looked down. He was holding a pint bottle of Jack Daniel's whiskey.

"Had it in my office," the sheriff said quietly. "Thought you might need it. Settle your nerves a bit."

Ricky Earl gave him a wolfish grin. "Sure as hell will. Appreciate it."

"You just try to relax, then. See you a bit later," the Sheriff said as he slammed the cell door shut.

CHAPTER 39

On the Monday the trial began, the Square resembled a fall Saturday hours before an Ole Miss football game. Crowds of noisy people milled about outside the courthouse, some ardent supporters of Tillman Jessup there to show the flag on his behalf, others simply curious and fascinated by the unfolding of this unlikely drama.

Inside the courthouse, the teams of lawyers filled the well of the court, busily organizing files and girding for battle, while potential jurors, most visibly anxious and clearly unhappy over being thrust into this high-profile arena, packed the spectator benches. Hordes of media members were arrayed along the walls, casting inquisitive glances at the combatants and the nervous jury panel, scribbling notes and exchanging muted comments to their colleagues.

Jeff and Travis Murray sat in the first row directly behind the prosecution table, along with a number of assistants from the district attorney's office. Ella was stationed in the rear, within the ranks of journalists waiting for seats to open once the jury had been selected.

While she waited for the court session to begin, Ella found her focus once again drawn to Kendra Leigh Jessup, perched immediately behind her husband on the defense side of the courtroom. Although she was surrounded by friends and supporters, Mrs. Jessup seemed somehow removed from the proceedings, her gaze strangely vacant, her attention wandering. She appeared even more slight and fragile than the last time they had all been in court, her long-sleeve blue dress hanging off of her slender frame, her face slathered in makeup in an attempt to preserve her fading glamour. Once again, Ella wished that she could speak with her, to seek out her reactions to the claims against her husband, and to talk intimately about her feelings and the private repercussions of the case. Her reporter's intuition told her that, in some ways, the most compelling story might be found within the emotional barricades constructed by Kendra Leigh.

Suddenly, the door to the judge's chambers flew open and a court attendant emerged.

"Please rise," the attendant announced. "Court is in session. The Honorable Rogers Langston presiding."

Behind the attendant, Judge Langston appeared, robes flowing, clutching an assortment of files and law books. He took his place on the bench, arranged his files and books before him, adjusted his glasses on the bridge of his nose, and, finally, looked up, acknowledging the presence of the crowded courtroom. Taking a long moment to glance around magisterially, first nodding at the lawyers and then in the direction of the gathered potential jurors, he quickly and decisively established in the minds of all that this was unquestionably his fiefdom and he was most definitely in charge. With a small, regal wave of his hand, he directed all in the courtroom to be seated. It was now his theater, his stage, and time for his performance to commence.

"Ladies and gentlemen," he began solemnly, "I want to begin by welcoming y'all to this courtroom. This courthouse has a long and venerable history, something all of you, as residents of Lafayette County, should be proud of. It is here, since 1840—with a brief period of interruption thanks to our Yankee friends," he said, with a slight, ironic smile, "that the rule of law has prevailed for generations of citizens such as you. Indeed, our own esteemed neighbor, the Nobel

Prize-winning William Faulkner, describing in his book, *Requiem for a Nun*, a fictional courthouse that we all proudly know was a reflection of this magnificent building, wrote about the importance of what happens within these walls. I want to take a moment, as I do before all trials, to read to you Mr. Faulkner's words."

With the impeccable timing of a seasoned actor, the judge paused, briefly scanned the crowd, and then picked up a small, leather-covered book and began to read, his deep Mississippi drawl propelling the words across the packed courtroom.

"Talking about his courthouse, Faulkner wrote: 'But above all, the courthouse: the center, the focus, the hub; sitting looming in the center of the county's circumference like a single cloud in its ring of horizon, laying its vast shadow to the uttermost rim of horizon; musing, brooding, symbolic and ponderable, tall as a cloud, solid as a rock, dominating all: protector of the weak, judicate and curb of the passions and lusts, repository and guardian of the aspirations and the hopes . . . .'" He looked up. "That, ladies and gentlemen, is a description of this courthouse. That is Faulkner talking about the sense of justice and fairness and duty to the law that resides right here, in this very room, where y'all are sitting today." He offered a paternal smile. "Matter of fact, you may have noticed those very words written on a plaque right outside the front doors."

The potential jurors—a clearly anxious collection of men and women, white and black—sat still as statues, mesmerized by Judge Langston's performance, as were many of the out-of-town media members, who seemed enthralled by the theatricality of justice in the Deep South. Meanwhile, the lawyers and local journalists, who had heard this Faulkner symposium frequently—Judge Langston fancied himself as something of a Faulkner scholar and began each of his trials with the same lecture—busied themselves scanning the faces of the gathered jury pool, looking for any early clues of allegiance to either side.

"Now," the judge continued, directing his comments toward the jurors, this time in a more courtly manner, "I want to take a moment to thank y'all for taking time from your busy lives to exercise your duty as citizens and join us here today. Although only fourteen of you—twelve regulars and two alternates—will actually serve as jurors in this case, we certainly appreciate all of you appearing today. In a moment, we will start the process of choosing the jury that will hear this case. But, before we begin, a few additional thoughts about your presence here. I suspect that y'all know by now what case this is. No sense trying to make believe you don't. Been all over the news lately." His tone became stern and he gave them a hard look, one eyebrow raised. "But understand something. This case is certainly important to the parties involved. But it is no more or less important than any other case—and will be tried as any other case would. No difference at all."

When he was certain that he had made his point, he turned to the lawyers. "Mr. Haynes, is the prosecution ready to proceed?"

The district attorney stood. "Yes, Your Honor."

"Mr. Wallace, is the defense ready?" the judge asked.

Channing Wallace also stood. "Yes, Your Honor. Indeed, we are."

"All right, then. Let's get started." The judge turned back toward the jury panel. "Ladies and gentlemen, I'm going to ask y'all a few questions to get started. Then each of the lawyers—Mr. Haynes for the prosecution and Mr. Wallace for the defense—will talk a little bit about the case and also ask you some questions. Now, I need y'all to be absolutely honest with us. There are no right answers or wrong answers here—just your own answers. And we really need you to be up front with us about anything we ask. Understood?"

There was a collective nod from the panel.

"Good. Now, to begin, I need to ask a question that has been asked in Mississippi courtrooms probably for more than a century. It may sound a bit quaint, even strange, but it's something our law requires.

So, here goes: Are any of you either habitual drunks or gamblers?"

The judge scanned the courtroom as a few giggles and snickers worked their way through the crowd.

"Well, I don't see or hear any responses." A small smile curled the corners of his mouth. "That's certainly reassuring. Now, is anyone not capable of reading and writing?" He paused a moment. Again, no response. "Good. Then, let us proceed to some specific questions about this matter. First, I want to read to you the indictment in this case. Now, it's important that you realize that an indictment is merely the document that describes the nature of the charge against a defendant. It is not evidence and should not be viewed by you as such."

The judge held the indictment in the air.

"Just a piece of paper. Nothing more. I'm going to take a moment to read it to y'all. It sounds a little complicated, but we'll take some time to explain it better later in the case. So," he said, adjusting his glasses, "the indictment reads that 'the defendant, Tillman Jessup, did, on July 21, 1960, feloniously, willfully, and of his malice aforethought, kill and murder Elijah Hall.'" He placed the indictment down and looked up again at the jury panel. "Now, make yourselves comfortable for a spell. The lawyers and I have some questions for all y'all."

For the rest of the morning, the group was peppered with a series of questions, focusing first on their backgrounds, then on their familiarity with the case, and, ultimately, any opinions that they may have formed based upon what they had read or heard. Both District Attorney Haynes and Channing Wallace talked with the panel, offering previews of their cases, and inquiring about the backgrounds and beliefs of the potential jurors, each infusing his questions with his own personal charm, looking to connect with them at the outset, jockeying for position even at this early stage of the trial.

Following a lunch break, they all assembled again and the process continued. Not surprisingly, almost all acknowledged having either heard or read about the case. Many also admitted that they had formed opinions based upon what they had learned. And some of those proclaimed, some rather adamantly, that they just could not imagine that Tillman Jessup could ever have done such a thing.

Judge Langston, with the deftness of a skilled surgeon, gently probed, questioning whether they might be capable of putting aside these early opinions and impartially judging the case based on the evidence they would hear in the courtroom. Some indicated that they would certainly be willing to try. Others were not so sure they could, while a small number were unwavering in their belief in Jessup's innocence and declared that absolutely nothing would change their minds.

Finally, following a full day of exhaustive questioning, the lawyers gathered in Judge Langston's chambers and the wrangling began. After the district attorney offered his list of twelve acceptable jurors, they entered into a complex and curious dance, with the lawyers striking certain names from the list and those names being replaced by others until, at last, both sides took a deep breath, exhaled, and announced that they were satisfied with the panel. Tillman Jessup's fate would be decided by a jury of seven women and five men. Four of the jury members were black—two women and two men.

Judge Langston took the final list and handed it to the court clerk.

"Let's bring the folks in and give them the news," he said, standing and donning his robes. "I'll tell them that we'll start with opening statements first thing tomorrow morning." His gaze swept the lawyers in the room. "I suggest that y'all be ready."

CHAPTER 40

The medical wing of the county jail was nothing like the rest of the facility. A large, open space, it had a common room with chairs and small tables scattered throughout, surrounded by a number of additional rooms, some providing medical treatment while others offered sleeping space for the inmates who were residing there. It resembled a college dormitory far more than a jail. Some of the prisoners were there for treatment of medical conditions while others, including Ricky Earl, were being isolated—for a variety of reasons—from the general jail population.

Ricky Earl was sprawled in a ratty old armchair, parked in front of the television, spellbound as he watched a murder trial unfold on Court TV. There was a buzz as the corridor door opened and a jail trustee from the kitchen wheeled in a trolley carrying dinner trays and individual milk and juice containers. The five other inmates currently residing in what was referred to, in jailhouse vernacular, as "The Penthouse" scurried over to the trolley and quickly laid claim to the plates of broiled chicken and mashed potatoes, rolls, and some mysterious-looking pudding.

Despite the dinnertime commotion, Ricky Earl's attention seemed to remain riveted on the television while the other inmates had retreated with their stashes of food to the small tables. The trustee shot a quick, furtive glance around the room, and then turned his back to the others, who were busily diving into their dinners, while he slipped a small, clear glassine bag from his pocket. He swiftly slid the top open and sprinkled a white powder across the mound of potatoes on the last platter of food.

A hand appeared like a flash of lightning and seized the trustee's arm in an iron grip.

"Whatcha doin' there, bud?" Ricky Earl said angrily, yanking the man's arm away and spinning him around.

"Ain't doin' nothin'," the man stammered. "Just puttin' a little salt on them potatoes. Everybody been complainin' 'bout 'em."

The trustee was a slight, stooped white man with a pockmarked face and a few strands of steel gray, greasy hair combed over from his ear. Beads of sweat began to pop out on his forehead as he looked anxiously around the room and tried to free his arm from Ricky Earl's vise-like grip.

"Don't really need no extra salt," Ricky Earl snarled, pulling the man closer to him. "How come you only spicin' up my food?"

The other inmates, noticing the confrontation, stopped eating mid-bite and turned toward the drama that seemed to be building, hopeful for some entertaining diversion from their mundane jailhouse existence. Drawn by the raised voices, two jail guards stationed near the door began to walk toward the struggling men, as the trustee tried again to squirm out of Ricky Earl's grip.

"Answer me! Why you fuckin' with my food?" Ricky Earl yelled.

"Hey, man," the trustee pleaded, "leave me alone. I wasn't doin' nothin'."

"Okay, then," Ricky Earl said, his lips curled in a cruel sneer, as he grabbed the trustee by the neck and pushed his face down toward the plate. "If you weren't doin' nothin', then why don't you go on and eat a little of that shit you dumped on my food?"

With his other hand, Ricky Earl grabbed a fistful of potatoes and tried to stuff it into the trustee's mouth. The man tried futilely to wrestle himself free, clamping his mouth shut, twisting his face away, a low, plaintive wail escaping from his clenched lips.

The two jail guards moved quickly now, grabbing Ricky Earl and pulling him away from the shrieking trustee, who, once free, had snatched a napkin and was frantically wiping the food from his face.

"The motherfucker tried to poison me," Ricky Earl screamed, as the guards forced him back against the nearest wall.

"What're you talkin' about?" the guard asked angrily.

"I caught him puttin' shit on my food," Ricky Earl said, gesturing toward the trolley. "Go ahead, make him take a bite."

"What the fuck's this all about?" one of the guards demanded, now facing the trustee.

"This is bullshit. I don't know what the fuck he's talkin' 'bout," the trustee muttered, still swabbing his face with the napkin.

The guard looked suspiciously at the trustee and then turned toward the plate of food perched precariously on the edge of the trolley.

"Well then," he said coldly, "if there ain't no problem, why don't you just take a little nibble of them potatoes and let's see how they go down."

The trustee looked around desperately, his eyes now wide with fear, as he tried to back away toward the door. The other guard released Ricky Earl and blocked the trustee's path.

"Well?" said the first guard, bending to grab a spoonful of the food.

"I ain't eatin' nothin'," the trustee said, now seized by panic. "And I ain't sayin' no more. I want my damn lawyer."

Ricky Earl lunged for the man, managing to grasp him by the throat for a split second before the guard yanked him away.

"You fuckin' little son of a bitch," he screamed.

"Keep him away from me," the trustee begged, trying to hide behind the other guard.

"Back off," the guard barked, wrestling Ricky Earl back toward the wall. "We'll take care of this."

Ricky Earl pulled away from the guard, raised his hands in a gesture of surrender and stepped back, still glaring at the trustee who was now huddling in fear behind a table.

"Don't nobody touch nothin' till we find out what the fuck's goin' on here," one guard ordered, directing the trustee to sit in a chair in the corner of the room, while the other guard radioed for assistance.

CHAPTER 41

It was nearing midnight when Jeff hung up the telephone. He looked over at Ella who was tucked into the couch in the living room of his apartment, her computer in her lap as she worked on her story for the next day.

"So," she said, a puzzled look on her face. "Who was that? And what was it all about?"

"Sheriff Poole," Jeff answered, his face twisted in thought.

"And . . . ?" Ella asked again.

"Someone tried to kill Ricky Earl."

She sat up, shocked. "Is he okay?"

"Yeah, he's fine."

"What happened?"

"Caught someone trying to poison his food."

"Who?"

"Another inmate. A trustee from the kitchen. Fortunately, Ricky Earl spotted the guy before he ate anything."

"How could that happen? I thought he was in some kind of safe wing."

"Sheriff just spent the last two hours grilling the guy," Jeff said, shaking his head slowly. "Sounds like our friend A. J. Hollingsly has a pretty long reach."

"Hollingsly? How could he get into the jail to do something like this?"

"Well, after Poole scared the shit out of the trustee, he confessed. Seems that someone—Poole's convinced it was Hollingsly, or else somebody doing his dirty work—reached out to the trustee's wife. First, left an envelope with ten thousand bucks in cash under her door. Then called a few days later and warned her that if her husband didn't do what they asked, they'd both be the victims of unfortunate accidents. He claims they promised another ten thousand if he did the job right. Poole said the trustee was scared to death—still is—and was afraid not to follow the orders."

"But where did he get the poison?" Ella asked.

"He said he found it under the pillow in his cell, in a small bag tucked into a pack of cigarettes. His instructions were to find a way to get the stuff into Ricky Earl's food. Fortunately, he didn't want to hurt anybody else so he waited for a time when he was sure that only Ricky Earl would eat the poison." Jeff shrugged. "Just lucky that Ricky Earl caught him in time."

"But how did they get it into the jail and then into his cell?"

"That's the problem," Jeff said gravely. "Poole believes that somebody inside the jail is dirty. Must be a guard. That's the only possible way that someone could've gotten the stuff to him."

"So if somebody inside is working for Hollingsly, how do they keep Ricky Earl safe?"

"Poole's investigating, trying to figure out who the inside guy is. In the meantime, he's assigned a special group of guards—guys he knows and trusts—to protect Ricky Earl. And all of his food is being brought in separately by sheriff's officers."

"Jesus," Ella muttered. "These guys really play for keeps."

"Does that surprise you? Given our experience with Mr. Hollingsly and his friends?"

Ella was quiet for a moment. "No, I guess it shouldn't," she said softly. "I'm just a little surprised how easy it was for them to almost get their hands on Ricky Earl."

Jeff sighed. "Well, we've got the opening statements tomorrow and the trial should be over in about a week or so. Hopefully, Poole and his boys can keep him safe until then."

"But what about after the trial? Won't they still try to get to him?"

"Maybe. Maybe not. Might depend on what happens. Guess we'll just have to deal with that when we get there."

Jeff stood, walked over to the couch, and took Ella's hand.

"Meantime, we need to get some sleep. Busy day tomorrow. For all of us."

CHAPTER 42

A criminal trial is, in many ways, like a Broadway show. The opening statements by the lawyers are the overture, soaring sounds full of anticipation and promise, at a time when the audience—the jury—is on the edge of their seats, anxious to be entertained. What follows— usually two acts on stage, but often many more in the courtroom— tells the story, an intellectual rollercoaster ride complete with the tension and uncertainty that marks great drama. And it all wraps up with the grand finale. On stage, it's the foot-stomping, show-stopping final number, a rousing song that reverberates within the minds of the audience all the way home; in court, it's the closing arguments— passionate appeals to the jurors that reverberate within the walls of the jury room throughout their deliberations. Now, a Broadway show was coming to the courthouse in Oxford.

The sun rose swiftly on the morning of the opening statements, the startlingly blue sky promising a bright, clear Mississippi day. The majestic old courtroom was packed once again. The first row held family and friends of the accused and the legal teams, while the next three rows were reserved for the media. The remaining seats were jammed full of spectators. An overflow room was set up on the first floor of the courthouse, complete with a closed circuit video feed, for those who were not able to find places in the main chamber.

At precisely nine o'clock, Judge Langston took the bench. The twelve jurors and the two alternates—some farmers, some Ole Miss employees, some local business folks, some government workers, all dressed in their Sunday best—were ushered into their seats in the jury box. An electric, anxious silence fell like a heavy curtain across the entire room. It was time for the lawyers to make some music.

The judge nodded solemnly toward the district attorney. Gibb Haynes, dressed in a shapeless blue suit, white button-down shirt, and Ole Miss blue and crimson tie, stood and sauntered over toward the jurors, instantly assuming his most charmingly down-home "I'm-just-one-of-y'all-from-Oxford, please-pass-the-barbeque" personality.

"Ladies and gentlemen," Haynes began, in his soft, easy drawl. "I want to thank y'all for being so kind as to give up your precious time to come here and fulfill that most important of public duties. To serve as a juror. And not just any juror, mind you. No, sir. And no, ma'am," he added, making a point to smile at each of the female jurors, who politely nodded in return. "Y'all have agreed to serve as jurors in, let's face it, the biggest case this town has seen in decades." He paused thoughtfully. "Maybe ever. But, you see, the fact that this case has gotten so darn much attention really shouldn't mean anything to all y'all. I know it probably sounds a bit silly, especially after all the questions we asked you, but we need you to just treat this like any other case called to trial. Don't matter who the defendant is. Don't matter who the lawyers are. Don't even matter who all these good folks from the press are, or why they've traveled all this way to come visit with us," he said, gesturing toward the media gathered in the room. He shook his head. "Don't make no difference at all. That's because," he continued, his voice rising, "justice is blind. Y'all have seen the statue of the blindfolded goddess holding the hanging scales of justice, haven't you?" The jurors all nodded. "Well, what that shows you is justice just doesn't care who's on trial: rich man, poor man; white man, black man; young man, old man. All the same. The law is the law. But," he paused dramatically, drawing the moment out, "justice might be blind, but she most definitely is not stupid."

Pursing his lips, he let his gaze slide up toward the magnificent chandeliers hanging from the high ceiling, which were catching the dazzling early morning light and reflecting it back in a thousand shimmering arcs. He remained silent for a moment, and then turned his lanky frame back toward the jury.

"There was an ugly time in our history, a time that we wish we could just wash away and forget about." He scanned the faces of the jurors. "But we can't. And we shouldn't. Some awful things happened 'round here back in the fifties and sixties. Things we're not proud of. Racism at its worst and its most violent. We've tried hard to move past those times, to somehow make up for the terrible things that were done. And we've done a pretty good job. Y'all only need to take a stroll through the Ole Miss campus to witness the strides we've made in real, meaningful integration. Black and white students taking classes together, tailgating together before football games. Black athletes and white athletes competing as teammates. Heck, just look at y'all here in the jury box. Wasn't that long ago that this box would've been full of only white males. Nobody else." He nodded his head vigorously. "Now that's progress. But," he said, dropping his voice, "sometimes the sins of the past rear their ugly heads. And when they do—if we ever want to truly move on—we need to deal with them. Honestly and fairly. And that, ladies and gentlemen, is why we're here."

Haynes stepped back from the jury box and turned to face Tillman Jessup, who sat stoically, appearing almost uninterested, facing the front of the courtroom.

"Late at night on July 21st, back in 1960," he said, his booming voice now filling every inch of the sprawling courtroom, "this defendant murdered the Reverend Elijah Hall. He cowardly gunned him down—a double-barreled shotgun blast to the back—and left him to die in a ditch by the side of the road. And what was Reverend Hall's crime? What had he done to deserve such a horrible fate?"

Haynes let the question hang in the air as he stepped closer to Jessup.

"I'll tell y'all what he'd done. He had the *nerve* to come here to Lafayette County to encourage black people, young and old, to register to vote. To stand up for their rights. For their freedom. And for that, this man," he paused, pointing directly at Jessup, who refused to make any eye contact with the district attorney, "this man sentenced Reverend Hall to die. This man became his judge, his jury . . . and his executioner."

Over the next hour, Haynes wove his story of hatred and violence for the jurors, prowling about the courtroom, his voice rising and falling like the crash and retreat of waves breaking on a rocky shore, as the drama unfolded. Finally, emotionally spent from the power of his monologue, his deep drawl raspy from the effort, he approached the jury box and leaned on the railing.

"Ladies and gentlemen, this case will test your courage. It will test your sense of decency. It will test your sense of justice. I'm sure y'all will hear a great deal in just a few minutes from my friend, Mr. Wallace, about this case being a travesty. About the prosecution relying on the testimony of a lifelong felon in order to try to take down a great man, a pillar of this community," he said, in a tone slathered with sarcasm. "Well, here's the truth for y'all to consider: Only two people still alive on this earth know what happened the night that Reverend Hall was murdered. Tillman Jessup and Ricky Earl Graves. Yes, Ricky Earl Graves is a career convict. Yes, you should weigh very carefully everything he says and compare it to the other evidence we present to you. And, yes, you should think long and hard before you believe him."

Haynes leaned closer to the jurors.

"But here's the real truth for you," he said solemnly, his voice now barely a whisper. "The real truth is that in order to catch the devil, sometimes you need to go straight to hell to find your witnesses. And make no mistake about it, this man," he pointed toward Jessup, "despite everything y'all will hear about his fine family and his charitable works, and about all his political contributions to this state—this man, back on July 21st of 1960 was, in fact, the devil. He gunned that young man of God down in cold blood. And all the charitable donations in the world don't give you a free pass on murder."

Haynes took a deep breath and stepped back from the railing, his gaze slowly sweeping past all of the jurors, locking eyes, for a fleeting moment, with each of them.

"We're counting on your courage, on your willingness to do the right thing. We're counting on you, all these years later, to tell this defendant—and everyone else who is watching and listening—that it's not too late for justice in the state of Mississippi."

CHAPTER 43

The district attorney remained standing, facing the jurors, as still and silent as the statue of the Confederate soldier that stood guard outside the entrance to the courthouse. Finally, he nodded once, solemnly, and returned to his seat.

There was immediately a low, thrumming murmur that rippled through the courtroom. Reporters continued their frantic scribbling in their notepads, while spectators whispered and shook their heads in affirmation of the marvelous performance by Gibb Haynes.

Judge Langston rapped his gavel twice to demand quiet and then, satisfied with the restoration of order, turned toward the defense table.

"Mr. Wallace?"

"Thank you, Your Honor." Channing Wallace, resplendently attired in a finely tailored charcoal-gray, vested suit, white shirt, shimmering blue tie, and white silk pocket square, rose from his seat and strolled to the jury box. Elegant and languid, he seemed almost royal in his carriage as he smiled and half-bowed in welcome to the jurors.

"Well, ladies and gentlemen, I'm sure you'd agree that we were just treated to a magnificent presentation by my good friend, Mr. Haynes," he said, smoothly and sincerely. "And, if you had any doubt as to why he has been the district attorney here for so many years, well, I think now you most certainly should understand."

Wallace took a moment to turn and offer a slight smile and brief nod of appreciation to Gibb Haynes.

"But, you see," he continued thoughtfully, "there is much more to a criminal trial than just the drama of the lawyers' arguments. And that's because we are not the stars in this courtroom." He smiled self-deprecatingly. "As much as we, with our egos, like to think we are. No, ladies and gentlemen, you are the stars here. You are the ones entrusted by the law with the fate of all who enter the confines of this spectacular temple of justice," he said, gesturing at the chamber surrounding them. "You are the ones—not the district attorney, not the defense attorney, not even Judge Langston, in all his wisdom—*you* are the ones who decide if someone charged with a violation of the law is actually guilty.

"This is an enormous obligation we place upon you," he said, as he promenaded from one end of the jury box to the other. "You act, in reality, as the conscience of our community. And, as our conscience, we ask you to decide if a defendant—in this case, Senator Tillman Jessup—should be convicted and punished."

Wallace shook his head slowly. "To make this decision is an enormous obligation," he repeated. "But," he said, his voice now rising, "we ask you to do that because we trust you. We trust each and every one of you to withstand any pressure you might feel—for instance, Mr. Haynes's inappropriate and unfortunate suggestion that, somehow, you folks are the ones who should be responsible for rectifying the racist conduct of others in the past—and to follow the law when it tells you that no person shall ever be convicted of a crime unless and until the prosecution has proven their guilt to you, beyond any reasonable doubt," he said, emphasizing the last words with a rhythmic pounding of his fist on the rail of the jury box. "Beyond any reasonable doubt," he repeated, waving his arm above him to accentuate the burden on the prosecution. "And that means that you must demand from this prosecution not just suspicions or conjectures—or in this case, absolute lies—but good, solid, believable, truthful testimony. Beyond any reasonable doubt."

Wallace took a deep breath and then exhaled slowly as he stepped away from the jury box and turned toward the prosecution table.

"Sometimes, even the best of us can get hoodwinked. Sold a bill of goods by a charlatan, a flim-flam man who knows little of the concepts of honesty and integrity and cares less. And that's exactly what you'll see has happened here. Ricky Earl Graves," he nearly spit the words from his mouth in contempt, "is as low and corrupt a career criminal as you'll ever meet. As despicable a creature as, I'll venture to say, has ever placed his hand on a Bible and sworn to tell the truth. As if he even knows what it's like to tell the truth," he said scornfully.

"And yet," Wallace continued, pausing to make eye contact with each and every juror, as if he was sharing some deeply personal secret with them, "this is the man the prosecution will rely upon to attempt to prove their case. In fact, this man is their entire case. He's all they've got."

Wallace paced back and forth, silent, shaking his head, seeming to wrestle with some profound internal struggle. Finally, he stopped pacing and faced the jury, his face distorted in what appeared to be a kind of anguish.

"Look around this courtroom. What is wrong with this picture?" He paused a moment. "I'll tell you what's wrong. Sitting right over there," he said, pointing to Tillman Jessup, "is one of the great men in the history of this state. A man who has devoted his entire life to helping others. A man who has given extraordinary amounts of both his time and his fortune to improve the lives of all people—black and white—here in Mississippi.

"And, now, this good man finds himself sitting here as a defendant in a murder trial, forced to try to prove his innocence, to defend himself from a detestable pack of lies."

The anguish in Wallace's face morphed swiftly into anger, as his voice rose, thundering off the walls of the immense chamber.

"Oh, yes, Reverend Elijah Hall's killer will be here in this courtroom. All of you will get to look him right in the eye. But that killer is not Senator Tillman Jessup. No, ladies and gentlemen, the man who killed Reverend Hall, the man who knows all the grisly details because he was there, the man who is the real coward who snuffed the promising life out of that young preacher with a shotgun blast forty years ago—that man is Ricky Earl Graves. And that cold-blooded murderer is now grasping at his last straw, trying desperately to save what's left of his miserable life by yet another cold-blooded slaying—this time it's the assassination of the good name and character of Senator Tillman Jessup. And the prosecution should be ashamed of itself for aiding and abetting in that assassination."

Wallace stepped back from the jury box, his fingers steepled, prayer-like, before his face. He took a deep breath and once again looked imploringly at each juror.

"A 'travesty,' the prosecutor said? No, ladies and gentlemen, this is much more than a travesty. This is a shameless perversion of our justice system, the worst nightmare for any honest and God-fearing man. His good name slandered, his freedom placed in jeopardy. And all because of the self-serving, desperate lies of the worst kind of criminal. But this travesty, this perversion, stops right now. It stops here in this courtroom. Because you, ladies and gentlemen, will stand up for this good man." He gestured toward Jessup, who gazed intently at the jury, the ghost of a tear in each eye.

"We have placed our trust in you. We will challenge the testimony of this evil man. We will prove to you that he is lying. And then, Senator Jessup—despite the fact that, as Judge Langston will tell you, he has no obligation whatsoever to testify in this case—will take that stand and will place his hand on that Bible and will swear to you that he had nothing whatsoever to do with this horrible murder." Wallace paused dramatically. "And then we will trust you, at the end of this trial, to stand up and say: 'This is not justice—and we will not let this happen to this good man.'"

Wallace turned and walked back to the defense table, placing his hand reassuringly on Jessup's shoulder as he dropped into his seat. Once again, a murmur of appreciation floated through the courtroom as the spectators absorbed yet another masterful opening statement, much like the crowd at a heavyweight boxing match stands and cheers to express its admiration for both fighters' skills as they enter the final round of a close and well-fought battle. It was now clear to all inside the courtroom that this would, indeed, be an epic battle fought by two extremely talented and combative heavyweights.

"Ladies and gentlemen," Judge Langston said, after two quick raps of his gavel. "We'll take our morning break now. Give y'all a chance to stretch your legs a bit. When we return, we'll get started with the prosecution's first witness."

He turned to the district attorney.

"Mr. Haynes, we'll return in twenty minutes. Please have your first witness ready." He smacked his gavel once more. "We're in recess."

CHAPTER 44

"Do you solemnly swear to tell the truth, the whole truth, and nothing but the truth, so help you God?" the court officer intoned.

"I do."

Reverend Calvin Butler, dressed in a black suit, white shirt, and dark tie, settled into the chair adjacent to the judge's bench, the first witness called by the prosecution. Despite his age and wizened frame, his reputation, together with the grace and quiet strength of his demeanor, lent a strong aura of power and respect to his appearance. Most of the jurors seemed to shift in their chairs, sitting up straighter in deference to his presence.

"Reverend Butler," the district attorney said in his warmest, friendliest drawl, as he rose from his seat and meandered to the front of the courtroom, opposite the witness chair. "Although we all certainly know who you are, I'd ask you, sir, for the record, to please state your profession."

Reverend Butler nodded.

"Certainly," he said, his voice deep, rich, and lyrical. "I am a minister, currently the senior pastor of the Morning Star Baptist Church."

"And how long, sir, have you been employed doing God's work?"

"Well, Mr. Haynes," Butler said, smiling. "I've never actually considered it 'employment.' Always found it to be more of a blessing, actually. Been doin' it now about fifty years or so."

"How long have you lived in Lafayette County?"

"Been here all my life. Born here, raised here, ministered here, and hope to leave this good earth from right here." Another gentle smile.

"Now, Reverend," Haynes said, his tone becoming more businesslike, "I'd like to take you back to July 21st of 1960. Were you the pastor of the Morning Star Baptist Church at that time?"

"Yes, sir. Been there for about three years or so, after takin' over for old Reverend Clay."

"Can you tell us, sir, if Reverend Elijah Hall visited your church on that date?"

"Yes, sir, he did."

"And can you tell us how that visit came about?"

Butler leaned forward in his chair. "Well, sir, it was a troubled time, back then. Some of you," he nodded toward the jurors and the spectators, "are old enough to remember. Very troubled," he repeated. "Anyways, I'd received a phone call from a friend of mine—a minister from Atlanta who was workin' with Dr. King—who was reachin' out to the local churches to try to convince more black folks to register to vote."

He turned once again toward the jurors and offered a sad shake of the head.

"Was a bit dangerous 'round here those days to be encouragin' black folks to vote. But I agreed to allow a minister from up north— that was Reverend Elijah Hall—to come preach at our church and to try to convince more of our flock to register. A whole lot of folks showed up that night. Must say, I was a bit surprised how many turned out. Reverend Hall was a wonderful preacher. Got my folks all excited 'bout voting. Yes, sir, it was a good night."

"Can you tell us some more about Reverend Hall's visit and what he had to say?" Haynes said.

Butler looked off into the distance for a moment, his eyes narrowed, his lips pursed in thought. Finally, he turned back to the jury.

"It was like some sort of magic had taken over inside my church. At first, everyone was sort of quiet, not really sure what to expect. Not really sure if it was even okay for them to be there listenin' to this man they didn't know talk to them about somethin' that seemed so distant, so unobtainable in their lives. He talked about Dr. King. He talked about the law and the Supreme Court. He talked about our journey from slaves to free men and women. He told them that standin' up and voting was the next step in that journey. And slowly he got them to understand, to trust him, to trust his message. Then, one by one, led by some of the oldest folks, they began to stand, and to clap, and to sing."

He shook his head, a bemused look creeping across his face, as if now, forty years later, he still couldn't believe what had taken place inside his church that night.

"They believed that night," he said softly, almost to himself. "They believed that it was time. *Their* time. To stand up and vote just like any other man. They all left there that night believin' in Reverend Hall, believin' in themselves. Yes, indeed, they did." He paused. "And then, the next morning, when his body was found lyin' out on that road, all blown to pieces—well, it seemed that it was all just torn away from them again."

The district attorney let the heavy silence linger for a moment before he asked his next question.

"Now, Reverend, you mentioned some singing that night?"

"Yes, sir."

"Do you remember what song y'all were singing?"

"Yes, sir, I do."

"Would you tell us what song that was?"

"We were singin' an ol'-time spiritual called 'Ain't That Good News.'"

"As you sit here today, some forty years later, are you sure that's the song?"

"Yes, sir, I most certainly am. Was always one of my favorite songs," he said, a sad smile seeping through. "Haven't sung it since."

"Reverend," the district attorney said, twisting his face in thought, signaling to the jurors that the next question was important, "do you recall if you ever told anyone—anyone at all—the name of that song y'all were singing?"

"No, sir," Butler said firmly. "Nobody ever asked."

"So, you never mentioned it to the police?"

"No, sir."

"The newspaper reporters?"

"No, sir."

"Anybody at all?"

"No, sir. Never. Not until recently when this investigation got started."

"So, would you agree with me, Reverend, that if someone knew *exactly* what song was sung that night, chances are that person was actually there?"

Reverend Butler nodded solemnly. "Yes, sir. I believe that's a fair statement."

"Well, Reverend, I thank you," Haynes said respectfully, and then turned toward Judge Langston. "Your Honor, I have no further questions for this witness."

CHAPTER 45

Channing Wallace rose from his seat, a concerned and sympathetic look etched across his face as he approached the witness.

"Reverend Butler, we also thank you for being here today. And I want to assure you that I don't intend to make you relive that terrible day, in any great detail, yet again."

Wallace paused for a brief moment, and then continued. "But I do have just a few questions for you, sir, if you don't mind?"

"Certainly," Butler answered.

"Thank you, Reverend. First, about that song. Now, you've told us that you don't believe you ever talked about what song was being sung inside your church until recently, correct?"

"Yes, sir, that's correct."

"But, there were others in addition to you at your church that night, were there not?"

"Yes, sir."

"As a matter of fact, as you yourself have stated, there were dozens of people—men, women, and children—there that night, correct?"

"Yes, indeed."

"And you would agree with me, Reverend, that you couldn't possibly know, during all these years, whether or not someone else who was there ever talked about the songs you sang that night, could you?"

"No, sir, I couldn't know that," Butler said.

Wallace nodded in agreement.

"Just a few other questions then, Reverend. After the murder, there were several attacks upon your church, were there not?"

"Yes, sir."

"Two instances of a cross being burned on the property?"

"Three, actually. The third one didn't really burn very much."

"All right, three cross burnings. And a firebombing, correct?"

"Yes, sir. Fortunately, my wife and I were able to put the fire out before any real damage was done."

"So, then, you would agree with me that, apparently, there were still people out there—racist, ignorant, and very dangerous people—who were angry about what you and Reverend Hall had been doing at your church that night?"

"Yes, sir, I believe that's true."

"People who were very angry—angry enough to burn crosses on your lawn?"

"Yes, indeed."

"Angry enough to try to burn down your church?"

"Yes, sir."

"Perhaps angry enough," Wallace said, lowering his voice, "that some of them had actually been the ones who murdered Reverend Hall, correct?"

"Objection," the district attorney challenged, leaping to his feet. "That would be complete speculation and it's unfair to ask that question of this witness."

"Sustained," Judge Langston said. "Mr. Wallace, this witness couldn't possibly know the answer to that question."

Wallace simply dipped his head in deference to the judge.

"Your Honor, I agree entirely," Wallace said, and then turned back toward the witness. "Thank you, once again, Reverend Butler. I have no other questions."

CHAPTER 46

The first witness following the lunch break was to be the medical examiner. Since the doctor who had actually conducted Elijah Hall's autopsy had passed away some time earlier, the current medical examiner would rely upon the official autopsy records from July of 1960 to testify about the cause and manner of Hall's death.

Before the jury returned and the doctor took the stand, Channing Wallace cleverly attempted to circumvent the powerful emotional impact that a discussion of the shotgun wounds would have upon the jurors. The attorney indicated to Judge Langston that, since the defense was only contesting the *identity* of the killer and not the fact that it was a murder, they were willing to stipulate to both the cause and manner of Reverend Hall's death, thus eliminating the need for any testimony by the medical examiner.

Gibb Haynes, recognizing the tactical ploy, graciously thanked Wallace for his consideration, but nevertheless declined the offer, advising the court that he felt it was incumbent upon him, as the prosecutor, to provide the jurors with the opportunity to review and consider all of the facts surrounding the case, including the details of the killing. Judge Langston agreed, explaining to a frustrated Wallace that he could not compel the prosecution to accept the defense's offer.

Wallace, like a boxer attempting to deflect powerful blows as he danced around the ring, next urged that the autopsy photographs should not be shown to the jury, arguing that the prejudicial impact of the gruesome photos would far outweigh any evidentiary value, especially since the defense was not challenging the cause of death. This time, despite vehement opposition by the prosecution, Judge Langston sided with Wallace, agreeing that the photographs were so vivid in their depiction of the wounds—wounds that were not the subject of dispute—that the potential to improperly sway the jury mandated their exclusion. However, in Solomon-esque fashion, the judge then provided an important victory to the prosecutor by ordering that, even though the jurors would not see the autopsy photos, they would be allowed to view the crime-scene photos, since the location of the body following the shooting was a significant element of the prosecution's case.

Following the legal sparring, the jury was brought back to the courtroom and the medical examiner finally took the stand. In a fairly brief, yet emotionally arresting, dissertation, he described the devastating shotgun wounds suffered by Elijah Hall, finally offering his conclusion that the wounds, although ultimately fatal, would not have caused death instantaneously. The message was clear: Elijah Hall would have suffered extraordinary pain from his wounds before he died.

There was no cross-examination by Channing Wallace. The next prosecution witness was the woman who had seen two vehicles speeding down the road around the time of the killing. Using a walker as she gingerly navigated a path through the crowded courtroom and up to the witness box, the nearly ninety-year-old woman was surprisingly alert and assertive as she began her testimony. Displaying a friendly and unexpectedly relaxed attitude, especially in light of the enormous tension radiating throughout the chamber, the woman described how she and her husband had taken their dog out for his walk somewhat later than usual that night, when they heard what sounded like a gunshot. Minutes later, two vehicles went speeding by, the first, "one of those new-fangled, two-color sedans"; and the second, "a beat-up old pickup truck." She indicated that they thought it was just some teenagers "cuttin' up" so they "didn't think nothin' of it" at the time. A few days later, after hearing about the murder, they contacted the police and told them about the gunshot and the vehicles. And that was the last involvement they'd had with the case—"No questions from the police, no interviews, no nothin' for forty years"—until just recently, when she was contacted by members of the sheriff's office.

Channing Wallace did his charming and amiable best to suggest that the darkness that night and the passage of time might have dimmed her recollections, but the witness was adamant in her testimony.

"I know what I saw, Mr. Wallace. And I'm not too old to remember!" she said, seeming more than a little upset at his suggestions.

Following the conclusion of her testimony, Judge Langston excused the jury for the day. Once the jurors had been escorted out, the judge asked the district attorney about the witness schedule for the next day. When Gibb Haynes responded that his first witness would be Ricky Earl Graves, there was an audible murmur throughout the courtroom. The stage had been set for real drama.

CHAPTER 47

The next morning, the blue skies and mild temperatures gave way to a sky smeared by slate-gray, roiling clouds and constant drizzle. But the dreary weather did nothing to dampen the intense interest in the trial—or the enthusiasm of those members of the public hoping to witness the explosive theater guaranteed to occur inside the courtroom that day. The line began forming before dawn, starting at the doors on the South Lamar Boulevard side of the building and twisting like a wriggling serpent around the courthouse grounds.

Across the street, inside the district attorney's office, the tension was as thick as the dank, heavy air of an August night down in the Delta. Gibb Haynes was in his office, along with Sheriff Poole and Jeff Trannon. They were once again trying to predict just how Channing Wallace would try to attack Ricky Earl Graves, when his assistant poked her head in the door and announced that Ricky Earl had been brought over from the jail and was waiting in a conference room down the hall.

Jeff stood and announced that he would go speak with his client alone one last time to review his testimony and how the day would proceed.

"This way," Jeff said, "the defense can't argue that the DA was prepping him for his testimony as recently as this morning. Ricky Earl can say he talked to me but, since I'm his lawyer, they can't ask what we talked about."

Haynes nodded his agreement and Jeff left the office and found his way to the small conference room, where Ricky Earl and Terrell Jackson were seated at a small table. Ricky Earl was dressed in khaki pants, a white shirt, and an ill-fitting blue blazer.

"You okay?" Jeff asked, noticing immediately that Ricky Earl looked terrible. Sweat was dripping from his face and pooling around his shirt collar, his complexion was a worrisome shade of grayish-yellow, and his eyes seemed to have been sucked back into their sockets.

"Shit, yeah," Ricky Earl mumbled. "Just nervous, I guess. Ain't got any sleep for two nights. Stomach's off, ain't had much to eat. Just wanna get this shit over with."

"Terrell," Jeff said, gesturing toward the door, "can you give us a couple of minutes?"

"Sure," Jackson said, lifting his bulk out of the chair and heading toward the door. "Be right outside if y'all need me. When you're done I'll bring him over to the courthouse."

As the door closed, Jeff looked over at Ricky Earl, concern etched across his face.

"You sure you're okay?"

"Yeah, man. I told you, I'm fine. Just nervous—scared shitless, actually. Be better for sure once this damn thing's over and done with."

"You'll be fine," Jeff assured him. "Just remember what I told you. Listen carefully and only answer the question that's asked. Don't go volunteering anything. If the lawyers want more, they'll ask you. And listen up—here's the most important thing: Whatever happens, don't let the defense attorney get to you. Don't let Wallace get you angry. He's going to call you a whole lot of things, all of them bad. Just take a deep breath and answer honestly and calmly. Got it?"

"Yeah, man, I got it," Ricky Earl said wearily. "I got it. Trust me. I know how to handle any bullshit he can throw at me. Let's just finish this fuckin' thing, once and for all." He paused and looked searchingly at Jeff. "You really think these jurors gonna believe me?" he said softly. "You really think we got a chance?"

Jeff nodded. "Yeah, I really do. Just be honest with them. Just tell the truth."

Ricky Earl chuckled.

"What's so funny?" Jeff asked.

"'And the truth will set me free,'" Ricky Earl smirked. "Sorta ironic, ain't it?"

CHAPTER 48

"Your Honor, the prosecution would call Ricky Earl Graves," District Attorney Haynes said.

"Mr. Graves," Judge Langston said solemnly, looking toward Ricky Earl, who was seated between Terrell Jackson and a jail guard in the row immediately behind the prosecution team, "please come forward and be sworn."

Ricky Earl stood, shot a quick glance at Jeff, who nodded reassuringly, and walked to the witness stand. After being sworn in, he settled into the chair, took a brief, curious glimpse at the gathered crowd, and then turned his attention back to Gibb Haynes.

"Mr. Graves," Haynes began, "are you nervous this morning?"

"Yes, sir, I surely am," Ricky Earl answered, using a handkerchief to wipe the sweat from his forehead.

"Can you tell us why?"

"Ain't never been in a courtroom before. As a witness, I mean," he added hastily. "Been in one for sentencin' plenty of times, unfortunately. But ain't never testified."

"Well, Mr. Graves, since you mentioned those sentencings, we might as well talk about them now. Get it all up front and out of the way. I'm sure Mr. Wallace will have some questions about your record, so let's just let these good folks," Haynes drawled, gesturing to the jurors, "hear about all the bad stuff you've done in the past."

"Yes, sir."

Haynes grabbed a sheaf of papers from the prosecution table and began leafing through them, pausing to question Ricky Earl about each of the convictions that were listed. Constantly shifting around in his chair, repeatedly wiping the perspiration from his face with shaking hands, Ricky Earl seemed progressively more uncomfortable as he recited the details of the litany of crimes that had littered his life's journey.

Dismayed by Ricky Earl's appearance, and puzzled by his demeanor since they had rehearsed this part of the testimony a number of times, Jeff turned slightly toward the media section behind him and caught Ella's eye. She raised an eyebrow and shot him a questioning glance but all Jeff could do was offer a slight, perplexed shake of his head in return.

"So, then, Mr. Graves," Haynes said, his tone a delicate balance between conveying just the right amount of scorn for his witness's criminal past while still embracing his truthfulness. "Have we about covered all your criminal transgressions?"

"Yes, sir, best of my recollection, that'd be all of 'em."

"And, as you sit here today, you are presently incarcerated, are you not?"

"Yes, sir. Drew twenty to forty years for attempted armed robbery. That'd be the last charge you mentioned. Doin' my time up in Parchman, now."

Haynes flipped the papers back onto the table and edged his way toward the defense table.

"Mr. Graves," Haynes said, raising his voice dramatically, "do you know the defendant, Tillman Jessup?"

"Yes, sir, I do," Ricky Earl said, turning his gaze toward Jessup.

For a moment, Ricky Earl seemed to regain his composure as he and Jessup locked eyes, an angry, wordless tug-of-war between the two, with neither man apparently willing to be the first to break off the hostile staring contest. Swiftly, not wanting Ricky Earl to show any weakness by being the first to blink, Haynes stepped between the two men and reeled his witness back in.

"Tell us, Mr. Graves," Haynes asked as he ambled back toward the jury box, "how is it that you know the defendant?"

"Well, sir, I grew up right outside of Oxford. We all went to the same high school, couple years apart. Didn't much run in the same social circles, if y'all know what I mean," Ricky Earl added, with a small, self-deprecating grin. "I was just a redneck cowboy and he was one a them rich college kids. But we'd bump into each other once or twice. Was a pretty small town back then."

"Were the two of you friends?"

"No, sir, not really. Just kinda knew each other to say 'hey' when we passed."

"Now, Mr. Graves, I want to direct your attention back to the night of July 21st of 1960. Do you remember where you were during the course of that night?"

"I sure do."

"And do you remember who you were with?"

"Yes, sir."

"Okay, then. Let me first direct your attention to around eleven p.m. that night. Could you tell us where you were at that time?"

"Yes, sir. We were parked in a field outside of town . . . right near the old colored Baptist church," Ricky Earl answered, his voice faltering toward the end.

"Would that be the Morning Star Baptist Church?"

Ricky Earl stared at the district attorney, almost as if he had not heard the question.

"Mr. Graves? Would that be the old Morning Star Baptist Church?" Haynes repeated.

Ricky Earl glanced frantically around the courtroom, a look of unfocused puzzlement on his face. His right hand snaked up to the collar of his shirt, tugging on it as he opened his mouth wide and gasped for air.

"Mr. Graves . . . are you okay?" a concerned Haynes asked as he stepped closer to the witness box.

Rocking forward in his chair, Ricky Earl wrapped his arms around his chest, as a low, strangled moan barely escaped from his lips. He turned his head, his eyes wild, his chest heaving, and looked directly at Tillman Jessup.

"He . . . killed . . . him," he sputtered, pointing a trembling finger toward the defendant.

Ricky Earl tumbled to the floor, rolling onto his back. His hands clenched at his throat, desperately struggling to draw a breath.

There was a rush of sound through the courtroom, like the whoosh of a passing train. Some spectators gasped in astonishment, a few let out shrieks, while many jumped to their feet to try to catch a better view of the drama playing out near the witness box.

"Objection, Your Honor!" roared Channing Wallace, springing to his feet.

Jeff also leapt up and dashed toward the writhing figure of Ricky Earl, as Judge Langston ordered the nearest court officer to call for an ambulance. At the same time that Jeff reached his client, another officer dropped to the floor and quickly checked Ricky Earl's pulse.

"Think it's a heart attack. Grab the med kit," he yelled, as he immediately started chest compressions. "And tell the ambulance to hustle!"

Judge Langston pounded his gavel. "Take the jury out—right away," he ordered.

A third officer immediately ushered the jurors toward the door to the jury room, all of them straining to see what was happening as they were hastily jostled out.

"And clear the courtroom! Everyone out! Now!" the judge shouted, slamming his gavel repeatedly on the bench.

CHAPTER 49

The waiting room was nearly empty. Jeff and Ella sat huddled together on a small, vinyl-covered couch, while Terrell Jackson was camped out in an oversized armchair directly across from them. It had been more than an hour since Ricky Earl Graves had been rushed to the hospital, emergency medical technicians working frantically to keep him alive on the way to the emergency room.

Jeff looked up as the door separating the waiting room from the medical treatment areas slid open. A doctor, dressed in green hospital scrubs and a flowered surgical cap, spotted them in the corner.

"You folks here for Mr. Graves?" she asked, approaching them.

"Yes. How is he?" Jeff asked, as the three of them jumped up.

The doctor offered a weary shake of her head. "I'm very sorry. Afraid we couldn't save him. His heart just gave out. We tried to shock him back, but he was too far gone by the time he got here."

"Aw, Jesus Christ," Jackson mumbled, dropping back into his chair. "Jesus Christ," he repeated, shaking his head slowly.

"God damn it," Jeff said angrily. "This is my fault. I could tell he wasn't well. I should've done something."

Ella reached out and gently touched Jeff's arm. "You can't blame yourself for something like this," she said soothingly. "You couldn't have known."

Jeff shook his head. "He kept saying he was just nervous. But he looked awful."

"She's right," the doctor interrupted. "You couldn't have known what was coming. With a case like this—someone with such a bad heart condition—there's no way to tell when the heart is just going to fail."

Jeff looked at the doctor, obviously puzzled. "A heart condition?"

"Pretty serious one. Must've had it for some time," the doctor answered.

Jeff looked first to Ella, then to Jackson. "Ricky Earl ever mention a heart problem?"

"Nope. Not to me," Jackson said.

"I don't remember him ever saying anything about it," Ella added.

"Why do you say he had a heart condition?" Jeff asked, turning back to the doctor. "How do you know that?"

The doctor flipped open the chart she was carrying and scanned the documents inside.

"Well, first you've got the history we received from the EMS folks—chest pains, breathing problems, excessive sweating, vomiting, decreased consciousness. His heart was in an arrhythmia, racing uncontrollably when he arrived. All classic symptoms." She peered at another note in the file. "Then, of course, you have the medication he was taking."

"Wait," exclaimed Jeff. "What medication?"

"Digitalis," answered the doctor.

"Digitalis?" asked Ella.

"Right. It's a medication prescribed to certain heart patients as an antiarrhythmic agent to control the heart rate. It's used often for patients diagnosed with congestive heart failure."

"So, you need a prescription for it?" Ella asked. "Not over-the-counter?"

"Absolutely. And the levels need to be carefully monitored."

Terrell Jackson, who had been listening to the conversation, nodded at Jeff as he grabbed his cell phone from his pocket. "I'll check it out," he said, moving off into another corner of the room.

"How do you know he was actually taking this digitalis?" Jeff asked.

"Right here." The doctor tapped her finger on a page in the chart. "We run blood tests immediately when the patient arrives. Helps with the diagnosis and treatment. Shows here that Mr. Graves had digitalis in his blood when he got here. Must've taken his meds fairly recently."

The doctor paused as she looked at the test results. "Hmm," she mumbled, almost to herself. Something had obviously caught her attention.

"What's the matter?" asked Ella.

"The numbers," she answered, frowning, "seem awfully high."

"What does that mean?" asked Jeff.

"The digitalis level. Didn't have the numbers while we were working on him. But now that I see them, they're way higher than you'd expect. Actually," she added, scanning the page, "they're dangerously high."

"But how can a medication meant to control your heart rate be dangerous?" asked Ella.

"It's called 'digitalis toxicity.' If a patient takes too much—either from chronic overmedication or a single exposure—it can cause a whole host of problems."

"Such as?" asked Jeff.

"Irregular pulse, loss of appetite, nausea and vomiting, difficulty breathing," the doctor rattled off, without a second thought.

"Is that the worst that can happen?" said Ella.

The doctor shook her head as she looked back at her charts. "Worst case," she said, ominously, "it can actually cause arrhythmias, even heart failure."

"Isn't that exactly what you're saying happened to Ricky Earl?" asked Ella.

Before the doctor could answer, Jackson rushed over, cell phone in hand.

"No prescriptions," he said, straining to control his anger. "No digitalis, no nothin'. Ricky Earl's been in the joint—first Parchman and now here—for more than six months now and there ain't no record anywhere of him havin' any prescriptions or gettin' any kind of medications that whole time. *Nothin'*!"

CHAPTER 50

Jeff and Ella sat in the back booth of a small café on the Square, trying unsuccessfully to force down a late dinner. Following the news of Ricky Earl's death and the discovery of the digitalis in his system, Terrell Jackson had rushed from the hospital to make arrangements for an immediate autopsy by the medical examiner. In the meantime, Jeff had spoken to District Attorney Haynes and had filled him in on the suspicious findings. Haynes then told Jeff that Judge Langston had agreed, despite the vehement objection by the defense, to adjourn the trial for two days while the prosecution determined if it was possible to continue the case without the testimony of their chief witness.

"So?" said Ella.

Jeff stopped picking at the food on his plate and looked up at her. "'So' . . . what?"

"So . . . what happens now?" she asked.

Shaking his head, Jeff took a deep breath and let it escape slowly.

"I just don't know. Can't imagine that the prosecution can continue without Ricky Earl's testimony . . ."

"But what about the other evidence?" Ella interrupted. "The woman who saw the cars. The details about the gathering at the church that night and the song they were singing. The location of the body. Doesn't that all help?"

"Yeah, it *helps*," he said, his voice laced with frustration. "But only to corroborate Ricky Earl's testimony. Without him, there's nothing to directly implicate Tillman Jessup. And since the defense didn't get to cross-examine him, nothing that he said on the stand—including accusing Jessup of the murder just before he collapsed—can be considered by the jury. It's like it never happened. I can't think of any way the judge could let the case continue without Ricky Earl." He sighed. "Afraid we're done," he said bitterly.

"So, that's it? A killer gets to walk away? Just like that? Case closed?"

"Yup. Case closed."

They sat in silence for a few minutes, until Ella reached across the table and took his hand.

"Nothing we can do right now. Let's go home and try to get some sleep. What's the famous Scarlett O'Hara line from *Gone with the Wind*?"

"'Tomorrow is another day!'" Jeff answered. "A good little Southern belle like you should know that line by heart," he added, a small, sad smile creeping across his face. They stood and Jeff threw some money on the table. They left the café, Ella's arm looped through Jeff's, her head touching his shoulder. They strolled slowly across the Square, down the street, and up the stairs to his apartment. Jeff dug around in his pockets until he found his keys, unlocked the door, and flipped the light switch as they stepped inside, closing the door behind them.

"Well, by tomorrow—*Jesus Christ!*" Ella blurted, a flash of fear in her voice.

Instinctively, Jeff swept Ella behind him as he whirled toward the shadow seated in the armchair on the other side of the living room.

"Whoa! Easy there, cowboy," said the dark figure, in a deep, raspy drawl. "Don't go doin' nothin' stupid," he added, raising a long-barreled Smith & Wesson .357 revolver and pointing it directly at Jeff's chest.

The shadowy figure reached over and flicked on a lamp perched on a small table next to the armchair.

Jeff glared at A. J. Hollingsly.

"What the hell're you doing here?" Jeff snarled.

"Just thought it was time we had ourselves another little chat. Last one didn't really go too damn well. Thought it'd be better if I just waited in here awhile instead of hangin' out in the hallway. Didn't think y'all would mind." Hollingsly shrugged.

"Yeah, well, I do mind when somebody breaks into my place. Especially someone like you."

"Fair enough. Next time I'll call first."

"There won't be any 'next time.' Now you better get the hell out of here. I'm calling the cops," Jeff said, reaching for his cell phone.

Hollingsly cocked his head while he kept the gun trained on Jeff and Ella. "Ain't y'all even just a little bit curious 'bout why I'm here?"

Jeff glared at him. "You come back to finish the job your boys messed up out in the woods? Figure now that you killed Ricky Earl you might as well get rid of us, too?"

Hollingsly chuckled, a deep, malevolent rumble. "You givin' me way too much credit, boy. Wasn't me got to that redneck bastard snitch. Tried once to get him in the jail," he shrugged again. "No luck. Don't get me wrong. I'm happy as hell that sumbitch keeled over dead. But he's no notch on my gun."

"You expect us to believe you?" Ella chimed in. "After what you tried to do to us?"

"Don't give a shit, little lady, if you believe me or not," Hollingsly said scornfully. "Anyway, I heard the bastard died of a heart attack?" He peered questioningly at Jeff. "Somethin' I don't know 'bout goin' on?"

Jeff stared at him. "You really had nothing to do with Ricky Earl's death?"

"Nope." Hollingsly chuckled again. "Even I can't make a fella have a heart attack. Looks like the Good Lord lined up on our side this time."

"Well then, why don't you just finish up your gloating—if you're not gonna kill us—and get the hell out of here!" Jeff said angrily, now emboldened by the idea that Hollingsly wasn't actually planning on shooting them.

"In good time," Hollingsly said, a cold grin creasing his face. He pointed the gun toward the couch. "Y'all have a seat, first. Somethin' I got to say. Think y'all will find it real interestin'."

Jeff looked at Ella and nodded. They crossed the room to the couch and sat, Hollingsly's revolver still pointed at them.

"We're listening," Ella said coolly.

"Good," Hollingsly said, the cold grin now a full-blown, evil smile. "So, let me fill y'all in on some details 'bout the shootin' of that ol' nigger preacher back in '60. First of all, like I told y'all back in the woods, Ricky Earl was right. Tillman Jessup was the one blew that fucker away out there on that road. Yep," he nodded, "pumped both barrels into that boy. It's funny. Wouldn't a thought the rich little pansy-ass had the balls to do somethin' like that. Never know, do ya?

"Anyways," he said, leaning forward and staring hard at Jeff, who returned the stare, "there was, in fact, four of 'em out there that night. Ain't you just a bit interested in who those other fellas were?"

"Sure," said Ella quietly, trying to ratchet the tension level down. "But Ricky Earl would never tell us. Said they were both dead now so he didn't want to get their families involved."

Hollingsly smirked. "And y'all just believed him?"

"Why shouldn't we?" Ella asked.

"Because he's a lyin' son of a bitch. Always been a lyin' son of a bitch. No different now."

"What do you mean?" Jeff interrupted.

"I mean that bastard lied to y'all. Ain't both dead."

Jeff shot a quick glance at Ella who raised an eyebrow slightly, sending a signal to just stay calm and listen.

"Well, actually, one of 'em is dead. Went and got hisself killed in Vietnam back in '68. But the other one—well, he most certainly ain't dead."

Hollingsly leaned back in his chair, the annoying smile still plastered across his dark, craggy face.

"So, the fourth boy isn't dead?" Ella asked, clearly taken aback by this new revelation. "Is he still around?"

"Sorta."

"What is this, some kind of damn guessing game?" Jeff barked. "I think you're full of shit and just trying to play with us. So why don't you just get the hell out, take your damn games with you, and leave us alone!"

Hollingsly said nothing for a tense moment, firing a riveting glare at Jeff. Finally, he slid forward in his chair, looked first at Ella and then at Jeff.

"Okay, mister nigger-lovin', justice-for-all crusader. If y'all are so damned interested in justice for that nigger's killer," Hollingsly paused as his upper lip curled into a sneer, "why don't y'all just go on up to that big ol' mansion you grew up in and ask your daddy who else was there that night?"

CHAPTER 51

The room was as silent as a tomb; the only sound was Hollingsly's tobacco-ravaged, ragged breathing. Jeff continued to glare at him, his expression unchanged, as if he hadn't heard the astonishing words. Ella looked at the two men, puzzled, as she struggled to process what Hollingsly had just said. Slowly, Jeff's hard gaze began to soften, the anger seeping out, replaced by a swelling surge of confusion.

"What . . . what are you talking about?" he stammered.

Hollingsly, his face flushed with a sardonic grin, rocked back in his chair, enjoying himself as he locked eyes with Jeff.

"Boy, I damn sure got your attention now, ain't I?" he cackled. "I said, why don't you go ask your daddy who all else was there when that nigger got hisself introduced to the wrong end of a shotgun?"

Jeff sat staring, stunned, paroxysms of fear and disbelief seizing at his chest, washing over him like a rising tide.

"Why should I ask him?" he finally said, his voice barely audible.

"Why d'ya think?" Hollingsly said, his face now contorted into a cunning, contemptuous sneer. "Well then, I'll just tell you why, since you apparently ain't smart enough to figure it out your own self. There were four boys out there that night, awright? Tillman Jessup, Ricky Earl Graves, boy by the name a Jimmy Raye . . . and Willie Trannon."

"Bullshit!" Jeff spat indignantly.

"No, sir. Ain't bullshit. God's honest truth. The great Justice William Trannon. Champion of the poor downtrodden niggers. Patron saint of the civil rights movement. And—oh, yeah—accomplice to the murder of that damn nigger preacher." He cackled again. "Now, ain't that a bitch!"

Hollingsly glanced over at Ella.

"Real interested in what yer headline'll be when you write that there story, little lady."

Ella just glowered at him.

"Why're you telling me this?" Jeff asked, still stunned. "Why not just go public with it yourself?"

"Shit, ain't nobody gonna believe me if I tell the damn story. But you? Hell, they gotta believe it if it comes from you."

Jeff's eyes narrowed. "What makes you think—even if I did believe your ridiculous story—that I'd ever tell anyone?"

"'Cause I know you," Hollingsly smirked, "and your kind. All holier-than-thou while you shout about integrity and justice. Well, here's some real fuckin' justice for you. Once you talk to yer daddy, you'll know I'm tellin' the truth. And then you're gonna hafta tell. 'Cause if you don't—if you try to bury the truth—then yer life'll be one big fraud, too. Just like yer daddy's."

Slowly, Jeff's face twisted into a mask of sheer hatred, his lips trembling, his jaw clenching.

"You're a fucking liar!" he exploded, starting up from his chair toward the old man.

Hollingsly swiftly raised the revolver, pointing it directly in Jeff's face.

"Nothin' I'd like better, boy, than to blow a big fuckin' hole in you. One more step and they gonna be cleanin' up your splattered brains for a week. Now sit the fuck down. I ain't finished."

"Yes, you are," Ella said calmly, standing and placing herself between a seething Jeff and a menacing Hollingsly. "You're not going to shoot us. Didn't do it when you had the chance out in the woods—left it to your idiot henchmen—and you're certainly not going to do it now. You've said what you came to say. Now leave."

No one spoke as an anxious moment passed. Eventually, Hollingsly lowered the gun, his malevolent glare transforming back into his sardonic grin.

"Okay, little lady. Yer right. Guess I am 'bout done here." He looked at Jeff. "So, you just go on up there and ask. See what your daddy has to say. An' soon as you reckon that I'm tellin' the truth—and you will—well, I just can't wait to see you or that damn DA stand up in that ol' courtroom and announce to the whole goddamn world that the next witness—the only witness left against Tillman Jessup—is William Fuckin' Trannon. Might even just stay around to see that!"

Hollingsly stood, the gun still held loosely at his waist, as he edged around Ella toward the door.

"Can't say you wasn't warned, boy," he said, pausing as he opened the door. "Told you to stay outta this or you'd be sorry. Next time, you might wanna listen up."

He slammed the door behind him.

CHAPTER 52

Elizabeth opened the door as Jeff was climbing the front porch stairs. Dressed in her typical evening attire of a skirt, neatly pressed blouse, and apron, there was a look of real concern spread across her dark, ageless face. Jeff had called a few minutes earlier and told her that he was coming over to see his father. She had sensed immediately, by the tone of his voice and the time of the call, that there was some sort of problem.

"Y'all okay?" she asked tenderly, touching his cheek.

"I'm fine," he answered. "Dad still awake?"

She nodded. "Just getting ready to help him upstairs to bed when you called. He's in his usual spot in the library."

Elizabeth started, noticing Ella, who had lagged behind and was still standing on the porch. She tossed a questioning glance at Jeff.

"Sorry," Jeff mumbled, somewhat absently. "Elizabeth, this is my friend, Ella. Could you keep her company for a few minutes while I talk to my father?"

Still puzzled, Elizabeth nodded. "Certainly," she said, her deeply engrained sense of propriety overtaking her confusion, as she extended her hand to Ella. "Sometimes Jefferson forgets his manners—despite his upbringing. It's a pleasure to meet you, Miss Ella. I was thinking about a cup of tea. Will you join me?"

"Thank you," Ella smiled. "That would be very nice."

"We'll be in the kitchen, if you need us," Elizabeth said to Jeff. Ella gently brushed his arm and offered a tiny, hopeful smile before Elizabeth led her off toward the rear of the house.

Jeff waited until they had disappeared into the kitchen, and then walked down the hall to the library. He stopped before the closed, arching double doors, his hand on the polished brass handle, unsure what he should do next. He pulled his hand away. This is foolish, he thought. Why should he ever believe anything that A. J. Hollingsly said? The man wasn't just a liar—he was also a killer. A pathological maniac still fighting guerrilla hit-and-run skirmishes in a war of hatred and bigotry that should have ended decades ago. What better way for this twisted, rage-filled sociopath to attempt to wreak vengeance on Jeff than to accuse his iconic father of an unthinkable act of racist violence, an allegation that it was now impossible for him to defend? Besides, it was extremely unlikely that his father would even comprehend the conversation, much less actually be capable of denying the allegations or responding to any questions.

Jeff stood before the doors, paralyzed with fear and indecision, unable to believe that Hollingsly's claim about his father could possibly be true. Yet he was unable to force himself to walk away, despite being deeply afraid of both asking the question and hearing what the answer might be.

He turned the handle and stepped into the library. Dimly lit and darkly paneled, with a Brahms violin concerto softly flowing from a CD player tucked within the bookshelves, the room had the comforting feel of a medieval chapel, at once both deeply spiritual and profoundly safe.

William Trannon was at his usual post, propped in a wing chair, staring blankly out into the shadows of the darkened gardens. As always, Jeff was struck by the cruelly painful irony of the still-healthy body of a former great athlete playing host to the vastly diminished vestiges of a once-great mind.

"Hey, Dad," he said softly, dragging a small chair to the window and placing himself within his father's line of sight. "Sorry to come by so late, but there's something I need to talk to you about."

Jeff leaned forward, staring directly into his father's eyes, looking for some glimmer of recognition. There was nothing but an empty gaze.

"Dad . . . Dad, look at me. It's Jeff. Please look at me," he begged.

Nothing.

"Dad," Jeff continued, inching even closer, trying somehow to penetrate that enshrouding fog that held his father's mind hostage. "Dad . . . listen to me."

Still nothing.

"I need to ask you something," Jeff went on, this time his voice louder and more demanding. "I need to ask you about the murder of Reverend Elijah Hall back in 1960."

Jeff stopped and peered deep into his father's eyes. He wasn't sure, but he thought he'd seen some brief flicker of response in his father's face, some fleeting sign of comprehension.

"Dad, this is important," Jeff said, his voice challenging some lost element of the spirit that once bravely inhabited his father's body to fight its way to the surface, if only for a few moments.

"Were you there that night?" Jeff asked. "Dad . . . were you there when Elijah Hall was murdered?"

There was no response, just the same opaque, impenetrable gaze. Whatever Jeff thought—or hoped—he had seen in his father's face had retreated back into the wilderness of confusion. Jeff sighed and fell back into his chair, staring at the elegantly molded ceiling in frustration, convinced that he would never know the truth of Hollingsly's accusations.

He was about to stand when he thought he heard a sound, not

actually a word but just a wisp of something that resembled a soft sob, from deep within his father's chest. He sprang forward, searching for something—anything—that suggested he'd somehow penetrated the mystifying haze.

For a long moment, there was nothing—no look, no sound. Jeff thought that, perhaps, he'd been mistaken. Then, his father's head turned, ever so slightly, toward him.

"Dad?" Jeff said softly.

Slowly, barely perceptible, the shroud that had fallen over the soul of William Trannon rose and there was some spark of life once again in those once-luminous eyes. But there was not just life—there was also pain. Haunted, bottomless, chastened, overwhelming pain.

And then there were tears. First a single drop, then a stream, coursing down from those agonized eyes, flowing across his wrinkled cheeks and cascading down onto the crisp white shirt and tie; his body, now a mere ghost of the great athlete, wracked by deep, shuddering sobs.

Jeff stared, at once astonished by the appearance of long-ago vanished emotions while also both angry and grief-stricken at the realization of what these emotions signified.

Now, he knew. His father, for decades the grand beacon of wisdom and rectitude, had been there that awful night. The great and legendary William Trannon had, indeed, been an accomplice to the brutal murder of Elijah Hall. Jeff sat motionless in the hushed and breathless room, unsure of what he should do, how he should react.

Finally, as the sobbing subsided into soft, whispering sighs, Jeff leaned forward and wrapped the lost and shattered figure of his father in his arms.

CHAPTER 53

Jeff and Ella sat next to each other, swaying gently in wicker rocking chairs perched in a corner of the old wrap-around porch. The only sound was the murmured chorus of the denizens of the dark and the only light was the shimmering, milky glow from a nearby streetlight sheathed in a soft nocturnal mist. Neither had spoken for nearly ten minutes since Jeff had left his father in the library inside the house.

After a while, Ella reached over and took Jeff's hand, entwining her fingers with his. They rocked silently for a few more minutes, Ella casting concerned glances toward Jeff, who had retreated somewhere far away from her.

"What happened there?" she asked quietly, finally breaking their conspiracy of silence, inclining her head toward the charred, skeletal remnants of the far corner of the porch.

Jeff shifted his glance in the direction of the corner, a bitter, ironic smile creeping across his face.

"A souvenir from the Klan," he said.

"What?"

"Sometime back in the late sixties, Dad was a young lawyer representing the members of a black church up near Jackson in a lawsuit he brought against the KKK. Claimed they were responsible for a firebombing that destroyed the building. Got a lot of attention, as you might imagine. Anyway, I guess the boys in the white hoods weren't real happy about it, so one night a few of them cruised by, burned a cross on the lawn, and tossed some Molotov cocktails on the porch. Kind of a subtle message to warn him off."

"So, what happened?"

"Well, this was all before I was born, but the story goes that Dad and Mom were able to put the fire out before it spread. He won the case and convinced a federal jury to award $100,000 in damages against a local Klan klavern. Forced them to declare bankruptcy and put them out of business. At least for a while. Started a whole new way for blacks to fight back in court."

"But why . . . ?" Ella began, looking quizzically at the scarred ruins.

"A badge of honor, I guess," Jeff said. "Made a lot of enemies back then. He refused to repair it. Kept it that way all these years as a sign that he wasn't going to back down, no matter what. As a lawyer or a judge." He shrugged. "At least, that's what I always believed. Now, I'm not so sure."

"Maybe he kept it that way as a reminder," Ella said, stroking his hand. "A reminder of a terrible mistake he made when he was very young. A reminder of his own need for redemption."

"Maybe," Jeff whispered.

"So . . . what now?" Ella asked after a few more minutes of silence crept by.

Jeff sighed deeply. "Don't know."

He stopped rocking and leaned forward, his hands clasped prayer-like in front of his face.

"I'm not a very religious man," he began, his voice so muted that it was almost as if he was talking just to himself. "Never have been. Always struggled with the notion of having faith in something that was beyond my grasp or understanding. The one thing—the *only* thing—I truly worshipped was my father. Like I told you, he wasn't always that easy to get close to. And it sure as hell was impossible to live up to him. But he was the one thing, the one person, I could always believe in. And now . . ." he stopped, his voice choked and faltering.

"But you can't just ignore all the goodness . . ." Ella began.

"Don't you see?" Jeff interrupted, his voice strained. "All those great things, all the accomplishments? Were they real? How can they still count for something, now that we know he was there that night?

"It wasn't just him that I worshipped," he continued. "Not just the great William Trannon. It was the *idea* of him, the hero who stood strong in the face of all the overwhelming obstacles and always did the right thing. Always. Just because it was the right thing to do."

Jeff turned and faced Ella, his eyes etched in pain. "I worshipped him because he was about honor. He was about the power of hope and the power of wisdom and the power of goodness and courage and honesty. I didn't have a religion or church—I had him. He was my faith." Again, his voice wavered, aching with the sting of betrayal, as he shifted his focus once again off into the distance.

"Jeff," Ella said cautiously. "Are you really sure he was there? I mean, he never actually said that he was out there that night. That he was with them. So how can you really be certain?"

"I'm certain," Jeff answered evenly. "If you'd seen his reaction, the look in his eyes, the pain, and the tears—if you knew him like I do, you'd be certain, too." He was silent for a moment. "The only question now is what do I do about it?"

"What do you mean, 'what do you do'? What *can* you do? You can't prove he was there. There's no confession, no witnesses, just what you believe. You, of all people, should understand that. So why should you do anything? Why should you tell anybody? Do you want to destroy his image and all he's done over a lifetime? For what?"

"I don't know," he confessed, his hands covering his face. "I just wish he could tell me what I should do."

CHAPTER 54

It was dark and quiet inside the Morning Star Baptist Church. Jeff had called Reverend Butler first thing in the morning and asked if he could come talk to him about something important. On the drive out from Oxford, Jeff explained to Ella that he wanted to share the last night's revelations about his father's presence at the murder scene with the minister. Still profoundly perplexed over what to do, Jeff hoped that the minister might offer some perspective and guidance.

The three of them sat tucked away in a corner of the church, sipping from the glasses of iced sweet tea that Reverend Butler had waiting for them when they arrived.

"Shame the Lord decided to bring Ricky Earl home right then and there in the courtroom," the minister, dressed as always in a dark suit, said, shaking his head sadly. "And after he'd finally found some meaning in his life, too. Darn shame."

"Once again proving, as we know, that God works in mysterious ways," Ella said.

"Amen to that, Miss Ella," he answered. "So now what?" he asked, turning toward Jeff. "Case closed?"

"Looks that way," Jeff answered dejectedly.

"So then, what brings y'all out here this early to visit with me? Don't take this the wrong way, but y'all don't strike me much as the early mornin' prayin' type," Butler said with a gentle smile.

"Well, there's something I'd like to tell you," Jeff began.

"Listen, Jeff. No need for any explanations or apologies. Y'all tried. You took on a powerful man because it was the right thing to do. Almost cost y'all your own lives but you didn't back down. If you grew up during the civil rights years like I did, you learned that victories over evil come in all different shapes and sizes. Maybe we didn't win in the courtroom, but y'all can rest assured that just resurrecting this case and, finally, after all these years, shining a light on Elijah Hall's murder, surely was some kind of victory. Yes, indeed."

"Thank you, Reverend. I understand what you're saying and, hopefully, someday I'll feel the same way. But . . . there's something else."

Jeff paused, looking uncertainly at Ella, who nodded and gave him an encouraging half-smile.

"It's about my father," he continued haltingly. "And Elijah Hall's murder."

"Your father?" Butler said, leaning forward in his chair, clearly confused. "I . . . don't understand."

"Let me explain it to you. Remember how Ricky Earl told us that there were four boys out there that night?"

"Right," the minister said. "He, Tillman Jessup, and two others he wouldn't name, who'd since died."

"Well, that's what we all thought. That the other two had died. Turns out what he actually said—Ella here checked her notes—was that they 'were no longer with us.' And we all just assumed that they were dead."

"They're not?" Butler exclaimed. "They're still alive?"

"Actually, one is dead," Jeff answered. "But the other . . . well, we think the other is still alive."

"Still alive?" Butler's eyebrows shot up in surprise. "Can he testify?"

"Well, there's a problem."

"What kind of problem?"

"The fourth boy, the one who's still alive . . . we have reason to believe he is my father," Jeff said.

Reverend Butler stared at Jeff through his thick glasses, his deeply creased face twisting into a mask of confusion.

"I don't . . . think I understand," Butler said hesitantly.

"Remember the old guy from the Sovereignty Commission? Hollingsly?" Jeff asked.

"The one who tried to kill you?"

"Yeah. Well, he showed up last night at my apartment. Claimed that the other two people who were there that night were a boy named Jimmy Raye, who died in Vietnam . . . and my father."

"But, you can't possibly believe . . ." the Reverend began.

Jeff held his hands up to silence him. "Please, just listen to me, first. So, Hollingsly, who we know had talked to Ricky Earl right after the shooting and claims to have talked to at least one other boy, showed up last night and told me that I should go ask my father who was there that night."

"And?"

"And, I did."

"Did he say anything?"

Jeff shook his head. "He doesn't really talk anymore. But when I asked him, he got upset."

"Upset? How?"

"Well," Jeff said, his voice now strained. "You know how they say that sometimes Alzheimer's patients can remember things from a long time ago but can't remember what happened yesterday? I think that's what took place last night. When I asked him, I could see something, some flash of understanding in his eyes. And then . . ." Jeff stopped and tried to compose himself. "And then . . . he started to cry."

There was no sound inside the church, other than the faint growling of a tractor from the farm across the road. Finally, Reverend

Butler took a deep breath and slowly exhaled, the noise a soft rattling in his frail old lungs.

"So . . . do you truly believe, in your heart, that your father was part of the killing?" Butler asked, with more than just a tinge of incredulity.

"I do," Jeff answered, his voice barely a whisper.

The minister closed his eyes and shook his head gently from side to side.

"I can't believe this," he mumbled. "This can't be true."

"I'm afraid it is," said Jeff. "If you could have seen the look—the guilt and the pain—in his eyes. And then the tears. If you'd seen that, you'd know."

After a moment, Butler leaned forward in his chair and looked searchingly into Jeff's eyes.

"What do you plan to do about this belief of yours?"

"I'm not sure. I was hoping that you could help me decide."

Butler nodded, seeming to emerge from his doubt and wonder as he assumed his role of minister and spiritual guide.

"What are your choices?" he asked.

"I guess I could tell the district attorney. Of course, then he'd have to tell the defense," Jeff mused. "Maybe I could just talk to Judge Langston about it. See what he thinks."

Reverend Butler contemplated this for a moment.

"But, I thought you said your daddy doesn't talk anymore?"

Jeff shook his head. "Not sure if he can't or if he just doesn't. Bottom line is, I don't think he's said a word for more than a year."

"Well then, if he can't talk, what good would it do to bring it up to all those folks? Not gonna be able to put him up on a witness stand to tell his story. So, what's there to be gained?" He peered carefully at Jeff through his thick glasses. "Seems to me, there's nothing to be gained at all."

Jeff seemed puzzled.

"What about justice?" he asked.

"Justice?" echoed the minister. "Justice for who? Not for Tillman Jessup. Said yourself that your father couldn't testify, so it surely wouldn't help to put Jessup in jail. Only thing coming from that, then, would be the destruction of your father's image and reputation. Certainly not gonna hurt Jessup. That what you want?"

"But what about justice for Elijah Hall? Isn't that worth something?" Jeff pleaded.

"How would all this provide any justice for him? Jessup'll walk out that courtroom, still be a free man. Some folks might believe he's a killer," he shrugged, "but chances are he'll probably go on and become the next governor anyway. And Elijah Hall? He'll still be dead after all these years. So, the only thing that you'll do is make people forget all the good your daddy did over the years." He shook his head sadly. "Don't seem like a very fair trade-off to me."

Jeff rubbed his hands over his face, anguishing over the dilemma that had invaded his soul, tears forming in the corners of his eyes.

"But Dad always believed that justice was absolute. Something was either right or it was wrong. There was no question, no indecision. He often said that justice was the one moral certainty in a world that would otherwise fall into moral chaos." He paused. "And what he did was wrong. I know he didn't mean for it to happen like that. I know he tried to stop it. But he was there. And that was wrong."

Jeff looked first to Reverend Butler, and then to Ella, who had sat silently, bearing witness to his torment.

"What would he do if this all was reversed?" Jeff asked. "If I'd been the one out there on that road? Would he tell me we had to keep quiet? And let the truth stay hidden until it dies?"

Reverend Butler leaned forward, his hands grasped prayerfully in front of his face, his eyes sharing Jeff's distress.

"Jeff," he said soothingly. "I've known your daddy for forty years.

First met him when he and a few Ole Miss kids came to me and volunteered to drive some of my church folks to the polls to register to vote. This was a year or two after Elijah's murder. Not a real popular thing for all them to do back then. Surprised the hell out of me, tell you the truth.

"We became good friends over the years," the minister continued, a hint of a sorrowful smile working its way across his face. "We talked often about the civil rights movement and what we could both do to help. After he became a judge, he'd sometimes talk to me about cases he was handling. I think I knew him pretty good, probably better'n most. And I see an awful lot of him in you, son. And that's somethin' you should be real proud of."

"So, you think he'd tell me to keep quiet? To just let it all fade away?" Jeff asked softly.

"I wish I could tell you I was truly sure what he'd say to do. But I can't. But there is something I am truly sure about," the minister said, his look still compassionate, but his tone more firm. "Sometimes we need to hold on to our heroes. No matter what. Lord knows, Dr. King was no angel all the time. But the good that he did, the leadership and hope that he provided . . . well, that was worth sometimes lookin' the other way. We needed to believe in him. Seems to me it's the same with your daddy. He did so much good for so many over the years. Yes, if he was there the night of the murder—even if he tried to stop it—that was surely wrong. But we still need our heroes. And your daddy—well, he's a hero. And we need to still believe in him, too."

Jeff looked at the minister, his eyes pooling, his faith shaken.

"I just want to do what's right," Jeff sighed softly.

"The thing about justice," the minister said, "is that it's not always perfect. But we do what we can. Does your father need to be punished somehow for justice to prevail?" He shook his head. "I can't believe that a just God would demand that of him. Or of you, as his son.

Sometimes we make a man pay for his sins with his life. Seems to me your father used his life to pay for his sins."

Jeff took a deep breath and exhaled slowly, wiping the tears from his eyes with his shirtsleeve.

"Thank you, Reverend," he said.

The minister stood and placed his hand tenderly on Jeff's shoulder.

"I think, son, that you need to let this go. You need to trust that, when the time comes, the Good Lord'll sort it all out."

CHAPTER 55

"He's right, you know," Ella said.

They were in Jeff's car, driving back to Oxford. Both had been quiet since they had left Reverend Butler back at the church. Jeff just stared out the windshield, both hands locked in a vise-like grip around the steering wheel.

"Jeff? You okay?" she asked.

Jeff nodded.

"Then talk to me. Please."

"Part of me knows he's right," he said softly. "I understand what he's saying—that revealing this won't help anyone. And will only destroy everything my father's done. I get that."

"But . . . ?"

He turned to face her, anger flaring in his eyes.

"But, if I do that, if I keep quiet . . . then Hollingsly's right. Then I'm part of a fraud. A horrible, hypocritical fraud. The same fraud that's haunted my father all these years."

Ella reached out, her fingers lightly brushing Jeff's cheek.

"I'm so sorry. No one should ever have to make this kind of decision. If you go public, you validate your father's ideals and values while, at the same time, you destroy his legacy. If you keep quiet," she sighed, "well, you know the pain that comes with that decision."

"So?" Jeff said, turning to her, a questioning look in his eyes. "What do you think I should do?"

"Like I said, I think Reverend Butler's right. It's the old 'greatest good for the greatest number of people' argument. You tell the story and it has a devastating impact on many. You stay silent and it's devastating to you alone." She raised her eyebrows and tilted her head. "Seems to me the answer is clear. You have to take the hit. For the good of so many others."

Jeff gnawed on his lip, deep in thought, again staring straight ahead.

"And, one more thing," Ella said. "I think you owe your father that much. He's earned it."

Jeff took a deep, fluttering breath and slowly exhaled.

"I know. You're right. And so is Reverend Butler. I guess I just need some time for the idea to settle in. The problem is I just can't get Hollingsly out of my mind. I keep seeing his leering, evil grin and thinking that if I don't tell, then, somehow, he wins. And it's killing me."

"Jeff, you can't let him get to you. That's exactly what he wants. His whole life has been about hatred and destruction. And trying to play people against each other. And now, he's trying to play you, too— against yourself."

Jeff nodded, his face hardening, now resolute. "I've got to forget about him. I know that." He paused. "I've got one more person I want to talk to. I think it'll be helpful. In the meantime," he said, turning and shooting her a curious glance, "at least this might make a great story for you."

"Story?" she said, puzzled. "What story?"

"About the fall of the legendary William Trannon." He shrugged. "In some ways, might be an even better story than if Jessup was convicted."

Ella glared at him for a full minute, an angry storm filling her eyes, and then the storm receded, leaving behind just a troubled cloud. She shook her head.

"No story there. Certainly not one that we could ever go with."

"What do you mean?" Jeff said uncertainly. "It's a huge story."

"Might be . . . if we could ever confirm it." She shook her head again. "Do you think the *New York Times* would ever run a story of that magnitude—challenging the heritage of a civil rights hero and accusing him of being an accomplice to murder—based solely on the ravings of a racist lunatic? With no confirmation or additional sources? I'd be out of a job right quick if I ever went to the editors with that one. I'm afraid, as far as I'm concerned, this whole thing never happened."

Jeff looked at her and, for the first time in a while, a small, thankful smile found its way across his face.

"I've lost a lot the last few days." He sighed. After a moment, he turned toward her. "Hopefully, you don't have to leave real soon?"

She reached out, took his hand, and grinned.

"Not much chance of that. I remembered why I really like it down here. Guess I'm still a Delta girl at heart. Talked to my editor yesterday and she agreed there's no reason why I can't work from down here. It's not like the old days anymore where you need to be in the newsroom to file a story. You can file from anywhere, now. So, I think I might just stay awhile."

CHAPTER 56

The chambers of Judge Rogers Langston mirrored the life of their occupant. Strong and masculine, with dark wood paneling, heavy carved furniture, and plush leather chairs, the stately men's club décor reflected the deep traditions of the judiciary of the Old South. The walls held a panoramic vista of the trappings of a successful legal career. Ornately framed degrees from the University of Mississippi and Harvard Law School were surrounded by photos of the judge with a staggering array of local and political figures. Plaques and award citations attesting to his judicial accomplishments were deployed like sentinels at strategic locations, adorning the walls and tabletops. Woven throughout the office were photos of the judge with his wife and children, sharing vacations and other happy family occasions.

Jeff sat across the vast expanse of the judge's desk, struck by the order and structure of its contents. Although the desk was covered with papers and law books, all were neatly distributed in a precise and systematic fashion. Again, a reflection of the man.

Judge Langston rocked back in his swivel chair, dressed in a dark suit, white shirt, and crimson and blue striped tie, his judicial robes hung regally on a brass hook behind him.

"So, Jeff," he began, "I was curious about your request to see me. You sure that the DA and defense lawyers don't need to be here, too?"

"No, sir," Jeff said. "I don't believe that's necessary."

The judge nodded. "Okay. I trust your judgment. So, what's this all about?"

"Well, Your Honor, I wanted to run something by you. I'm looking for some advice."

"Happy to help, if I can."

Jeff took a deep breath and began hesitantly.

"Let me give you a hypothetical situation. Then, perhaps, you can give me your thoughts. Okay?"

"Certainly," the judge said, leaning forward in his chair.

"Suppose a possible witness comes to light in the midst of a trial. Neither side knows anything about this witness, but someone who's peripherally involved with the case receives information that this witness might have direct knowledge of certain important facts."

"Is this hypothetical witness available to testify?"

"That's the problem. At least, it's part of the problem."

Judge Langston looked at Jeff quizzically.

"Let me explain," Jeff said quickly. "This hypothetical individual, if the information is true, is the only person left who may have witnessed certain events. But, because of the person's medical condition, the facts can't be confirmed."

"What kind of condition?"

Jeff paused. "Let's just say that the person's impaired cognitive functions and inability to communicate would prevent anyone from being able to positively confirm the allegations."

The judge looked carefully at Jeff, his focus now sharp and penetrating.

"So," he said, his eyes narrowing, "this hypothetical person can't actually confirm the suggestion that he may be a witness?"

"No, sir."

"And there's no other available evidence to confirm it?"

"No, sir."

"And he's not capable of communicating? Couldn't testify under oath?"

"No, Your Honor."

Judge Langston stared for a long moment at Jeff, and then leaned back in his chair, his chin tilted toward the ceiling.

Finally, he grunted and turned to Jeff.

"Well—hypothetically speaking—it doesn't seem to me that this should be a real problem. There's absolutely no independent confirmation of the suggestion that the witness is actually in possession of relevant and material facts. And clearly he would not presently be competent to testify in any event." The judge leaned forward, his hands folded on the desk, a spark of sympathy in his eyes as he looked knowingly at Jeff.

"In my opinion—in this hypothetical situation—a person could not then be considered a material and competent witness. And," he added, "as a result, there'd certainly be no need to bring any of this to the attention of any of the parties."

Jeff took a deep breath, let it out slowly, and nodded thankfully to the judge.

"Thank you, Your Honor. I appreciate your time and your thoughts."

"Not a problem," the judge said, rising from his chair. "And since this was just a hypothetical conversation, seems to me we can just assume that this talk never happened."

As they got to the door, the judge placed his hand on the polished silver knob and paused.

"I ever tell you, Jeff," he said kindly, "how much I've respected your father over the years?"

"No, sir," Jeff said, his voice faltering with emotion.

"About time, then, that I did. A truly great man. Send him my regards, will you?"

"Yes, sir. I surely will."

CHAPTER 57

The prosecution team, including Jeff, was gathered Friday morning in the conference room in the hallway outside of the courtroom. The room was quiet and tense, barely masking a roiling anger over the fact that they were about to lose the most important case brought by the district attorney's office in decades. Gibb Haynes stood at the head of a small conference table, sullenly shuffling through some notes while his staff sat quietly around the table. Sheriff Poole had parked himself in a chair in the corner, a deep scowl creasing his square face. Jeff sat in the other corner, absently fidgeting with a pen, anxious to get the court session over with, knowing that once Judge Langston was told the prosecution no longer had any witness who could directly tie the defendant to the killing, he would have no choice but to grant the defense motion to dismiss the charges against Tillman Jessup.

The door flew open and Terrell Jackson burst in, waving a sheaf of papers in his massive hands.

"He was murdered!" he exclaimed.

Everyone looked up.

"What?" asked Haynes.

"Ricky Earl! He was murdered!"

There was an odd, puzzled silence for a moment, and then everyone began shouting questions at the same time.

"Hold it! Quiet down!" Haynes hollered. He turned toward Jackson. "What're you talking about?"

"Ricky Earl didn't have a heart attack," Jackson said, nearly breathless. "He was murdered!"

"Murdered? How?" asked Sheriff Poole, his face tight with anger.

Jackson threw the papers down on the table.

"It's all right here. Just got off the phone with the medical examiner. The cause of death was digitalis toxicity."

"What the hell does that mean?" growled the sheriff.

"It means he was poisoned!" said Jackson.

"Slow down a minute," Haynes ordered. "Gimme the details."

Jackson took a deep breath and looked toward Jeff. "Remember when the ER doc at the hospital told us that digitalis showed up in Ricky Earl's blood test? A lot of it?"

Jeff nodded.

"Well, the medical examiner says the amount was more—a whole helluva lot more—than would ever be prescribed. Said it must've been either chronic overdosing or a single massive ingestion. I checked all the jail records. Ricky Earl had been behind bars for almost a year. No prescriptions! No digitalis! No heart problems! No nothin'!"

"So, how . . . ?" Haynes began.

"Don't know for sure," Jackson interrupted. "Medical examiner said it can be ingested a lot of ways. In food. In somethin' he drank."

"Son of a bitch," Gibb Haynes muttered through clenched teeth. "How the fuck did they get to him?"

"I ordered everythin' from his cell boxed up for testing. Gonna take a look at all the security tapes from the jail, too. Hope to get some kinda answers back quick," Jackson said.

The room became silent once again, the earlier frustration now replaced by a seething rage.

"Any way we can use this to keep the case from being dismissed?"

asked one of the young staff members.

Gibb Haynes shook his head somberly. "Afraid not. Not for the murder charge. Without Ricky Earl, we're done."

"But what if Jessup, or someone on his team, was responsible?" asked the same staffer.

"First, we'd have to be able to prove it," said Haynes. "Even then, yeah, we could charge them with Ricky Earl's murder, but this case against Jessup is still gonna go away."

Haynes picked up the report that had been faxed by the medical examiner and rapidly scanned it. Disgusted, he tossed the pages back, scattering them across the table and onto the floor.

"Might as well go get this fuckin' circus over with," he said. "Then," he added, shooting a hard glance at both Sheriff Poole and Terrell Jackson, "y'all get out there and find me a damn murderer!"

CHAPTER 58

Inside the courtroom, every available seat had been claimed for more than an hour, most of them by restless members of the media. Ella was in her usual seat in the front of the chamber, her attention once again drawn to the powerful magnet of Kendra Leigh Jessup. While other friends and supporters seemed relaxed, some practically jubilant, she appeared somber and withdrawn, almost uninterested in her husband's fate.

At the defense table, Tillman Jessup and Channing Wallace were locked in whispered conversation, while Jessup's aide, Royce Henning, was leaning over the railing, amiably chatting up a gaggle of reporters.

The courtroom doors swung open and the prosecution team marched in, District Attorney Gibb Haynes and Sheriff Clayton Poole in the vanguard, faces hard as chiseled stone. Jeff, bringing up the rear, glanced in Ella's direction, raising an eyebrow and inclining his head as a signal that something very interesting was about to play out.

A moment later, Judge Rogers Langston took the bench. He carefully arranged the case file and a number of legal texts before him and then rapped his gavel.

"All right, folks. Y'all can settle down," he intoned, peering out at the crowd gathered in the courtroom before turning toward the lawyers.

"We've got some matters to resolve before I bring the jury in. Following our last session two days ago, and the unfortunate death of the prosecution's witness, Ricky Earl Graves, I had granted the prosecution's request for a two-day adjournment. Mr. Haynes, you had asked for the time to assess whether you were still in a position to proceed with your case. In the meantime, the defense has filed a motion seeking the dismissal of all charges, contending that, without the testimony of Mr. Graves, there is an insufficient factual basis for this prosecution to continue. So, Mr. Haynes," the judge said, focusing his attention on the district attorney, "let's start with you. Do you have any other testimony that, in some fashion, could link this defendant to the murder?"

Gibb Haynes rose deliberately from his chair. "Your Honor," he began, his voice soaked in angry, righteous indignation. "First of all, I'd like to advise the court that our witness, Ricky Earl Graves—the one person who has directly identified this defendant as the man who killed Reverend Elijah Hall—did not just 'unfortunately' pass away." Haynes paused dramatically, and then continued. "He was, in fact, murdered!"

There was a detonation of gasps and surprised cries as the seismic shockwave of the district attorney's accusation rolled through the courtroom. Judge Langston flailed his gavel once, twice, and then a third time before order was restored.

"That is a serious allegation, Mr. Haynes," the judge said.

"It is, indeed, Your Honor. But it is also true. The medical examiner has concluded that Mr. Graves did not die of natural causes—he was poisoned. We're talking about murder, obstruction of justice, tampering with a witness. And I assure Your Honor—and the good citizens of this county—that we intend to throw all of our resources into this investigation. We will find the killer—or killers—and I promise that justice will be swift and harsh."

"Your Honor," Channing Wallace cried, leaping to his feet. "This is an outrage! We object to any implication that this witness might have been killed—if, indeed, he was killed—because of his involvement with my client and this case. And I would demand a retraction of that statement by the district attorney."

Haynes first glared at Wallace and Tillman Jessup, and then turned toward the judge.

"A retraction, Your Honor?" the DA said cynically. "Does Mr. Wallace think this is the Old South of long ago and that, somehow, I've slighted his honor? What's next? A duel? Pistols at twenty paces?"

Haynes shifted his gaze back to the defense table.

"Seems to me," he added ironically, "the defense 'doth protest too much,' if I can borrow a line from Mr. Shakespeare. I'm not sure why they should be so upset. I haven't accused anyone. I wonder if Mr. Wallace—or, perhaps, his client—knows something that I don't know about Mr. Graves's poisoning?"

"This is completely improper," Wallace roared, "and Mr. Haynes should know better."

"Gentlemen, gentlemen," Judge Langston interrupted sternly. "That's enough. From both of you. Now y'all settle down. And sit down. Now!"

The judge waited for a moment until both lawyers—Wallace still fuming and Haynes still indignant—reluctantly took their seats.

"Now, then, Mr. Haynes," the judge began, "I certainly understand your concern over the medical examiner's findings. *And* your intention to pursue a murder investigation. But I'm concerned right now with this case—and this case alone. So, let me ask you this: Do you have any additional witnesses who can, either directly or circumstantially, link this defendant to the killing of Elijah Hall?"

Gibb Haynes stood, took a deep breath, and exhaled slowly. He looked first at Tillman Jessup and then at Judge Langston.

"No, Your Honor. I'm afraid I don't."

"Am I correct, then, that you would have no additional facts to present to this jury?"

"That is correct, Your Honor."

"Well, then, in that case, since I am satisfied that there are no additional witnesses who would be competent to add any material evidence to the prosecution's case," the judge said solemnly, catching Jeff's eyes for a barely perceptible instant, "I must now render a decision on the defense motion to dismiss the case. You see, Mr. Wallace has taken the position that, without the testimony of Ricky Earl Graves, there is, as a matter of law, an insufficient factual basis to allow this case to go to a jury."

Judge Langston paused and rocked back in his chair, deep in thought. Finally, he looked to the district attorney. "Mr. Haynes, I'm afraid that, under the circumstances, I must agree with Mr. Wallace. Y'all have certainly proved that Reverend Hall was murdered, but, as we know, that fact was never an issue. Unfortunately, your other witnesses have merely served to provide some circumstantial corroboration for the testimony that you expected to elicit from Ricky Earl Graves. But without his testimony—regardless of how Mr. Graves died—there is no link to this defendant for them to corroborate. The essence of your case no longer exists."

Judge Langston took a moment to scribble something on his notepad, and then looked sympathetically toward Haynes, who was staring stoically at the Great Seal of the State of Mississippi, hanging majestically above the judge's bench.

"As a result, I am constrained to grant the defense motion. Accordingly, the indictment against the defendant is hereby dismissed, the bail order is vacated, any property pledged shall be released to the defendant forthwith, and the jury will be discharged."

The judge turned to face the defense table.

"Mr. Jessup," he said, "you, sir, are free to go."

The courtroom erupted in applause as Jessup's supporters leaped to their feet, clapping and shouting, pushing toward the former defendant, extending hands in congratulations.

In the midst of the celebration, Judge Langston quietly gathered up his books and papers and retired to his chambers. On the other side of the bench, Channing Wallace beamed as he embraced his client and then thrust a clenched fist into the air in celebration. Around the counsel table, the remainder of the defense team grasped hands and pounded backs as if they had just won the national championship in the Sugar Bowl.

Meanwhile, Gibb Haynes angrily tossed his files into his briefcase and led the prosecution team on a forced march through the surging crowd, spitting out a terse "No comment right now" each time a reporter asked for a reaction.

Jeff remained in his seat, watching the celebration unfold, as the media members struggled to get close enough to fire questions at Jessup. He saw Ella shouldering her way toward the railing opposite the defense table.

"Senator Jessup," a voice from the back of the room shouted. "How does it feel to have the charges against you dismissed?"

Tillman Jessup stopped shaking hands and turned toward the crowd, his arms raised like a triumphant boxer in the ring.

"I've said from the beginning that I was an innocent man," he said, offering his best and broadest campaign smile. "And this certainly proves it."

A roar of approval came from the throng of well-wishers.

"Senator? Senator?" Ella called out, raising her hand as she burst through the scrum and reached the railing. "What about the allegation that Ricky Earl Graves was murdered? What's your reaction to that charge?"

Jessup turned serious and looked out at the now-hushed crowd.

"It's a shame when any man dies. And it's certainly a shame that Mr. Graves died before my lawyers had a chance to show the world what a devious and despicable liar he was. But I'll tell all y'all what. I'm a great believer in the power of the Lord. I don't know what Mr. Haynes was babblin' about. But I do know that that damn liar had a heart attack right here in front of y'all. Right there on the witness stand as he placed his hand on the Bible and then proceeded to tell lie after lie." He paused and then added in a dramatic, evangelical preacher voice, "Perhaps that was the Lord rendering his verdict on the evil life of Ricky Earl Graves as he took him right here in this tabernacle of justice."

"Yes?" Jessup said, nodding toward another reporter who was gesturing wildly with both arms.

"But, Senator," Ella persisted, raising her voice over the other shouted questions, "what about the fact that you weren't found not guilty by a jury? No one in this courtroom—judge or jury—has actually determined that you weren't involved in the killing."

Jessup, his features now taut, directed a swift, icy glare at Ella, and then turned away, pointing instead in the direction of another reporter who was frantically waving his notebook.

"Yes, I think you were next," he said smoothly.

As Jessup spoke, offering up self-congratulations in response to every question, regardless of the various reporters' queries, Jeff finally stood and began to work his way past the swelling gathering inside the railing. Pausing to let two new revelers enter, he caught Royce Henning looking his way, a smirk curling the corner of his mouth. Fighting back a flash of anger and an urge to break the sleazy political aide's jaw, Jeff simply shook his head in disgust and turned away.

Navigating his way through the heaving horde, Jeff caught a glimpse of Kendra Leigh Jessup in the back of the courtroom. She was staring in the direction of her husband, an unlikely look of what appeared to be sorrow and revulsion engraved on her fragile face. He caught her eye for a fleeting moment and she nodded to him, a look of sadness creeping into her gaze.

As he watched, she took a deep breath, raised her chin high, and slipped silently out of the courtroom.

CHAPTER 59

Jeff and Ella had been sitting on his balcony above the Square, drinking beer, finishing off their dinner of pulled-pork sandwiches, and mulling over the courtroom events of the morning, when the marked police cruiser pulled up on the street below. A sheriff's officer jumped out and peered up into the darkness.

"Mr. Trannon? That you up there?"

Jeff stood and leaned over the railing.

"Yeah. What's up?"

"It's Officer Walls. Detective Jackson sent me to find you."

"There a problem?"

"He didn't say. Just radioed in and told me to find you. Said—and these're his words, sir—'to find you, throw your ass in the car, and get you to him right away.'"

"Okay. Be right down."

Jeff turned to Ella, a puzzled look on his face.

"What's that all about?" she asked.

Jeff shrugged. "Don't know. C'mon, let's go find out."

They hustled out of the apartment and down the stairs to the waiting police car.

"Okay if she joins us?" Jeff asked, nodding toward Ella.

"Guess so," the officer said, opening the rear door.

"Where we headed?" Ella asked.

"An address outside of town," the officer said, jumping into the front seat and throwing the vehicle into gear.

Ten minutes later, after speeding along darkened country lanes, they pulled into a large circular driveway that fronted an impressive three-story, rambling, white-columned mansion. Two other sheriff's vehicles were parked in front of the house.

"What the hell . . . ?" Jeff muttered to Ella. "I think this is Jessup's place."

As they approached the house, Terrell Jackson appeared in the doorway, a look of deep concern etched across his face.

"What's going on?" Jeff said. "Why're we here?"

Jackson gestured for them to step inside. The entrance foyer was vast, with hallways radiating out in four directions. Jackson took Jeff by the arm, nodded to Ella, and guided them down the nearest passage toward what looked to be a large library.

"Need y'all to see this," Jackson said somberly. "One of my guys caught a 911 call about some kind of emergency out here. Soon as he arrived, he called me."

As they stepped into the room, Ella gasped and Jeff stopped in his tracks. Kendra Leigh Jessup was seated calmly at a small writing desk, a cup of tea in her hands. Across the room, sprawled in a leather armchair, was Tillman Jessup. There was a small, neat bullet hole in the center of his forehead. His eyes were wide open, staring vacantly into nothingness, a rivulet of drying blood meandering down along the bridge of his nose to his cheek.

"Oh, my God," Ella whispered.

"What . . . ?" Jeff murmured, turning to Jackson.

"Not sure," Jackson said, looking over at Kendra Leigh. "She was sitting right there when I got here. Just sippin' tea. Said she'd tell me what happened . . . but only if you were here."

"Me?" Jeff exclaimed. "Why me?"

"Not a damn clue," Jackson said, shaking his head. "Let's go find out."

Jeff and Jackson walked over to the desk, Ella lagging behind. Kendra Leigh, wrapped in a dark crimson, silk brocade dressing gown, turned toward them, a tight, joyless smile on her face. The corner of her lower lip was cut and swollen, a patch of blood smeared on her chin.

"Thank you for coming," she said to Jeff, sounding as if she was welcoming them to some sort of social affair. "You, too, Miss Garrity. I hope this isn't a terrible inconvenience for you."

"No, ma'am," Jeff said uncertainly.

"Are you okay?" Ella asked kindly.

Kendra Leigh touched her lip absently and tilted her head slightly.

"Oh, this? It's nothing." She let out a small, ironic chuckle. "Nothing compared to . . . well, never mind that, now. I'm fine. Thank you for asking."

"Mrs. Jessup," Jackson said gently, "now that Jeff and Ella are here, can you tell us what happened?"

Kendra Leigh sat still as a statue for a moment, her eyes fixed on the death mask of her dead husband. She turned back toward her teacup, raised it, took a demure sip, as if she were enjoying their companionship at a tea party, and then replaced the cup on the desktop.

"He was such a bastard," she whispered, as if sharing teatime gossip. Then she straightened, looked toward them, and began to speak, her voice now clear and firm. "I'd had enough. And today was the last straw."

"What do you mean?" Jeff asked.

"I couldn't take it anymore. The abuse. The beatings. The insults. The lies. And after what happened today in the courtroom, and then back here . . ."

"Wait a minute," Jeff interrupted. "Did you shoot him?"

Kendra Leigh looked at them, a strange bewilderment in her eyes, apparently puzzled as to why he'd ask the question when the answer was so obvious.

"Of *course* I shot him," she answered, matter-of-factly.

"Terrell, stop right now! No more questions! Her rights—you've got to give 'em to her now. Before she says anything else."

Jackson shot him an angry glance, shook his big head, and then pulled his Miranda card from his pocket and reluctantly proceeded to read the warnings to her. When he had finished, he asked her if she understood them.

"Of course I do," Kendra Leigh said, a slight tone of annoyance in her voice.

"And are you still willing to speak to us?" Jackson asked.

"Certainly. That's why I called you here."

"Mrs. Jessup," Jeff said. "I really don't think it's a good idea for you to be talking about this without talking to a lawyer, first."

Jeff turned toward an obviously frustrated Jackson. "Sorry, man, but I've got to tell her."

"Damn lawyers," Jackson muttered, a mix of annoyance and appreciation for his old friend in his voice. "Just can't help yourself, can you? Always buttin' in."

"It's all right, Mr. Trannon," Kendra Leigh said soothingly. "I appreciate your concern, but I really would prefer to tell you what happened. And when I'm finished, I think you all will be very happy that I did." she added.

CHAPTER 60

"The perfect couple. The beauty queen and the rich politician," Kendra Leigh said, a mocking smirk curling her damaged lip. "The perfect marriage. At least, that's what everyone thought. Maybe it was, early on. But then it all went bad. His political star was rising and he was traveling a lot. We were trying to have children but nothing worked so, of course, he blamed me. He started having affairs—a bunch of them. Then I started having affairs to get back at him. He started drinking. I started drinking. Sounds pretty much like a textbook case, doesn't it?"

Ella nodded sympathetically while Jeff and Jackson stood by quietly.

"Anyway," Kendra Leigh continued, "before long, the screaming and the nasty words just weren't enough for him. First, it was just a push or a shove to make a point. Then, one night, after a particularly bad argument—I'd found a woman in my bed when I got home early from a trip—he slapped me. Somehow, I think he got some kind of cheap thrill out of it. Well, from then on I became a punching bag. Nothing that couldn't be covered over by a lot of makeup—had to protect the image of the 'perfect couple,' after all. I tried like hell to just stay away from him, only going out together to political events. But . . ." Her voice trailed off.

"Mrs. Jessup," Ella pleaded. "Jeff's right. Please let us get you a lawyer before you say anything more. I really think . . ."

Kendra Leigh raised her hand and stopped Ella mid-sentence.

"Thank you, no. I promise you, I know what I'm doing." She looked them each carefully in the eye. "I know you're all probably thinking, 'Why didn't she leave him, if it was really that bad?' Well, I certainly thought about it." She shrugged. "I know this sounds terribly simple, but my generation was raised to stay married. We didn't divorce. We stayed together and worked through our problems. Does sound pretty silly, nowadays, doesn't it? And, I'll be honest, I didn't really want to give all this up," she said, gesturing at the splendor of her surroundings. "I know that sounds awful, but I guess it was just the pact I made with the devil. My own personal Faustian bargain."

She stopped and took another sip of tea. Ella reached out to touch her arm and Kendra Leigh patted her hand gently and reassuringly.

"So, what happened tonight?" Jackson asked.

"After the case was thrown out this morning," Kendra Leigh began, her face hardening, "and all the sycophants had finished sucking up to him like he'd just won some heroic battle, he ended up back here. I stayed upstairs. Didn't want to be anywhere near him. He was down here with that disgusting aide of his, Royce Henning. I could hear a lot of other people coming and going and, after a while, it sounded like everyone had left. So I came downstairs to get something from my desk before I went to bed—I always kept a bottle hidden there and figured I'd need it tonight—and was surprised that he and Henning were still here, just sitting around drinking. When I walked in, he told me to get out, that they had business to discuss. So I came over here to my desk, got what I needed, and left."

Pausing for another sip of tea, she looked up. Her hard, angry expression had changed, replaced by a sly, mirthless grin.

"But I didn't go back upstairs. I snuck around to the sunroom—it connects to this room through that door," she said, pointing to a closed door on the far wall of the library, "so I could listen to what they were saying."

She paused once again, a faraway look on her face, as she seemed to be wrestling with something within herself. Then she took a deep breath and looked directly at Jeff.

"He did it, you know."

"What do you mean?" Jeff asked.

"He killed that preacher."

"How do you know that?"

"I heard him say so. When I was listening at the door. 'Can't believe that shootin' a damn nigger forty years ago almost got me put in jail'— those were his exact words. Then he and Henning started laughing. Then Henning said that maybe the trial ended up being good for his campaign, that now he'll probably get more votes from the old racist rednecks out there."

"Did you know?" Ella asked. "I mean, before you heard him admit it to Henning, did you know that he was the killer?"

Kendra Leigh thought a moment. "I had my suspicions. The way he talked about the case. His attitude. Even asked him directly one time. Got a smack in the face for being so nosy. I guess, deep down, I think I knew. Just didn't want to admit it. It's one thing to be married to a wife-beater, quite another to be married to a murderer."

"But you're sure that he admitted it to Henning?" Jeff asked.

"Absolutely."

Jeff exchanged a knowing glance with Ella, and then turned to Jackson.

"What do you think?" Jeff said to the detective.

"Think it's time we have a little 'come-to-Jesus' talk with Mr. Henning," Jackson said.

"Before you do," Kendra Leigh said, "there's something else you need to know. I also heard them talking about that Ricky Earl Graves fellow. About how he died."

"What'd they say?" Jeff asked.

"Seems that they were the ones responsible for his death."

"What?" Jeff said. "How?"

"I didn't hear a lot of details. They just laughed about God taking him when he did, right there in the courtroom. And then Henning said something about God, 'with a little help from our friend.' That's the term he used, 'our friend.'"

"Did either of them say who that 'friend' was?" asked Jackson.

Kendra Leigh shook her head. "Not right then. But a little later, just before Henning left, he told Tillman to make sure he came up with the money right away because he'd promised to deliver the rest of it soon."

"Deliver the money? To who?" Jeff asked.

Kendra Leigh looked directly at Terrell Jackson.

"Henning's exact words were: 'Once he gets the rest of his money, my guess is that's the last we'll see of the sheriff. Probably spend the rest of his life off fishing somewhere in the Florida Keys.'"

Jackson looked like he'd taken a shoulder to the ribs. His jaw dropped open and his face was a twisted mask of confusion.

"'The sheriff'?" he stammered. "Sheriff Poole?"

Kendra Leigh nodded sympathetically, as if consoling a child after giving bad news. "I'm sorry, dear, but that's what he said."

Jeff looked at Ella, stunned by the revelation.

"I'm afraid it makes sense," Ella said. "The sheriff could get access to Ricky Earl anytime. And Ricky Earl probably trusted him."

"But Clayton Poole?" Jeff said, his voice wrapped in painful bewilderment. "He's one of the good guys. Always has been. How could . . . ?" His voice trailed off.

"Money," Kendra Leigh said. "My guess is a lot of it. They say that everybody has a price. Sounds like Tillman found Sheriff Poole's. He was very good at that."

"Did they say anything else about the sheriff or the money?" Jeff asked.

"No," Kendra Leigh said. "They just laughed some more, and then I heard Henning leave."

"Then what happened?" asked Jeff.

"After what I'd heard, I decided right then that I was leaving him. No matter what. I came into the room—he was standing over by the window with a drink in his hand—and I told him I was packing my bags and leaving. He laughed at me and told me to get on up to my room and drink myself to sleep. Then I told him that I'd heard what he'd said to Henning. That I knew he killed that poor preacher."

Kendra Leigh paused and placed her hands over her face. A quiet sob shook her frail body once, and then again. She sighed, gathered herself, wiped a tear from each eye, and continued.

"Before I could move, he lashed out at me, punched me in the face and knocked me down. He stood over me, shaking his fist, and said if I ever said that again, to anybody, they'd be fishing my body out of the lake."

"What'd you do then?" Jeff asked gently.

"I picked myself off the floor and pushed past him. He sat down in that chair—he still had his drink in his hand—and started laughing at me, calling me a run-down, drunken whore. So, I walked over to my desk and grabbed these."

She pulled open the top drawer and removed a small .22-caliber revolver. Terrell Jackson swiftly reached out and grabbed it from her.

"I'm so sorry," she said. "I should have given that to you right away."

Then she reached back into the drawer and pulled out a small, dark object and held it out to them. They all stared at it, puzzled.

"A tape recorder," she said. "Voice activated. Been here in the drawer forever. When I'd gone to my desk earlier to get my bottle—after

Tillman told me to get out—I reached in and flipped the 'on' switch. Not sure why, really. Maybe it was just some kind of premonition, I don't know. Anyway, I held this up and told him that I'd taped everything he and that weasel Henning had said. And that I'd make sure everyone heard it if he didn't agree to let me go."

"What'd he do?" asked Ella.

Kendra Leigh looked over at the body and slowly, sadly, shook her head.

"He said he'd kill me first, and he started to stand up." She paused and took a deep breath.

"So I shot him."

CHAPTER 61

Silence filled the room. No one spoke while Kendra Leigh sat at her desk, tape recorder in hand, staring again at the body of her dead husband. Finally, Jeff broke the spell.

"Mrs. Jessup?"

Kendra Leigh turned toward him, her eyes misty.

"Mrs. Jessup, did you check the recorder? Are the conversations there?"

She nodded.

"All of them?" asked Ella. "Talking about killing Elijah Hall and the sheriff poisoning Ricky Earl?"

Kendra Leigh nodded again.

"May I have that, please, Mrs. Jessup?" Jackson said, gently taking the device from her hands.

Jeff gestured for Ella to stay with Kendra Leigh while he grabbed Jackson and guided him over into the corner. Ella pulled a chair next to Kendra Leigh and they began a quiet conversation.

"So, now what?" Jeff asked.

"We grab Henning right away. Play the tape for him. Grab him by the balls and squeeze him hard. Get him to confirm what's on the tape." He looked at Jeff, anger flaring in his eyes. "And then I go take down the sheriff. Or, I should say, the soon-to-be former sheriff." He shook his head. "Damn, Jeff. I would've bet my life on that man."

"Me, too. Good thing we didn't."

"Yeah, right. Anyway, I'm on this. I'll call the DA and fill him in on the way. Y'all can stay here with her until we bring her in. I'll send my men in to seal the scene and keep an eye on her. The crime scene folks'll be here soon."

"Okay. Let me know what happens."

Jackson stopped in the doorway and turned back toward Jeff.

"Looks like we wrapped up two big murders in one night."

Jeff nodded. "Looks that way."

"So how come I ain't happy 'bout it?"

Jeff shrugged and shot a tired, grim look at his friend. "I know what you mean."

As Jackson rushed out and his officers entered, staking out positions around the room, Jeff walked over toward Ella and Kendra Leigh, who seemed to have completely deflated as she slumped in her chair. Ella rose and stopped him before he got to the desk.

"How's she doing?" he asked.

"Not too good. I think it's all starting to sink in."

"I know it's hard on her. But that tape recording—and her testimony—just solved two major murder cases."

"Jeff," Ella said, "she just killed her husband! I know he was a murderer and a wife-beater—but he was still her husband. And . . ."

"I know, I know," Jeff interrupted. "We'll make sure she gets help to deal with it. And I'll find her a good lawyer. Someone who's done spouse abuse cases. I think there's a good chance she can get off on some kind of self-defense . . ."

"Jeff," Ella said, grabbing his arm. She looked at him, deep sadness washing over her face. "Jeff, she doesn't need a lawyer."

Jeff stared at her, perplexed.

"Of course she does."

"No. She doesn't."

"I don't understand."

"She's dying, Jeff. Ovarian cancer. Stage four. Spread all through her body."

"What?"

"She got the diagnosis a few months ago, right before the case broke. The doctors said there was nothing they could do. It was too advanced. She didn't tell Jessup about it. And he never asked. Never even noticed that she was wasting away, dying slowly right before his eyes. What a bastard!"

"But we have to do something for her," Jeff said, a note of desperation mixed with sorrow in his voice. "There must be something we can do. After all she's been through. After all this," he said, gesturing toward Jessup's body.

Ella let out a long, low sigh and shook her head. "The doctors say she'll be dead in a month."

Jeff placed his arm around Ella as they turned toward the desk where a sheriff's officer stood guard over the fragile, dejected figure. Kendra Leigh sat, arms wrapped tightly across her chest, trembling slightly as she gazed forlornly at the body of Tillman Jessup, a whiskey glass in his lap, a bullet in his head.

EPILOGUE

It was Sunday and the Morning Star Baptist Church was ablaze with color and alive with noise. The members of the congregation, dressed in their church-going best—the women wearing vibrant, multi-hued dresses and hats, the men in suits and ties—had spent the last hour lifting up their souls with a succession of traditional hymns and spirituals.

Jeff and Ella were seated in the front row, invited guests of Reverend Butler. Surrounded by worshipers old and young, they felt warmly welcomed and at peace. The past few days since the murder case against Tillman Jessup had been dismissed had been a dizzying whirl of developments. Royce Henning had, in fact, been squeezed by Terrell Jackson and, faced with the nightmare of life in prison, had immediately confessed and agreed to testify about the roles played by Jessup and Sheriff Poole in the death of Ricky Earl Graves.

Dealing with the sheriff was initially a bit more problematic. He indignantly denied any involvement in Ricky Earl's killing and claimed that Henning was lying just to protect himself. However, the search of Ricky Earl's cell had turned up a nearly empty bottle of Jack Daniel's, and forensic tests revealed the residue of a significant amount of digitalis inside the bottle, together with two fingerprints, smudged but readable, that matched those of Sheriff Poole. After a search of the sheriff's home resulted in the discovery of $250,000 in cash hidden in two shotgun cases—a cache that coincided with Henning's claim that he had delivered that amount to Poole as a down payment for his betrayal—Poole's lawyers were now desperately negotiating a plea deal to save him from the potential of a death sentence. The likelihood was that Clayton Poole would spend the rest of his life in prison while Royce Henning, as a result of his cooperation, would do five to ten years on a conspiracy charge.

The apprehension and arrest of A. J. Hollingsly had proved more difficult. A warrant had been issued for his arrest but, so far, he had managed to elude capture. Although a rumor had him retreating deep into the North Carolina woods, an interstate task force headed up by Terrell Jackson was confident that, eventually, they would track him down.

As for Tillman Jessup, the once-rising star of Mississippi politics, the public now knew that he was, indeed, a murderer. District Attorney Gibb Haynes had played Kendra Leigh's recording of Jessup's confession at a press conference attended by a mass of local and national media. Lead stories and headlines across the nation blared that the four-decade-old murder mystery had finally been solved.

Meanwhile, Kendra Leigh had been arrested and charged with her husband's murder, triggering yet another eruption of media coverage. Once the details surrounding the shooting were made public, a flock of top lawyers had volunteered to defend her. Judge Langston, after being advised of her dire prognosis, released her to home confinement as a condition of her bail, with a fervent prayer that when she passed away, it would be peacefully in her own bed.

As the music and voices in the Morning Star Baptist Church faded, Reverend Butler stepped to the podium, his aged, graying head held high, and his eyes radiant with the joy he felt in his heart.

Looking down at Jeff and Ella, he smiled as a proud father would when acknowledging that his children had persevered through difficult times and accomplished something of value. Ella reached over and took Jeff's hand, tucking it between both of her own.

"Brothers and sisters," Reverend Butler began, "we gather this morning to celebrate the triumph of justice, a justice long delayed but, finally, not denied."

A chorus of "Amen" rippled throughout the church, as the members nodded their heads in approval.

"Some forty years ago—a few of you were here with me back then," he said, scanning the sea of uplifted faces, "I stood here in our old church and embraced a brother who had come to shed a light on our lives. A brother who brought us good news about our fight for freedom." He paused. "A brother who, later that night, sacrificed his own life for that freedom.

"Today," he continued, his voice rising, "we are here to finally lay the soul of our brother, Elijah Hall, to rest."

"Amen!" came the shouts.

"Dr. King told us many times," Reverend Butler said, his voice now stronger, louder, and pulsing with rhythm and raw energy, "that the arc of the moral universe is long." He paused for a dramatic moment. "But it bends always toward justice."

"Yes, Lord!" came the cries from the congregation.

"And that arc has bent and twisted along its path for many years, but it finally found the justice it sought right here this week in Oxford."

"Praise the Lord!"

"The forces of good rose up and circled the ancient citadel of evil and racism, blowing their horns and praying that the Lord would help them prevail."

"Yes, Jesus!"

"And the Lord heard their prayers," the minister cried, his voice soaring. "The Lord heard the sound of the trumpets of truth! And the walls of Jericho have fallen once again!"

The congregation exploded into a raucous, impassioned symphony of "Amen!" and "Praise the Lord Jesus!"

After letting the wave of sound wash over the room for a full minute, Reverend Butler raised his hands and a reverential silence slowly descended upon the old building.

"Brothers and sisters," he solemnly intoned, "the soul of our long-departed friend, of our brother, Elijah Hall, can finally rest in peace. Justice has been done!"

Reverend Butler turned toward the members of the choir and nodded, smiling broadly, as they launched into a hand-clapping, foot-stomping rendition of "Ain't That Good News"—a song that had not been heard inside those walls for forty years—their voices raised to God, tears streaming down their cheeks.

I got a crown in that kingdom—ain't that good news?
I got a crown in that kingdom—ain't that good news?
I'm gonna lay down this world
I'm gonna shoulder up my cross
I'm gonna carry it home to Jesus—
Ain't that good news, my Lord, ain't that good news?

ACKNOWLEDGMENTS

I have had something of a love affair with Oxford, Mississippi, for more than a decade. As Oxford resident William Faulkner recognized when he noted that his "own little postage stamp of native soil was worth writing about," the history, the traditions, and the people of Oxford, all of which I've come to appreciate, combine to provide a marvelous tableau from which a wealth of compelling, complex, and engaging stories can emerge.

The story I have written had its genesis in an actual unsolved civil rights-era murder that I came across as I was doing research for a course I teach at Yale. The 1955 shotgun slaying of Reverend George W. Lee, as he drove home in his car following a voting rights rally in Mississippi, was never solved; indeed, it was barely investigated after his death was initially deemed to have been the result of "a traffic accident." I was struck by how different *that* Mississippi—the one that embraced the Sovereignty Commission, Citizens' Councils, the KKK, and burning crosses—was from the Mississippi that I had come to know. And I wondered how the new Mississippi would confront the specter of the old Mississippi. The result of that curiosity is *The Walls of Jericho*.

I have been fortunate to develop a great many wonderful relationships in Oxford and at the University of Mississippi, relationships that have helped shepherd me through the research and writing of this book. Initially, I must thank Langston Rogers, the esteemed long-time Sports Information Director at Ole Miss, for his constant guidance and great friendship over many years. Also, I owe an extraordinary debt of gratitude to the Ole Miss legend, and good friend, Archie Manning, for his insight and introductions to so many of the good citizens of Oxford who graciously took the time to impart their own special knowledge of this lovely town and its history to a writer from New Jersey. Among these new friends are: former Ole Miss Chancellor Robert Khayat; former Law School Dean Sam Davis; noted journalist and author Curtis Wilkie; Campbell McCool; Ken Coghlan, Esq.; and Court Clerk Mary Alice Busby and her staff.

In addition, I would like to thank my friend, Judge Evan Broadbelt, for his observations and suggestions following an early reading of the manuscript. And my thanks also to my daughter, Dr. Ashley Ford Haggerty, for her assistance navigating through my maze of medical questions.

My agent and friend, Paul Fedorko, has been a steadying source of direction and inspiration throughout the life of this book. I am also particularly grateful to the entire team at Bascom Hill for their creativity, enthusiasm, and invaluable contributions to the editorial and publishing process.

I am especially thankful, as always, to my wife, Dorothy Ann, for her ideas, patience, and candor throughout the writing process, and to my children, Ashley and Colin, for their unfailing support and enthusiasm.

ABOUT THE AUTHOR

Jack Ford is an Emmy and Peabody Award-winning television journalist and former prominent trial attorney. Since leaving the courtroom and entering the world of journalism, he has served as an anchor/correspondent for NBC News, ABC News, Court TV, and CBS News, and is recognized as one of the top legal journalists in the country. A graduate of Yale University and the Fordham University School of Law, Ford is a Visiting Lecturer at Yale, NYU, and the University of Virginia. His debut novel, *The Osiris Alliance*, was published in 2009. He lives in New Jersey.